D0974575

The Dark Warrior series

"The world of the Immortal Warriors is a thoroughly engaging one, blending powerful ancient gods, fiery desire, and touchingly human love, which readers will surely want to revisit." —*RT Book Reviews*

"[Grant] blends ancient gods, love, desire, and evil-doers into a world you will want to revisit over and over again." —*Night Owl Reviews*

"Sizzling love scenes and engaging characters." —*Publishers Weekly*

"Ms. Grant mixes adventure, magic, and sweet love to create the perfect romance[s]." —*Single Title Reviews*

The Dark Sword series

"Grant creates a vivid picture of Britain centuries after the Celts and Druids tried to expel the Romans, deftly merging magic and history. The result is a wonderfully dark, delightfully well-written [series]. Readers will eagerly await the next Dark Sword book." —*RT Book Reviews*

"Another fantastic series that melds the paranormal with the historical life of the Scottish highlander in this arousing and exciting adventure." —*Bitten By Books*

"These are some of the hottest brothers around in paranormal fiction." —*Nocturne Romance Reads*

"Will keep readers spellbound." —*Romance Reviews Today*

ALSO BY DONNA GRANT

THE HEART OF TEXAS SERIES
THE CHRISTMAS COWBOY HERO
COWBOY, CROSS MY HEART

THE SONS OF TEXAS SERIES
THE HERO
THE PROTECTOR
THE LEGEND

THE DARK KINGS SERIES
DARK HEAT
DARKEST FLAME
FIRE RISING
BURNING DESIRE
HOT BLOODED
NIGHT'S BLAZE
SOUL SCORCHED
PASSION IGNITES
SMOLDERING HUNGER
SMOKE AND FIRE
FIRESTORM
BLAZE
HEAT
TORCHED
DRAGONFIRE

THE DARK WARRIOR SERIES
MIDNIGHT'S MASTER
MIDNIGHT'S LOVER
MIDNIGHT'S SEDUCTION
MIDNIGHT'S WARRIOR
MIDNIGHT'S KISS
MIDNIGHT'S CAPTIVE
MIDNIGHT'S TEMPTATION
MIDNIGHT'S PROMISE
MIDNIGHT'S SURRENDER

THE DARK SWORD SERIES
DANGEROUS HIGHLANDER
FORBIDDEN HIGHLANDER
WICKED HIGHLANDER
UNTAMED HIGHLANDER
SHADOW HIGHLANDER
DARKEST HIGHLANDER

MY
FAVORITE
COWBOY

DONNA GRANT

St. Martin's Paperbacks

This is a work of fiction. All of the characters, organizations, and events portrayed in this novel are either products of the author's imagination or are used fictitiously.

MY FAVORITE COWBOY

Copyright © 2019 by Donna Grant.

All rights reserved.

For information address St. Martin's Press, 175 Fifth Avenue, New York, NY 10010.

ISBN: 978-1-250-16902-0

Our books may be purchased in bulk for promotional, educational, or business use. Please contact your local bookseller or the Macmillan Corporate and Premium Sales Department at 1-800-221-7945, ext. 5442, or by e-mail at MacmillanSpecialMarkets@macmillan.com.

Printed in the United States of America

St. Martin's Paperbacks edition / March 2019

St. Martin's Paperbacks are published by St. Martin's Press, 175 Fifth Avenue, New York, NY 10010.

10 9 8 7 6 5 4 3 2 1

Acknowledgments

A very special thanks to everyone at SMP for this book from the art department, to marketing, to publicity, to production. I'd also like to thank Mara Delgado-Sanchez for being such a big help for so many things. It goes without saying that a shout-out is directed to my editor, Monique Patterson.

More thanks to my agent, Natanya Wheeler, who is always so supportive in whatever direction I happen to be headed in.

A special thanks to my children, Gillian and Connor, as well as my family for the never-ending support and love.

Hats off to my incredible readers who have fallen for my cowboys!

Chapter 1

July

Another one.

Audrey sighed as she removed the plastic gloves and ran a comforting hand over the too-still mare that stared blankly at the wall. The strawberry roan was a gorgeous specimen to behold, and it killed Audrey that the horse was ill.

"I'm going to help you, baby," she said softly, passing long strokes down the mare's neck.

Audrey pulled out her iPad and jotted down notes, including the symptoms she had seen in three other horses. The fact that none of the animals came from the same owner, and each had arrived at the auction house on different days meant that whatever was making the horses sick had happened at the auction house.

The mare didn't even swivel her ears as David Warner approached. Audrey looked over to the owner of the auction house. His stomach protruded, obscuring his belt buckle. He removed his cowboy hat, turning it around in his hands as he gazed anxiously at the horse with his hazel eyes. No one could fake that kind of concern for an animal.

He ran a hand through his thinning, graying, blond hair. His gray mustache twitched atop his lip like a long, thick caterpillar. "I'd hoped for good news, but I can see by your face that isn't going to happen."

Audrey closed her tablet and dropped her arms to her sides. She'd known David all her life and had always liked him. He loved equines and was well known in the community for coming to the aid of any horse in need. In fact, most of the animals in his barns were those he had rescued.

David's narrow-set eyes watered as he blinked at her. "Audrey, are you sure it's as bad as you feared?"

"Without a doubt," she replied.

He dropped his head and looked away to hide his distress.

She walked to him and put a hand on his arm. "You need to speak to every employee. More importantly, you need to turn on the cameras you installed years ago."

"They don't work," David admitted, still gazing at the ground.

She frowned as she looked around to see if anyone was close. "Who knows that?"

Finally, he lifted his head to her. David shrugged helplessly. "Everyone."

Audrey closed her eyes, biting back an angry retort. She had to remember that David was a gentle soul. He'd married young and lost his wife just a few years afterward when she fell from a horse and broke her neck. Forty years later, he was still alone, preferring to give his time to the beautiful creatures he loved.

She shot him a reassuring smile because he'd do the same for her. "We'll figure this out."

"Knowing you're on my side is a huge relief. Thank you."

"Don't thank me yet. I've not found exactly what is happening to these animals. I need to rule out everything before I can give a definitive answer."

David replaced his hat atop his head. "You will. You have the same tenacity as your father."

The mention of her father brought back the ache in Audrey's chest that she'd lived with for the past year. She watched David walk away before turning back to the roan. Four horses were counting on her to heal them. After years of veterinarian school and learning every nuance of equines, she didn't like being stumped.

If she gave any of them the wrong medicine, it could do more harm than good. She didn't want to chance doing that until she knew for certain what was causing such a reaction in the animals.

Audrey looked at the stall. The wood was Southern Yellow Pine, an inexpensive and durable material that worked well for barns. David had applied a finish to help stop mold and splintering.

At least that was in this barn, which was used for injured horses or those just coming in to the auction house. Most of the animals were kept in the larger, covered corrals with steel fencing separating them.

If she hadn't been coming to the auction house her entire life and seen for herself just how well treated the animals were, she would test the wood from the stalls and even the metal of the corrals to see if something might have leaked into the horses' skin or tongues. Since only four of the twenty horses had been listless and refused to eat or drink, she didn't believe wood or metal had anything to do with it.

The food and hay, however, was another matter. Audrey let her gaze run over the other horses in the corrals. Why just four? That's what it kept coming back to. Four.

She squatted beside her bag and pulled out some supplies. After opening the alcohol-soaked gauze, she stood and wiped the jugular furrow of the roan while talking gently to the animal to keep her calm. She then pressed her thumb against the base of the horse's neck and felt the vein throb. The pressure also caused it to bulge, which made it easier to collect the blood.

Audrey kept talking to soothe the animal while she inserted the needle into the vein and began to draw the blood. Once she had enough, she withdrew the needle and placed another alcohol-soaked pad over the injection site to stop the bleeding.

The roan jerked her head up and tried to shy away at the contact. Audrey quickly removed the gauze and gently massaged the area while humming a gentle tune. It took only a few seconds for the horse to calm once more.

Audrey spent another few minutes with the mare before she repeated the process another three times with the other ill horses. Audrey marked each tube carefully and put them all into her bag.

But she wasn't finished. She chose four random horses and drew their blood as well for comparisons. One way or another, she was going to figure out why the equines were sick.

It physically hurt Audrey when an animal was in pain, and she couldn't help them. There was no way she was going to rest until she got to the bottom of the issue.

And learned what—or who—was doing this to the horses.

Audrey didn't believe that David was involved in any way, but she couldn't be so certain about any of the others he employed. David had a good heart and was always giving jobs to those in need. While he had the patience of Job, the moment he even suspected that anyone might think of harming the animals, they were fired.

The mystery of the ill horses took precedence over anything else Audrey had. She walked into the blazing heat and squinted from the bright sunshine. As she made her way to her SUV, she churned everything round and round in her head, hoping that she might be able to somehow figure out the mystery.

Just before she got into her vehicle, she paused and turned her head to the long, metal building David used as his office. She closed the door and tightened her grip on her bag as she walked through the gravel parking area toward the structure set off to the side.

She walked in to find David sitting as he leaned his arms on the desk, his gaze directed out the window to where the horses were. Audrey quietly closed the door behind her.

"I've had this business for over thirty-five years," he said in a voice filled with hurt, anger, and worry. "In all that time, only one horse has died while in my care."

Audrey inwardly winced at the reminder of that horrible day. She had been with her father and David when they found the gelding lying unmoving on the ground. The death had been natural, but David had never gotten over it.

His hazel eyes swung to her. "Do you think someone is doing this? Do you think they want to hurt the horses? Or could they be after me?"

"I don't know anything yet, and I'd hate to speculate."

He swallowed as he nodded, looking away. "Of course, of course. I didn't mean to put you on the spot."

"You're worried. It's perfectly all right for you to feel a whirlwind of emotions right now."

David blinked rapidly and went back to looking out the window. "I'm going to stay here with the horses until all of this is figured out and they're better."

"That's probably a good idea. I have some tests I want to run on the blood I've drawn. I'll be back as quickly as I can."

He didn't appear to hear her as he continued looking out the window.

Audrey licked her lips and took a step toward the desk. "David."

"Hmm?" he said as he glanced her way.

"You need to get the cameras working. And do it without anyone else knowing."

He bobbed his head slowly. "I know someone I can call that might help."

"Good. Get it done today once everyone has gone home. Also, I'm going to send Maddy over to help you keep an eye on the horses until I get back."

David's head swung to her as his brow furrowed. "Audrey, you need to be careful. You work exclusively for two well-known ranches. If they find out you're helping me, things won't go well for you."

"They can kiss my ass," she stated. "Besides, they don't need to know about this."

"I never should have asked you to come."

"Stop," she told him. "I'd be pissed if you hadn't called. Now, I need you to trust me. I also need you to promise me the cameras will get repaired."

He blew out a breath, exhaustion evident in the droop of his shoulders. "I will. You have my word."

"Good. I'll be back."

Audrey shot him a smile and turned on her heel. In moments, she was back in the heat, walking to her vehicle. She glanced toward the red pickup truck that rolled to a stop next to David's office.

She didn't recognize the vehicle, but then again, she didn't spend as much time at the auction house as she used to. Maybe if she had, she would have a better idea of what was going on with the horses. She'd focused on her career and let this—among other things in her life—fall by the wayside.

After she was inside her SUV, she glanced over at the other vehicle and spotted the outline of a cowboy hat through the tinted windows. It wasn't until she started up her engine that the door of the red truck opened, and a man stepped out.

He was talking to someone inside the truck, so she didn't get to see his face. She put her SUV in reverse and backed up before driving away. A quick look in her rearview mirror showed her nothing but a lean-framed body walking in the opposite direction. Even in the mirror, there was no denying the finely shaped ass. Too bad she hadn't gotten a look at his face.

She snorted. As if she'd do anything about it. Nothing was more important than her career. It had been the only thing that mattered for a while, and then it became a habit that was impossible to break.

There was a clinic at each of the ranches she worked for, but Audrey also had one of her own. That's where she headed to test the blood. She didn't want anyone to know what she was doing, mostly because she didn't trust anyone.

Audrey noticed her sister's car at their house as she drove past it to park in front of the building she had built for her private practice. It had begun as storage for extra products and equipment, but it hadn't taken long for her to turn it into a mini-clinic for neighbors and friends.

She shut off the engine and opened the door. With her bag in hand, she turned to get out of the truck and found Maddy standing there.

"Dammit," Audrey gasped in surprise. "I hate when you do that."

Younger by three years, Maddy was a free spirit. She couldn't settle on a career, so Audrey paid her to work as an assistant.

"I know that look," Maddy stated with a raised brow.

Audrey wished she could pull off the messy bun, baggy sweatpants, and graphic tee look as well as her sister did. But Maddy had the tall, thin frame of models and could wear anything while still looking beautiful. She literally rolled out of bed looking gorgeous.

Maddy took the case from Audrey's hands. "What happened?"

Audrey slid out of the truck and closed the door before walking toward the clinic. "David has four sick horses, and I have to figure out how they're getting ill."

"What do you need from me?"

Maddy might have her head in the clouds most days, but she was also someone Audrey could always depend on.

"I need you to go to the auction house and stay with the horses until I get back. David isn't taking this well."

"On it." Maddy shoved the bag at Audrey and spun to hurry away. Then she called over her shoulder, "There's food on the table. You better eat it."

Chapter 2

Some days, nothing in particular screamed "wrong," yet the feeling hounded Caleb. Inevitably, his intuition ended up being right.

And he'd had a hunch since the moment he opened his eyes that morning.

"Want to tell me what you're thinking in that head of yours?" his brother, Brice, asked from the passenger seat of the truck once they reached the auction house.

Caleb watched a woman stride from the metal office building and climb into a charcoal gray sport utility vehicle. He couldn't take his eyes from her, and years of training in the military had him cataloging her straight black hair pulled into a ponytail, as well as the black bag she gripped as if it were a lifeline, despite its apparent weight. He eyed the plain, white button-up shirt she wore with the sleeves rolled to her elbows, the hem tucked into the waistband of a pair of jeans encasing trim legs he wouldn't mind wrapped around him. Her brown boots were well worn with the heels in need of repair.

This was no wanna-be cowgirl. This woman lived and worked the life.

"Caleb," Brice said, thumping him on the earlobe.

Caleb swatted his brother's hand away and glared angrily. "You know I hate that."

"Then answer me."

Caleb rolled his eyes and opened the door to get out, the same time Brice did. "I was about to."

"Bullshit."

Caleb shut his door and walked around the front of his truck to meet Brice. "You know, I don't kick your ass on a regular basis because I don't want to make you look bad in front of Naomi, but I'll be happy to change that."

"As if you could," Brice said with a snort as he took the two steps to the office door.

The sound of tires rolling on rock drew Caleb's gaze. He looked over his shoulder to see the woman driving off. He didn't know why, but he really wanted to know who she was. It wasn't because she had nice legs and he liked the sway of her hips as she walked. It had to do with the niggling feeling that had plagued him since he opened his eyes that morning.

"Seriously. What's going on?"

Caleb shook his head as he shrugged. "I don't know."

"Something has your attention. That makes me take notice. Because while I'm loath to admit this and make your already bloated ego bigger, your intuition is normally right on the money."

"Yeah." Caleb swung his head back to his brother. "I just wish I knew why that woman piqued my interest."

Brice's lips curved into a smile. "Perhaps she got your attention for another reason."

"She was a looker."

Brice raised his gaze to the sky and blew out a breath as he removed his sunglasses. He then locked his pale blue eyes on Caleb. "You couldn't see shit from just her profile."

"Obviously, they didn't train you right in the Marines, big brother, because I saw all I needed, to know how attractive she is."

"A woman is more than boobs, legs, and ass," Brice stated flatly.

Caleb grinned as they started toward the office. "Maybe to you."

"You're never going to change, are you?"

The teasing was gone. Caleb saw the shift in his brother's demeanor. Ever since Brice had fallen in love and married Naomi, he expected Caleb to follow suit.

Caleb didn't have the heart to tell Brice that while Brice might have gotten past his abandonment issues enough to marry, Caleb never would. Not after what he'd gone through.

Hell, their sister, Abby, seemed to have come to terms with his decision.

But not Brice.

"Don't," Caleb warned dangerously. This wasn't a conversation he *ever* wanted to have. "Just because you got hitched, doesn't mean everyone needs to."

"You have a different woman every time I turn around. I think you've slept with everyone in this county."

Caleb hooked his thumb over his shoulder, motioning back the way the woman they'd been discussing had gone. "Not everyone."

Brice narrowed his gaze, showing his irritation before

he jerked open the door to the office and turned away. Their conversations had been the same of late—Brice attempting to urge Caleb to settle down, and Caleb telling Brice no. Then his brother would get angry and storm off. Except, this time, he couldn't.

Caleb followed his brother into the office, the cool air from the A/C washing over them. He came to stand beside Brice, both of them noticing how distracted David was since the man didn't seem to take note of either of them.

They exchanged a look. Caleb shrugged.

Brice cleared his throat. When that didn't work, he called out David's name.

The older man turned his head to them, his narrow-set eyes widening when he spotted them. "Gentlemen," he said, though his smile was forced. "I forgot about your appointment this morning."

"Is this a bad time? We can come back," Caleb said.

David looked down at his desk covered with a variety of papers. He splayed his hands on them and pushed to his feet. "Actually, I was about to call your brother-in-law."

"Clayton?" Brice asked.

Caleb's attention sharpened as he crossed his arms over his chest. "What's going on?"

David Warner was one of those people who couldn't hide their emotions even if their life depended on it. The creases of worry on his forehead accentuated the lines of strain around his mouth. He was nervous and fearful.

"You can tell us," Brice urged.

David squeezed the bridge of his nose with his thumb and forefinger. "My security cameras are down. Do you think Clayton could come take a look?"

Neither Caleb nor Brice pushed David to tell them what

was really going on. While Clayton had one of the best security systems in the three surrounding counties, he hadn't installed it, even though he knew enough about them to do it himself.

Brice pulled out his phone. "Sure. I'll give him a call."

He turned on his heel, shooting Caleb a quick look before walking out of the building to make the call.

Caleb waited until Brice was gone before he moved to the coffee machine to the left of David's desk and poured some of the brew into two paper cups. He handed one to David and noticed the tremor in the man's hands as he reached for it.

"You know that Brice and I use the same security system on our ranch, right? We'd be happy to take a look," Caleb offered.

David lowered himself back into his chair and removed his hat. "You might as well since you two are here."

"Do you know what the problem is, exactly?"

David shook his head and met Caleb's gaze. "I can barely operate my computer, and I still have an old flip phone. I've never understood electronics."

"Don't worry. We'll take care of it."

For the first time, the beginning of a genuine smile appeared on David's face. His relief was palpable. "Thank you." Then, he shook his head in frustration. "You and Brice came to look at that filly."

Caleb held up his hand to stop David. "It can wait. I'll grab Brice, and we'll have a look at the cameras while we wait for Clayton."

"Your family is good people, Caleb."

He gave a nod of thanks and walked from the building. Caleb couldn't help but wonder if the feeling he'd been having had something to do with whatever was going on with David. Regardless, he was going to find out. There was only so much someone could hide. He and Brice knew just how and where to look to find answers.

Just as he was about to take a drink of his coffee, Brice took it from his hand.

Caleb raised a brow. "That was mine."

"It's mine now."

And just like that, they were five and seven again. "What did Clayton say?"

Brice glanced at the office as he sipped the hot liquid. "He was in town running some errands. He'll be here in about ten minutes."

"That will give us time to have a look around."

They turned as one and headed to the back of the office where the security system was routed. An initial look confirmed that no wires had been cut. Next, they moved from camera to camera.

"These haven't worked in over a year," Brice said in disgust as he looked at a set of disconnected wires that were covered in dirt and grime.

Caleb nodded. "Exactly. What has David so wound up that he wants these cameras working now?"

"Do you think someone stole something?"

Caleb looked over the corrals of cattle, sheep, goats, and the stables of horses. "The only thing David cares about is the animals. If one was stolen, he would've called Danny immediately."

"You're right. David wouldn't have hesitated to bring in the sheriff's department. That leaves . . . what?"

Caleb put his hands on his hips as he jerked his chin to the animals. "Them."

"You go left. I'll take the right."

They each went their separate ways. While they continued checking cameras, they also looked for any other signs that could indicate what had David so worked up.

Just as Caleb thought that there might not be anything to find, he saw the chestnut gelding. The lethargic way the horse had its head lowered and the way his eyes were glazed over let Caleb know that the animal wasn't well. It didn't take Caleb long to discover three other horses in the same barn that looked similar.

Caleb's mind immediately went to the woman he'd seen. The bag she carried, and the SUV all made sense now. She was a vet.

"There you are," Brice said as he walked up. "Did you find something?"

"Unfortunately."

His brother shot him a look of concern before his eyes swung to the sick animals. "Well, hell."

Caleb grunted. "Exactly."

"David's reaction makes sense now."

"Not entirely. That woman I saw was a vet, and I bet she was here to look at these horses."

Brice's brow furrowed. "I wonder what's wrong with them."

"I don't know, but it would explain why David is in such a hurry to get the cameras up. Whether it's to keep an eye on the animals or someone doesn't matter."

"I should've known you'd figure out about the horses," David said from behind them.

Caleb and Brice turned to find him standing with their brother-in-law, Clayton East, who happened to own the East Ranch—the biggest in the county.

The auction house owner shrugged, twisting his lips. "I noticed something wrong with the chestnut three days ago.

I thought it might be colic at first, but it soon became apparent that wasn't the case. The next day, two more horses exhibited the same symptoms. When I got here this morning and saw the roan, I called Audrey."

"Audrey Martinez?" Caleb asked in surprise.

Clayton jerked his gaze to him. "You know her?"

"We know *of* her," Brice explained. "She's a well-known and highly coveted equine veterinarian. We thought about bringing her on to work with us, but we learned she was already taken."

David walked to the stall and leaned against it. "Audrey's dad and I were friends. I've known her and her sister Maddy since they were born."

"And you knew you could trust her," Caleb guessed.

David nodded slowly. "She's the one who said I had to get the cameras working again."

"She's right," Clayton said. "Whether someone is doing this to the animals or it's some contagion, you need to figure it out. Otherwise, this could ruin you."

David opened the stall door and walked inside to run his hand down the chestnut's back. "I don't care about that. I care about these animals."

"But we care about you," Clayton said and motioned for Brice and Caleb to follow him.

Chapter 3

The ache in her neck caused Audrey to tilt her head from side to side, stretching the tight muscles. She leaned back from the microscope and squeezed her eyes closed in an effort to stop the burning.

After stifling a yawn, she grabbed the pen and wrote down the results. Finally, she was done looking at all eight samples. She was in the process of running a few more tests, but it would be several hours before she had the results. She really hoped that she wouldn't have to send the samples off to a lab for more extensive testing.

But if she didn't find anything conclusive, she wouldn't have a choice.

Audrey slid off the stool and gave in to the yawn. She hadn't slept well the night before. Then again, she rarely slept through the night. When she finally did drift off last night, her phone had soon woken her.

No matter how tired she was, she wasn't going to ignore a call from one of her father's oldest friends. She'd gotten up and gone straight to the auction house, never imagining that she might stumble upon something that she couldn't sort out easily.

This was Karma laughing at her. At least that's what Maddy would say. How many times had Audrey said that she wished for something more than the regular checkups, colic, and deworming of the horses?

Audrey sank back onto the stool and leaned an elbow on the table before dropping her head into her hand. How could she ever wish for such a thing? She loved animals, especially horses.

She worked tirelessly—and free of charge—at a horse rescue to help the abused animals. She never wanted any of them to hurt, but it seemed that lamenting the fact that things had been *easy* may have done just that.

Audrey didn't really believe in Fate or Karma, but when things like this happened, it made her pause and take stock of what she had said or done.

Or hoped for.

It was Maddy who always harped on Audrey to make sure to do good so no bad Karma could pile up. Why then did it feel as if that were exactly what had happened?

Audrey raised her head and took several deep breaths. She knew from experience that she would have to be the calm one, especially in an unknown situation like this. If she freaked out—like she was currently doing on the inside—so would everyone else.

It was best, especially for the horses, if everyone remained composed and unruffled.

She put her hands on her lower back and arched backward, popping her spine. After closing her iPad, she stuffed it into her bag, gathered a few other items she might need, and checked on the last blood test she was running.

"Three more hours," she murmured, hating to wait.

There was nothing else to do. She had to let it finish. But she wanted to get back to David and the horses. Audrey gathered her bag and flipped off the lights as she walked from the building.

She only got a few steps when her cell rang. Thinking it was her sister, she didn't look at the display before answering.

"It's not like you to not show up."

Audrey came to a halt, her eyes closing as she heard the voice of Robert Bremer. As the owner of Bremer Horse Farm and one of her employers, he wasn't the type of man she wanted to anger.

She didn't particularly care for him. But he had some of the best horses around. She quite liked being involved with such highly sought after animals as those from the Bremer Horse Farm.

She put up with Robert's arrogance and brashness because he took care of his horses. It also helped that he paid her quite well. That extra money allowed her to give aid to more equines through her charity work.

"Audrey."

She opened her eyes and adjusted her grip on her case. Sweat trickled down the side of her face from standing in the blazing afternoon sun. She continued on to her SUV and said, "I'm sorry, Robert. I had an emergency come up."

"More of your pro bono work?"

She hated that his voice fairly dripped with distaste, as if helping those less fortunate somehow sullied her.

Robert sighed loudly through the phone. "I know you feel as if you should help those poor animals, but if people can't afford to take care of their horses, then they shouldn't get them in the first place."

"I'm not going to have this argument with you again."

They'd already had it multiple times, and frankly, Audrey was tired of it. "Is there something that needs my attention?"

"I have thirty horses here. There is always something that needs your attention. And," Robert continued, deepening his voice to show his displeasure. "Per our arrangement, you are to be here on Mondays, Wednesdays, and Fridays and any day there is an emergency. Did you forget today is Wednesday?"

She climbed into her SUV. The heat only added to her anger. She started the engine and turned the A/C on full-blast. "Of course, I didn't. As I said, I had an emergency."

There was a long pause. "If you weren't so damn good at what you do, I'd have replaced you years ago."

It was on the tip of her tongue to tell him that she quit, but she didn't.

Instead, she said, "I'll be by later today."

"I sincerely hope so."

She ended the call and tossed her phone into the cup holder. "Smarmy asshole," she murmured.

Maddy asked her all the time why Audrey worked for someone she didn't like. Audrey tried to explain why, but her sister just didn't understand.

Just as Robert would never comprehend why she spent hours of her free time helping neglected horses and those who didn't have the means to pay for a vet.

She put on her seatbelt and drove off. A glance at the clock in the truck told her that she'd been gone for over six hours. The fact that Maddy hadn't called was a good sign. That meant the horses hadn't worsened.

It also meant they hadn't gotten any better.

All Audrey could hope for was that the cameras were fixed by the time night fell. Even if they weren't, she was going to be there. She not only had a gun in her bag, but she also knew how to use it.

Her father had been the one to push both her and Maddy to get weapons, but it was their mother who'd insisted that they learn how to defend themselves without a gun.

At this point, Audrey was ready and willing to handle anyone who crossed her path that night.

She came to the turn-off to the Bremer farm and decided to stop by now instead of later. Once she got to David's, she knew she wouldn't want to leave. Robert was already irritated with her. It was better to smooth his ruffled feathers now.

She told her hands-free to call her sister and waited for Maddy to pick up.

"You on your way?" her sister asked.

"I have to stop at Bremer's."

"Ugh."

Audrey grinned, practically hearing her sister's eye-roll. "I won't be long."

Maddy made a sound in the back of her throat. "He called you, didn't he?"

"I do work for him, and I not only didn't show up, I didn't call either."

"Whatever. You know how I feel about him," Maddy said quickly, shifting her attention from the subject. "But you are coming here?"

Audrey made a face at the dashboard. "Of course."

"Good. The quicker, the better."

Audrey slowed the SUV, ready to turn it around immediately if needed. "Why? Has one of the horses gotten worse?"

"I swear. Do you think about anything other than horses?"

"Yeah," Audrey replied as she sped back up. "I think about putting Nair in your shampoo on a daily basis."

Maddy gasped loudly. Then there was a long pause. "You're such a bitch."

"Back at ya, sis."

"And here I was going to tell you about a couple of cute guys. I think one's married, though."

Audrey should've known where her sister's mind had gone. "Do you ever think about anything but men?"

"I think about food a lot."

Maddy could eat anything she wanted and not gain an ounce. It was maddening. If Audrey happened to eat a slice of cake, she could actually feel her jeans getting tighter within moments of swallowing it.

"I've got to go."

Maddy laughed. "Love you, too."

The connection went dead, but Audrey had a smile on her face when she turned into the Bremer farm.

She wanted to hurry her way through everything, but she stopped herself. She went to every horse, doing her usual check of the animals. A few needed vaccinations. One had to have a bandage changed, and the wound examined.

Audrey was finalizing the last of her notes when she heard Robert's voice at the other end of the stables. She was in no mood to talk to him, especially when she wanted to get back to the sick horses at the auction house.

She waved to the trainer who was nearby and returned to her vehicle. As she drove away, she glanced in her rear-view mirror and saw Robert watching her.

There was no doubt that she would have to make up the hours she'd missed. Despite the fact that she always went over the time they had agreed upon, Robert wasn't someone you shortchanged. Ever.

Audrey half expected him to call again, and she was greatly relieved when he didn't. It wasn't long before she forgot all about Robert Bremer.

She pulled up next to her sister's bright red Mazda Miata and turned off the engine. Audrey gathered her bag and phone and hurried to the horses.

The heat was stifling without any movement of the wind. Thankfully, David had fans installed in the stables and covered areas for the animals in the paddocks. She wiped her arm across her brow as she spotted her sister sitting outside the stalls, meditating.

Audrey could only shake her head. At least the music Maddy played was soothing. Hopefully, that would help the animals.

Audrey looked around for signs of anyone else, but so far, all she'd seen was Maddy. There had been another truck next to David's when she arrived. It must be someone fixing the cameras.

Audrey set down her bag and looked in on the roan. The horse hadn't moved since morning. There was food and hay in the stalls, as well as water. None of the four ill horses had come near any of it. She wouldn't let them get dehydrated, though.

"You're here."

She looked over her shoulder to find Maddy getting to her feet. "I'm here. Anything happen?"

"Other than the cute guys? No."

Audrey turned to face her sister, who came to stand beside her. "Did you get their numbers?"

"You act like I'm some kind of ho or something," Maddy said, affronted.

Audrey shot her sister a dry look. "You forget. I know you."

Maddy suddenly laughed. "So what if I like sex? I'm an adult. I can have as much of it as I want."

"Sure. Just don't get some disease or pop up pregnant."

Maddy suddenly stood straighter. "It wouldn't hurt you to have more sex. How long has it been? A night or two of good lovin' would change your outlook. I bet I could find you a man who could help you relax."

Audrey opened her mouth to reply when she took note of her sister. Maddy wasn't just grinning, her gaze was directed over Audrey's shoulder.

Which meant, they weren't alone.

Well, two could play at that game. "So you didn't get their numbers? You losing your touch?" she asked innocently.

Maddy's gaze locked on her and narrowed. Then she said in a soft voice, "Score for Audrey. But the game isn't over yet, sis."

Chapter 4

Damn.

It was the first thought that went through Caleb's mind as he stared at the fine ass before him. He'd gotten enough of a look that morning to recognize the woman as the same one he'd spotted when they arrived at the auction house.

Audrey Martinez.

If he'd known what a fine specimen she was, Caleb would've made her acquaintance years ago.

He found himself smiling when he caught Audrey's whispered retort to her sister in Spanish. Caleb glanced over at his brother and Clayton to see both of them staring at him.

That wiped the grin from his face. He shot them a confused look and mouthed, "What?"

Neither said a word as they returned their attention to the women.

Caleb adjusted his cowboy hat atop his head as David ambled up. The strain around the older man's eyes had only intensified as the day progressed. He'd asked them not to tell anyone they were trying to fix the cameras, which had seemed like an easy request.

Until some of the employees asked what Brice and Caleb were doing. They were quick to come up with an explanation, however.

Audrey pushed away from the stall and turned to them. Her gaze landed on Caleb first but quickly slid to Clayton. Caleb tried not to be annoyed that his brother-in-law had been granted a smile.

But he was irritated.

"Hello," Audrey said as she walked up to Clayton and held out her hand. "I'm Audrey Martinez."

Clayton clasped her hand briefly. "I've heard a lot about you, Ms. Martinez. I'm Clayton East."

"Please, call me Audrey." Then large, dark eyes widened. "East? As in the East Ranch?"

David chuckled and slapped Clayton on the back. "The very one. I've sold a lot of horses for both Clayton and his father."

"And we've bought a lot of them from you," Clayton added with a grin. He then motioned to Brice and Caleb. "These are my brothers-in-law, Brice and Caleb Harper."

Audrey's gaze moved to Brice, who tipped his hat to her. "Ma'am."

Caleb waited until her eyes were on him before he reached up and touched the edge of his hat. "Nice to meet you."

He found himself awestruck, though he couldn't put a finger on why. He drank in her golden-brown skin, dark eyes, and black hair that denoted Audrey's Spanish heritage.

Her oval face was covered in a light sheen of sweat that

gave it a beautiful glow. He wanted to wipe his thumb over her wide, full lips before he kissed her.

Because he was going to kiss her.

Caleb had never walked away from someone he was attracted to, and he certainly wasn't about to start now. Audrey didn't just have a stunning face, she also had the hourglass figure that always brought him to his knees.

Audrey licked her lips and glanced away. Caleb nearly groaned at the sight of her pink tongue. Then he remembered that they weren't alone. And they were dealing with a very serious situation.

But once everything was in hand, he was going to pursue Audrey.

Caleb winced as Brice slammed his elbow into his ribs. Caleb looked at his brother to find Brice glaring at him.

"Did you find anything?" David asked, breaking the silence.

Audrey shook her head. "Not like I'd hoped. I looked at their blood compared to four other horses here, and while I didn't see anything definitive, I am running another test to see if it will tell me more."

"And if it doesn't?" Caleb asked.

Dark eyes landed on him. "Then I send the samples off to a lab for more in-depth testing."

"First things first," Clayton said. "We stop this from happening to more horses."

Everyone nodded, including Maddy.

"Are the cameras fixed?" Audrey asked.

Brice nodded. "Just about."

Caleb still wasn't happy with what they had discovered about the security system. No wires had been cut. Instead, they found several places where it looked as if someone had surged the lines with electricity—enough to burn them.

"Good. Since I'll be staying overnight," Audrey stated.

David took a step toward her. "Now, I—"

"You called me," Audrey interrupted him. "You brought this to my attention and asked for my help. Did you really think I was just going to take a look and then go about my day?"

David shook his head and lowered his eyes to the ground. "I didn't think you'd stay, but I should've known."

"Yes. You should have."

Maddy was quick to add, "I'll stay with my sister."

"You won't be the only one," Clayton said.

Brice jerked his thumb at Caleb. "He and I will both remain overnight, as well."

"That's not necessary," Audrey began.

"The hell it isn't," David said over her. "I'll feel a sight better knowing that two men will be able to keep you safe. Just in case."

Audrey fought to keep her temper in check. "You forget, David, both Maddy and I can handle ourselves."

He grunted in response. "I know you can, but Brice was a Marine, and Caleb was a Green Beret. They're both staying."

After his announcement, David turned and walked away with Clayton following. Silence grew as the four of them stared at each other.

Finally, Brice said, "I'm going to call Naomi and let her know what's going on."

Caleb nodded to his brother before Brice walked away.

Maddy suddenly looked at him, smiling brightly. "So, Caleb, are you married?"

"No," he said, hiding his smile since he knew what she was doing. "I'm not seeing anyone either."

Maddy cut her eyes to Audrey, who rolled hers and turned away. Caleb watched as Audrey squatted next to her bag and opened it, pulling out a tablet. Then she took it into the stall with the roan and began examining the horse.

"Harper," Maddy said, her eyes narrowed in thought as she stared at Caleb, her head tilted to the side.

Caleb glanced Maddy's way and nodded. "That's right."

"I've heard some of the other horse owners talk about the Rockin' H Ranch," Audrey said without looking at him. "Is that you?"

Pride welled inside him that their ranch was becoming so well known. "It is. Brice and I began it three years ago. He has an eye for horses, and I train them."

Audrey looked over her shoulder at him. She said nothing, which bothered Caleb.

"You started your own ranch?" Maddy asked before Caleb could pose a question to her sister.

He drew in a breath. "I can tell you're surprised by that. Most people are."

"It's just that you could have done it on the East Ranch and used their contacts," Maddy said.

Caleb noticed how Audrey had shifted so she could see him out of the corner of her eye. She had also stilled, as if waiting for his reply.

He lifted a shoulder in a half-shrug. "Before my sister, Abby, married Clayton, we were dirt-poor. We rarely had money to turn on the A/C to cool the house in the summers because we saved it to have heat in the winter. It was nice to live at the East Ranch, but the fact my sister loves and is loved by Clayton is what matters most. We learned a lot living at the ranch, but Brice and I wanted to strike out on our own."

"So you and Brice wanted to make a name for yourselves," Maddy said, smiling.

"Exactly."

Maddy cut her eyes to Audrey as another wordless look passed between the sisters.

As intrigued as he was by the pretty vet, Caleb was also very much aware that something nefarious was going on at the auction house. He was leaning toward someone having done this to the horses because for four of them to fall ill so quickly and at the same time was too coincidental. Which meant, Caleb needed to make sure it didn't happen to any of the other animals.

He walked to the stall and folded his arms atop the rail. "Do you think they were poisoned?"

Audrey turned to face him and lowered the iPad. "If it's a virus, I would expect to find it in more horses. Especially ones that have been in contact with the infected ones."

"But?" Caleb urged.

She shrugged. "If it's poison, it's something new."

"She thinks it's poison," Maddy said as she joined them.

Audrey gawked at her. "Maddy!"

"What?" Maddy asked innocently, shrugging. "You do. I know that look. Besides, if you thought it was a virus, you would have separated the animals who are ill from the healthy ones."

"They are separated," Audrey stated.

Maddy blew out a breath. "More than they already are then. I know you."

There was a tense moment before Audrey sighed loudly and threw up her hands in defeat. "Fine. I think it's poison, but I have to keep my mind open to other possibilities until the final test is finished. I don't want to focus on one thing and miss some detail that could show me it's something else."

The longer Caleb watched her, the more he came to realize why so many ranches fought to have Audrey work for them. There were many good equine veterinarians in the area, but Audrey went the extra mile.

"You'll figure it out," he said.

She looked at him, worry in her deep brown eyes. "I really hope so. These horses are suffering, and I can't stand that."

"Is there anything you can give them to help?"

She pressed her lips together briefly. "Since I've not discovered what it is yet, I could put the horses in danger if I give them something that reacts negatively to poison."

"The music helps," Maddy said.

Caleb saw her about to turn on the music again. "Wait."

"Why?" Audrey asked.

He nodded at the horses. "I want to ease them as much as both of you, but I'm looking at all the angles here. If whatever is happening with the horses isn't natural, then we have to consider that someone is doing this. Obviously, Audrey, that was already on your mind when you had David fix the cameras. But we're going to be here tonight, so let's use that to our advantage."

"That's a good idea," Audrey said.

"If it's a person," he agreed. "They won't know the cameras have been fixed, but more importantly, they won't know that we're all here."

Maddy frowned. "So why can't I turn on the music?"

"Because if whoever it is knows someone is here, they won't come in," Audrey replied.

Caleb smiled at her. "Exactly. We need to remain as quiet as we can."

"What if it isn't someone doing this intentionally?" Maddy asked.

Caleb chuckled softly. "Then we all spend a night watching over the horses."

"Until David closes for the night, I'm going to play music," Maddy stated.

A few moments later, the soft strings of an Asian-inspired song filled the air. Caleb wanted to stay with Audrey and talk to her some more, but he needed to get with Brice and Clayton to figure out a plan.

He nodded to the women and went to find his brother. Just as he suspected, Brice and Clayton were already in deep conversation.

"I was just about to come get you," Brice said.

Caleb looked between them. "What's going on?"

"The security system won't come online," Clayton announced.

"I thought we found the issue," Caleb said. "We can re-route the lines that have been burned."

Brice ran a hand down his face. "That was a ruse so we didn't discover what really took out the cameras."

Unease rolled through Caleb. "And what's that?"

"A virus," Clayton said. "I found it when I was going through the coding."

Brice cracked his knuckles. "Someone who goes to that kind of trouble wants to make sure the cameras aren't working."

"That means, someone is doing this to the horses," Caleb said and looked back to where Audrey was standing.

Chapter 5

"I told you he was hot," Maddy said with a knowing grin.

Audrey didn't look up from her tablet as she made additional notes before heading into the next stall. She needed to concentrate on her job, not think about the incredibly hot cowboy with the gorgeous brown eyes. "You did."

"Oh, come on, Audrey. Even you have to admit they were all pretty good-looking."

Audrey murmured soothingly to the bay gelding as she walked into the stall. After comforting him for several minutes, she said, "Are you including David in that?"

"I've known him all my life. He's more like an uncle. Besides, you know I'm not including him."

Audrey smiled, but it didn't last long as she spotted the swelling on the gelding's front left knee. It wasn't unusual for a horse to take some weight off one leg, which is why she hadn't noticed the swelling sooner.

She squatted down to take a closer look at the knee.

When she put her hand on the horse's leg, he snorted at the same instant his body tensed.

"It's okay, boy. I won't hurt you," she said.

Audrey was careful not to get near the affected area as she inspected it with her eyes. Once the gelding calmed, she managed to get her hand several inches closer before he twitched his head.

"I'm going to fix you," she promised. "You have to trust me."

Another few tense minutes passed before she moved with agonizing slowness until her palm was over the knee. She didn't feel any fluid, so it could just be joint pain. But since this was one of the ill horses, she wasn't sure of anything.

Audrey rubbed her hand softly over the leg again and again. The horse closed his eyes, letting her know that he trusted her. She sat cross-legged and continued to stroke him with one hand while adding notes to the chart on her iPad with the other.

Though she didn't want to leave the bay, Audrey knew she needed to get to the other two horses. She climbed to her feet and ran her hand down the gelding's head to the soft, velvety muzzle.

When she turned to leave, her gaze landed on none other than Caleb Harper. Audrey's heart skipped a beat when she saw his attention on her. She couldn't look away from his brown eyes. They were a unique mixture of dark and light with a band of gold around the iris.

Audrey realized that her breath was coming faster. Her fingers clasped the tablet tightly. How could she not react when faced with such an arresting man?

Because Caleb wasn't just any cowboy. He wore the hat, boots, and jeans like a second skin, but it was the way he stood, the way he took in everything around him that made her aware of him.

Learning he had been in the Army's elite fighting force didn't surprise her. He had that look about him. The bearing of a man who had seen and done a great many things. The look that said he was ready and willing to face any challenge put before him.

And win.

Eyes that had witnessed terrible things were in direct contrast to his sexy grin. His face seemed sculpted from granite with a firm jawline and chin and lips that could make her forget her name with just a smile. From his broad shoulders encased in a tan button-down shirt, to his slim hips and long legs, Caleb was utter perfection.

It was too bad he wasn't grinning at her now.

He opened the stall door and waited for her to walk out before closing it. When she turned to face him, they were inches apart.

"Wh-what's wrong?" she asked, trying to get her bearings with him so close.

He glanced over his shoulder to where Maddy meditated once more. "Is your sister right? Is your gut telling you this is a poison?"

"As I told her I—"

"Your gut," he insisted.

Audrey swallowed and reluctantly nodded. "I still won't rule out anything until the last test comes in."

"Follow your gut, doc," he said and pivoted to leave.

She quickly moved to stop him. "What aren't you telling me?"

"I think it might be better if you don't know."

"I disagree. My sister is here, and I need to know all the facts so we can protect ourselves."

His brow furrowed. "I'll do that."

"I appreciate the thought, but that's not how we Martinezes handle things. Maddy and I take care of ourselves."

Caleb stared at her for a long moment. "Shouldn't we bring her into this conversation so she knows what's going on?"

"No." As soon as Audrey answered, she realized Caleb had tricked her.

He didn't apologize, and she didn't attempt to explain herself. Caleb had a brother, so he knew what siblings would do for each other.

Audrey glanced down at Caleb's belt buckle and noticed the gun holster for the first time. It hadn't been there before. He put his palm on the butt of the gun, and she found her eyes drawn to his long fingers. She gazed up his hand to his bare, tan forearm, stopping where his shirt was rolled up to his elbows.

Never in her life had she ever thought a man's hands sexy. Until that moment.

Her eyes lifted to meet his. "Maddy is as skilled as I am at protecting herself, but she has a tendency to believe the best about everyone."

"While you see the worst?" Caleb asked, his brow quirked.

Audrey twisted her lips and wrinkled her nose. "I like to think I see reality. I've healed enough abused horses and other animals to know the cruelty of mankind."

"I know all about brutality and malice."

Her heart hurt for the pain Caleb allowed her to see before he tamped it down again. She walked to her bag and bent down. Her palm wrapped around the pistol she kept inside. Audrey straightened and showed Caleb the weapon.

"Keep that near you at all times," he cautioned.

She returned it to the bag. "I will. Where will you be?"

"Not far, but I'll be hiding. If anyone does come, they won't see me."

"Just us," Audrey said as she cut her gaze to Maddy. "They'll believe we're here alone."

Caleb walked to stand before her. He waited until she turned her head to him. "You're not alone. I'd offer to sit out here in your place, but I'm pretty sure I know how you'd respond to that."

Audrey couldn't help herself. She smiled at his teasing tone. It wasn't until they had that quick moment of light-heartedness that she realized how much she needed it.

"It's going to be fine," he assured her. "Clayton is guarding the entrance and will alert us if anyone arrives."

That comforted her until she thought about the acres of land the auction house sat on. "You're assuming they'll come from the road."

"We had a look around earlier and saw no signs of a vehicle approaching the area, and I seriously doubt someone would walk over forty acres of land just to get here."

"They could've ridden a horse."

Caleb drew in a breath as a muscle ticked in his jaw. "None of us thought of that. I'll be back."

She watched him as he strode away. When she turned around, Maddy was smiling at her. "Don't say it," Audrey warned her sister.

"I didn't say anything," Maddy said with a knowing smile, but then her smile dropped. "We have to be prepared tonight, don't we?"

"Yeah."

Maddy rubbed her hands together. "I'm ready."

Audrey returned her attention to the horses, but she

looked up frequently, hoping to find Caleb there again. Neither of the other horses had any inflamed joints. After she'd finished with the last animal, she went back over the records for the bay.

She'd done a quick look when she first spotted the swollen knee, but now she wanted to go back through the gelding's records more thoroughly to see if she'd missed something.

Thirty minutes later, she rubbed her eyes and yawned. It was going to be a long night. Normally, she hoped to feel tired so she could sleep. But wouldn't you know it, the one night she needed to stay awake was the one where she wanted to sleep.

Audrey walked from the stall, her gaze moving to where Maddy had set herself up, but her sister was nowhere to be found. Audrey rushed down the walkway, looking in the stalls, hoping to find Maddy.

"Trying to stay awake with some exercise?" Maddy asked as she walked into the stables.

Audrey ignored the question. "Where the hell did you go?"

"Hold up there," Maddy stated. "I told you exactly where I was going."

"No, you didn't."

"Yes, I did. You even grunted in response."

Audrey shook her head. "I would've heard you."

"You did. And you replied. Now, take your damn coffee," Maddy said and held out the brew.

Audrey didn't hesitate to wrap her hand around the cup. A look down confirmed that her sister had fixed it just the way she liked it when she had it—heavy on the milk and sugar.

"Thanks," Audrey said.

Maddy cut her eyes to her and shrugged as she sank to the ground to sit cross-legged. "You act just like Dad, thinking I can't take care of myself. I went through the same training you did."

"Yeah."

They'd had this conversation for the last six years. This was usually the part where Audrey mentioned that if Maddy had used the gun she kept in her purse, she wouldn't have been attacked.

Maddy would then reply that it was the self-defense skills they'd learned that stopped her from being raped that horrible night. Right after that, Audrey usually brought up their mother. And the conversation ended.

There was so much of their mother in Audrey's sister. Maddy, like their mother, didn't hate guns. They both knew how to use a number of them, but they preferred not to.

If only their mom had taken the small pistol from the console of her car. If only she had reached for it. Perhaps then, she could have stopped the men who robbed her and stole the vehicle, leaving their mother on the side of the road to suffer a stroke and die.

"Will you ever stop thinking about it?" Maddy asked angrily.

Audrey didn't pretend that she didn't know what her sister was talking about. "Mom had the weapon for a reason."

"You assume things would've turned out differently had she drawn it."

"They would have."

"She might have shot one of them," Maddy said, shaking her head in agitation. "You and I both know that would've destroyed Mom."

Audrey didn't try to hold back her ire. "Instead, Mom is dead, and Dad is the one who's so destroyed, he took off one day to God only knows where because his heart was so broken that he couldn't go on."

"He'll be back," Maddy stated confidently and gave a firm nod of her head to accentuate the point.

There was no more conversation as Maddy put in her earbuds. Audrey lifted the coffee to her lips and let the liquid slide down her throat as she put the discussion behind her and focused on the task at hand. Audrey wasn't particularly fond of the hot drink, but right now, she needed the caffeine to stay awake.

She turned and saw movement out of the corner of her eye. As soon as she recognized Caleb, she felt her expression softening. She met him halfway and immediately noticed the frown on his face.

"Brice and I brought in two of our friends to help keep watch. I wanted you to meet them, but there isn't time. Their names are Jace and Cooper," he told her.

"You trust them?"

"With my life," he stated.

She wondered what type of man it took to be Caleb Harper's friend. "Were they also in the military?"

"Yes, ma'am. Jace and Cooper have been friends with me and Brice for over fifteen years. I doubt either you or your sister will run into them tonight since they're posted farther out."

Audrey couldn't fathom that kind of friendship. Then again, she'd always found animals much nicer than people, so she generally preferred them.

She looked at the darkening sky. "The employees went home, didn't they?"

"The last one left ten minutes ago. My and Clayton's

trucks have been hidden. The only ones out there now are yours and Maddy's."

"So, it's really begun."

"There's still time for you to leave."

She shook her head. "Not going to happen."

He grinned. "Good."

Audrey didn't want to think about why that one word made her stomach flutter with excitement.

Chapter 6

There was no reason for Caleb to remain, but he still couldn't make himself leave. He hadn't meant to overhear Audrey's conversation with her sister. Now that he had, he couldn't stop thinking about it. He knew all about traumatic events, but since he didn't like talking about his, he wasn't going to ask her to do it.

Audrey looked down at the paper cup in her hand. "You heard me and Maddy arguing, didn't you?"

"It was hard to miss. I wasn't eavesdropping."

"Oh, I know," she hastily replied. "I wasn't accusing you of that."

Caleb looked around Audrey to Maddy, who for all intents and purposes, appeared to be deep in meditation—but he had his doubts. Free spirit or not, Maddy recognized the danger surrounding them. He didn't know her, but she didn't seem like the kind of person who wouldn't take that seriously.

He knew he put in earbuds just so his brother wouldn't

talk to him after an argument like the one he'd just over-heard between Maddy and Audrey, all while still listen-ing to everything Brice had to say. Caleb would bet his half of the ranch that Maddy was doing the same.

"I'm sorry about your mother," he said.

Eyes a deep, earthy brown met his. He saw flashes of copper there, adding more depth to her beautiful orbs.

Audrey drew in a breath, her shoulders rising. "Thanks. It's been hard. More so on my father. My parents had the kind of love you read about but never think to see. When she died, so did a part of him."

"I know the kind of love you speak of. My sister and Clayton found it. As did Brice and Naomi."

"Not you?"

Caleb had been asked that question dozens of times, but somehow, coming from Audrey, it made him really think about the answer for once. "Not yet."

The words came out before he realized it.

Yet?

Why the hell did he say that? He knew better than any-one that he had no intentions of ever settling down. He'd never be able to get past his abandonment issues enough to trust someone with his heart.

Caleb had recognized that when he was still a teenager. It was why he had never seriously dated anyone. The lon-gest he'd been with a woman was two weeks.

He cleared his throat and quickly changed the subject before he reflected any more on a past he wished he could forget. "Have you spoken to your father? Maybe he just needs you and Maddy."

Audrey lowered the cup after a long drink. "Mom passed away two years ago. The day after the funeral,

Maddy and I went to see Dad and found a note that said he was going away for a while. We've not heard from him since."

"What about his cell phone?"

"It's turned off. Believe me, we've tried all kinds of ways to locate him. We spoke to the sheriff's office, who is on the lookout for him, but since Dad left on his own, there isn't much they can do."

Caleb crossed his arms over his chest. "What about a private investigator?"

"It's about to come to that," she admitted. Then she let out a long sigh. "I have this fear—really, it's like a rock in my stomach—that Dad is dead and we just don't know it."

"You think he killed himself?"

She shook her head, the long length of her black ponytail swaying with the movement. "He'd never do that. No, I think if he's gone, it's because he died of a broken heart. My parents always said they couldn't live without each other."

"At least you and Maddy have each other. The bond between siblings can get you through anything."

She blinked, regarding him silently for a moment. "You say that as if it's a fact."

"Because it is. My father died when I was very young. I don't remember him. Mom didn't want to be a mother. She left Abby in charge of Brice and me. The day Abby graduated high school, our mother left. She even left documents giving Abby guardianship of us."

Audrey's face went slack with shock. "How old were you?"

"Six. Brice was eight." It was so damn long ago, but at times, it felt as if it had just happened. That's how Caleb knew he'd never get past it to trust someone enough to love them.

"I'm so sorry," Audrey murmured, sorrow filling her gaze.

Caleb shrugged as if it were nothing—which was a lie—and dropped his arms to his sides. "Abby didn't hesitate to step in and raise us. Life was hard. Every day was a struggle, but we knew we had each other."

"Maddy would say that Karma paid Abby for her good deed by giving her Clayton."

Caleb laughed softly. "Whether it was Karma or not, no one deserved it more than Abby. She sacrificed everything for us. Now, she and Clayton have three amazing kids."

"I'd like to meet her."

"Oh, there's no doubt that you will," Caleb said with a smile.

They looked at each other as the conversation halted. Caleb couldn't find a reason to remain, but he didn't want to leave. He wasn't even out of sorts after telling her about his mother, which was odd. Silence lengthened until they were just staring awkwardly at each other.

"I better get back to my post," he said, wishing there was a reason for him to stay. He liked talking to Audrey. And talking wasn't something he often did with women.

She nodded. "Yeah, of course. And I need to get back to. . . ." Audrey looked around and grinned. "I guess arguing with Maddy until I do another check on the horses."

He started to turn away and remembered the other reason he had come to see Audrey. "Also, don't worry about getting hungry. We have food coming."

She frowned and looked askance at him. "I thought we were trying to keep a low profile."

"Oh, we've got that covered."

"Care to share?" she asked, quirking a brow.

Caleb smiled and found himself moving closer to her. "David, of course."

"Of course," she said with a cynical nod. "Why didn't I think of that?"

Damn, but he liked how she wasn't afraid to say whatever was on her mind. "We're not hiding the fact you're here."

"I still don't see how that'll work. If I was sneaking onto a place, knowing someone was there would scare me off."

"Whoever this is has a mission. They want something, and they won't let you and Maddy being here stop them. Besides, there are plenty of other horses for them to get to."

She pursed her lips together. "I have to admit, you've got a point."

"I asked David where these horses were when they got sick. None were in the stables."

Audrey twisted her lips ruefully. "It was the first thing I asked him when I arrived."

Caleb wasn't at all surprised by her statement. Ranches all over the county tried to outbid each other to have her work for them. She wasn't just good at her job, she also had a way with horses. That was a true gift. "You worry about the horses. We'll do the rest."

"I'll do whatever it takes so that no more horses become ill."

Caleb fought the urge to touch her. He hadn't yet figured out what kept him coming back to her. It was an odd sort of feeling. The kind that fixed the beautiful vet in his thoughts whether he wanted her there or not.

And he wasn't sure he did.

He'd bedded more women than he wanted to admit. Each had something different that appealed to him—a wonderful smile, great hair, an amazing laugh, or an adventurous spirit. Not one of them had been able to hold his interests for longer than a day or so.

And *many* had tried.

He'd once tried to explain to a woman why he couldn't have a relationship, but she refused to accept anything he said. It became easier to make sure no one got the impression that he wanted more than one night with them. He hated hurting anyone, but he knew that's what it would come to if he stuck around.

Caleb glanced at the horses. "The rest of us are here so you don't have to do anything more than figure out what has made the animals sick."

"I will."

"Maybe we'll get lucky and catch the bastard tonight. I'll get him to tell us what was used."

Her lips curved into a wide smile. "Just make sure I'm there to help you get it out of him."

"Yes, ma'am," he said and tipped his hat at her.

Caleb made himself walk away this time. This was way out of character for him. Attraction, he knew well. He was a master at flirting and wooing women.

Yet when he was with Audrey, his mind switched between wanting to kiss her and needing to learn every detail about her.

He returned to his hiding place that gave him views of the girls in the stable as well as anyone approaching from the side. He'd just settled in when his phone vibrated in his pocket. Caleb withdrew it and looked down at the text from Brice that said:

NOW I KNOW WHY YOU WANTED THAT POSITION NEAR
THE STABLES.

Irritation spiked through Caleb, and he quickly replied
with: YOU KNOW NOTHING.

I KNOW QUITE A LOT, LITTLE BROTHER. WAIT UNTIL THIS
IS OVER BEFORE YOU MAKE AUDREY ANOTHER ONE OF
YOUR CONQUESTS.

Caleb blew out an angry breath. GIVE ME SOME CREDIT.
He put away his phone. Brice would rag on him for
hours if Caleb didn't put a stop to it. They could pick it up
later, but right now, his attention needed to be on the area
and anyone who approached.

Not that Caleb expected anyone this early. It would be
some hours yet before anyone showed up—because they
would. He knew it in his gut. And when they did, he was
going to be ready.

It might have been a few years, but doing this brought
back his time with the Army. To his surprise, he discovered that there was a lot he missed.

The men in his unit were amazing soldiers, and they
were a tightknit group. A small part of Caleb had found
the adventurous, grueling life as a Green Beret right up his
alley. But it wasn't long before the missions took their toll.

When Caleb realized that he was experiencing the very
things that had driven Clayton from the SEALS, he'd
known it was time to get out. The thing was, Caleb was
damn good at being a soldier.

He was even better as a rancher. Being out on the land
and working with the horses soothed the mental, emo-
tional, and physical wounds he'd sustained while in the

military. There was no other life for him than the one he had now.

But every once in a while, he was reminded why he'd become a Green Beret. Tonight was one of those times. It didn't matter how long it had been since he wore the uniform, the training he'd received would always be with him.

Just as Clayton kept himself in shape, so did Brice and Caleb. The three sparred regularly, often including Jace and Cooper. They might live in a quiet part of Texas, but they'd all learned the hard way that things came for them when they least expected it.

His phone buzzed again, but Caleb ignored it since it was probably just Brice. He focused on the night, listening to the animals as they moved around to learn what sounds were normal for the auction house so he'd be able to tell when something was off.

Two hours went by before he saw the flash of headlights from a vehicle turning into the drive. Caleb palmed his gun and swung his gaze to the stables. Audrey was with one of the horses, talking to it and brushing it.

Maddy yanked the earbuds from her ears and jumped up just as David strolled into the barn from the other side. He and Maddy exchanged a few words as she took the bags of food from him. Then, Audrey was with them. She looked over her shoulder, her gaze moving right over him. But Caleb knew she couldn't see him.

He had been designated as the one to get food from the girls and sneak it to the others, but he didn't move. He watched the friendly way Audrey interacted with David, and the genuine concern she showed for the horses.

Caleb wondered if any other equine vet would be as dedicated as Audrey was to the task of healing these horses before they died. His thoughts abruptly halted when Maddy walked out of the stables with David. A moment later, two vehicles drove off.

He kept to the shadows and made his way over to where Audrey waited. She held out the bags that had sandwiches and bottles of water inside.

"Maddy went back to the house to get the results of the last test I ran," she said before he could even ask.

Caleb grinned. "I was that obvious, huh?"

"Not at all. Since I need the results, it gave me the excuse I needed to get Maddy back home and away from all of this." Audrey's dark gaze slid away.

He took the bags from her, their fingers brushing against each other as he did. Something hot and electric ran through him, making it difficult to breathe. "I understand."

Their gazes met and held.

Chapter 7

Say something!

Yet, Audrey couldn't find any words. Then Caleb was walking away, disappearing into the darkness once more. Usually, she liked being alone with the horses, but she enjoyed having the hot cowboy near.

Caleb made her feel flustered and excited. But he also made her feel safe. Like she didn't have to constantly be on guard—and it was a wonderful feeling.

Not that she didn't stay alert, but with Caleb and the others out there keeping watch, Audrey was able to keep her attention on the horses. Though, to her surprise, she found her thoughts turning again and again to Caleb Harper.

Audrey finished up another check of the horses and discovered that each of their heart rates was above sixty beats per minute, which was an indication of dehydration. She then checked their gums by opening each horse's mouth and pressing gently on the soft tissue. When the color didn't return immediately, it was another sign that the animals were dangerously dehydrated.

She'd been listening for shallow breathing, which would have let her know that they needed water, but they had yet to exhibit that. Which could be an effect of the poison.

Since dehydration in horses could be deadly, she had to act quickly. Audrey had no choice but to give the four animals fluids intravenously. She worked swiftly, moving from one horse to the next until all four were seen to.

Since she'd arrived, the animals hadn't moved more than to shift from side to side. She checked the fluids often because while dehydration was dangerous, too much liquid had the same effect.

An hour later, Audrey noticed a remarkable change in the horses. They started to become more aware of their surroundings, their ears shifting with sounds. They still didn't move around or eat, but they did turn their heads toward her when she entered their stalls.

It was a vast improvement, and one she would gladly take. But it was also one she feared was a short fix, like a Band-Aid over a cut. Until she knew if it was poison causing the distress, whatever it was would continue to slowly kill the horses. She was just thankful that they were all still alive.

But her time was running out. Audrey was all too aware of that. If she didn't learn something tonight, there was a good chance that she'd lose one or more of the animals.

She yanked her phone out of her back pocket when it rang. Relief surged through her when she saw Maddy's name. "Hey."

"Hey," her sister said around a mouthful of food. "So, I'm here."

Audrey prayed for patience as she gripped the phone tighter. "Annnnnd?"

Without another reply, Maddy began reading off the results. Audrey rushed to her tablet and opened a blank document to quickly type in what her sister told her.

"Want me to come back out there?" Maddy asked.

Audrey frowned as she looked over what she had typed. "Let me read these back to you to make sure I got everything straight."

"Sure."

Audrey went through each line, waiting for Maddy to give the all-clear that she had taken the information down correctly. She hesitated.

Maddy asked, "What's wrong? I know that pause. You've found something."

"I've found nothing. That's the problem."

"Oh."

Audrey squeezed her eyes closed. "I need to look at this some more. Keep your phone with you and the ringer on in case I need you to bring me something."

"You've got this, Audrey."

Audrey smiled into the phone. "Thanks."

"Now, go eat while you're looking at this because I know you well enough to know that you've not touched the food David brought."

Audrey inwardly winced as she looked over at the sandwich still wrapped and waiting near her bag.

"Your silence says it all." Maddy sighed. "Eat, or else!"

The phone went dead. Audrey put it back into her pocket and made her way to the food. She lowered herself to the ground and leaned back against a stall as she reached for the sandwich. She unwrapped it and sank her teeth into it

as she tried to reconcile the results of the test with the information she had—and the symptoms of poisoning.

"She's here."

Phil smiled as he looked at the SUV parked at the auction house. "Everything is going to plan."

"But is she alone?"

Phil whipped his head around to face Zeke and glared
at him. Normally, the nineteen-year-old never hesitated to
do a job. The fact that he had any reluctance at all didn't
sit well with Phil. "Maybe I should've brought Ricardo
with me instead."

Zeke's nostrils flared in anger. "You're such an asshole."

"And you're still a kid. Learn how to have a comeback
without resorting to name-calling. It's childish."

Phil watched as the youngster fought not to release the
string of obscenities that likely filled his mouth. Even in
the dark, Phil could see the red blotches on Zeke's face
from his rising anger. The bright red matched his hair.

Phil had tried to make Zeke dye it, but he'd refused.
Oddly enough, Zeke was proud of his hair color. Something about his Irish heritage. Phil could not care less. The
simple fact was that it was a color that people remembered.

As a compromise, Zeke wore a beanie to hide the bright
hue. But all it would take was someone yanking the hat
off to reveal what was underneath.

"Let's get this over with," Zeke stated as he got to his feet.

When Zeke rose to cross the road to the auction house,
Phil grabbed his arm and jerked him back down. Phil eyed
the business. The vet was there just as they'd planned, but
was she alone?

Zeke tugged his arm free, his lip curling with his fury.
"Now you want to wait?"

"Do you know why I've never been caught? Because I'm careful. You said you wanted to learn from me, so stop giving me lip and learn. Otherwise, it will be Ricardo coming back with me."

Zeke snorted. "No, he won't. He can't stand the idea of hurting the horses."

Phil slowly turned his head to the kid. "Don't fuck with me. You won't like the consequences."

Immediately, the cocky smile vanished from Zeke's face. "Yes, sir."

Phil nodded, then went back to studying the building. After another ten minutes of not seeing any movement, he motioned for Zeke to go to the left.

They remained crouched and crossed the road. Phil pulled his facemask down while he skirted around an armadillo that was searching for food. Once in the parking lot, Phil ran to the vet's SUV.

She had no writing on the side of the vehicle proclaiming her name and profession as most mobile veterinarians did. But everyone still knew the charcoal gray SUV was hers.

"Audrey Martinez," he mumbled as he looked through the window into the cab.

Phil released a long breath and turned to the metal office building. He shook his head at the shabby structure. It was crude and simple. If this were his place, he'd have taken some of the profits and constructed something much grander.

Instead, Warner had used his money to help fund one of the places that rescued horses from all over the nation. Though, all the animals that came to the auction house were treated like royalty. David made sure only the best hay, feed, and structures were used.

His care for the animals was why everyone in the seven surrounding counties used the auction house to buy and sell their livestock. Warner had even gone so far as to install a security system after some feed had been stolen.

But Phil had made sure the system wasn't operational. It didn't matter to him that Warner often forgot to turn it on. He wanted to be sure that it couldn't be used.

Phil peered around the SUV and looked toward the stables. The lights were on inside. Audrey would have separated the sick animals. It was easy for him to dodge the beam of the security lights outside and make his way to the stables.

He couldn't see the vet when he looked inside, which meant that she was most likely in one of the stalls. There were no sounds of movement. At three in the morning, she was likely dozing.

His gaze landed on the case that she carried everywhere. Phil pulled out a small bottle from his pocket and wrapped his fingers around it. He cautiously slipped around the entrance, flattening his body against the wall. Slowly, he made his way toward the bag, glancing into the stalls as he went.

When he reached the horse, he couldn't help but smile at the sight. It wouldn't be long now before the first one they'd infected died.

When he reached the next stall, he found Audrey. She was propped up in the corner, her head lolling to the side as she slept. She was a pretty thing. Very pretty.

It was too bad Phil didn't have more time to spend with her. He turned to the open bag and held his hand over it. Just as he released the vial, he saw something out of the corner of his eye.

The fist came right for his face. He dodged to the side,

rolling to his feet. Pain exploded in his jaw, letting him know that he hadn't avoided the punch entirely.

Phil glared at the man who had surprised him. Years of such work made Phil hyper-alert to any sounds or movement. How the hell had he not realized that there was someone else there?

The man's brown eyes were full of delight at finding him. The way he stood, his feet planted and arms up at the ready, indicated his opponent was someone who knew how to fight.

One of the reasons Phil had never been caught was because he knew when to walk away—or in this case, run. At least he had delivered what he needed to. All he could hope for was that Zeke had done the same.

The splintering sound of a gunshot behind the stables pierced the silence and made Phil's blood run cold. The man didn't so much as flinch, but there was a gasp from within the stall, and Audrey jumped to her feet a second later.

She looked at the man, then her head turned to him. Phil knew he had to get away, and fast. He wasn't sure he could outrun his attacker, and the fact that there was someone else out there with a gun was troubling.

A loud neigh sounded, and then the ground trembled. The next second, a rush of horses roared past. Some came charging through the stables.

He waited until the man jumped into a stall to avoid being crushed, then Phil turned and ran from the stables alongside some of the horses. He didn't care that he might get trampled. He wasn't going to get caught. By anyone, much less the man who'd punched him.

The others would likely be trying to round up the horses, which limited the number of those who could follow him. He glanced behind him and saw nothing but a cloud of dust that would help aid his getaway. Phil really regretted the cigarettes he'd smoked for most of his life as his lungs burned from the exertion. Every beat of his legs made it feel as if his heart would burst from his chest.

But he didn't stop or slow until he reached the meeting place he'd designated in case he and Zeke ran into trouble. Phil's legs crumpled, and he fell to the ground, sucking in mouthfuls of air and wondering if Zeke had been caught.

But at least his mission had been accomplished. His employer would be exceedingly happy.

Chapter 8

He'd had him. It galled Caleb that he'd had the intruder, but the man had gotten away. Caleb had intended to go after him, but with the stampede and the dust that followed, it was impossible.

Without hesitation, both he and Audrey exited the stalls and began rounding up the horses. Within moments, Clayton, Cooper, and Jace were with them.

It took another forty minutes before the horses were back in the corrals. That's when Caleb realized that Brice hadn't been helping. Caleb glanced around, looking for some sign of his brother.

"He's fine," Jace was quick to say, even before Caleb could ask about Brice. "He headed off toward the back of the property."

Caleb looked into the darkness where Brice had been hiding. "What happened?"

"Someone tried to inject one of the horses with something."

Audrey hurried to them. "Did you say inject? Is the syringe still there?"

Jace shrugged. "Maybe. Couldn't see much in the stampede."

Caleb's gut twisted at the mention of the syringe. He pointed at his friend. "Stay here. We'll be back."

"Head toward the northwest side of the property," Jace called as Caleb and Audrey ran off.

Caleb blinked against the brightness of the light from Audrey's phone that she was using as a flashlight.

"Sorry," she said. "I can't see in the dark like you."

They shared a quick grin. He was still wound up from seeing the man looking at her. The mask might have covered his face, but there was no denying the need he'd seen in the intruder's eyes.

Caleb ran faster when he saw Brice kneeling on the ground, looking at something. His brother lifted his head as they approached. With one look, Caleb knew Brice wasn't injured.

"I'm sorry," Brice said to Audrey, his lips twisting with regret.

Caleb frowned at the words until his gaze lowered to the ground and he saw the syringe smashed to bits.

Audrey blew out a breath as she picked up the pieces that were left, examining each one. "Damn. So close."

That's when Caleb remembered something. "Your bag. The guy dropped something into your satchel."

"There were two of them?" Brice asked with a deep frown.

Caleb nodded, but his attention was on Audrey.

She took a step back. "He put something in my bag?"

"A small bottle."

Without another word, she turned and ran back to the

stables. Caleb had only taken two steps when he looked over to find Brice right beside him.

Somehow, Audrey's vet kit had only been kicked a few times. That was probably because it had been up against the stall and out of the way. The contents were still inside. Audrey paused when her phone started beeping loudly.

"It's the alarm to check the horses," she told them as she set aside what was left of the syringe and shut it off. She glanced at the bag, her lips twisting in concern.

Caleb stood next to her. "Want me to pull out the contents and tell you what each of them is while you check on the horses?"

"Yes, please."

Their gazes met, and she shot him a grateful smile. When Caleb squatted to begin, his brother went down on his knees, smiling widely.

"What the hell is wrong with you?" Caleb asked irritably. "Did you hit your head on something?"

Brice chuckled, the smile remaining. "Nope."

Caleb ignored his brother as he cautiously reached for the first item in the bag, calling out what it was and then setting it aside on the ground beside him. Alcohol wipes, bandages, sanitizing towelettes, iodine swab-sticks, exam gloves, a cotton roll, eye wash, pocket scalpel, and bandage scissors were some of the items he laid out. Brice joined in, and between both of them, they were finished emptying the bag fairly soon.

Audrey frowned at the items as she moved from one stall to another. "You said a vial. That means the rest of my things can go back into the bag."

"It was one of these," Caleb said and picked up a small glass container.

Brice rubbed a hand over his chin. "Do you think he

might have been trying to take it and returned it when he saw you?"

"No." Caleb looked at the vial in his hand. "I saw him walk into the stables and stare at Audrey."

Her face appeared over the stall. "He stared at me?" she asked, stricken by the thought.

Caleb nodded, anger rising each time he thought of the bastard looking at her with such hunger. The same craving Caleb felt. "Then he leaned over the bag and dropped one of these."

"Then one of them isn't mine," she said, indicating the glass bottles with a nod of her head.

Caleb gathered all six of them and got to his feet. He set them atop one of the empty stalls on the opposite side of the stables and stood back, crossing his arms over his chest.

"I had him," he said in a low voice as Brice walked up beside him.

His brother removed his cowboy hat long enough to scratch his head. "And I had the other."

"Mine shouldn't have gotten away."

Brice blew out a breath and hooked his thumbs in his belt loop. "We can do this all day."

"I laid hands on him. Well, one fist, but still." Caleb glanced to where the altercation had happened. "I shouldn't have let him get away."

"It wasn't your fault. The other intruder released the horses after I shot at him."

Caleb looked at his brother. "Did you find your mark?"

"I was sure I did. I saw the asshole spin around as if struck, but the next thing I knew, the horses were running free. I lost him in the stampede. So, I went looking for any signs of blood. That's when I spotted the syringe."

Audrey walked up then. She peeled off her latex gloves and stuffed them into her pocket. "Do you know if the guy got the dose into the horse? I'm hoping he didn't, but if there was any liquid left in the syringe, it got lost when the horses trampled it."

"I'm sorry, doc, I don't," Brice said.

She shrugged. "It's okay."

But Caleb knew it wasn't. Four horses were suffering, and their best chance of stopping the men had been foiled.

"Do you remember the horse the attacker was after?" Audrey asked Brice.

His brother nodded, and they walked from the stable across to the corrals. Brice opened the gate to the enclosure and brought a white gelding to him and Audrey. She climbed over the fencing and began looking the horse over using a flashlight.

After a few minutes, she smiled at them. "He appears okay, but I'd like to keep him with the other four just in case."

Caleb opened the gate for Brice to walk the gelding out. Once Audrey was clear, he closed it and fell in step with her behind his brother.

"Are we sure there were only two intruders?" Audrey asked.

Brice pushed his hat back on his head. "Clayton saw two men cross the road. Neither I nor Jace or Cooper saw anyone else come toward us."

Caleb wished he'd used his gun on the guy, but he hadn't wanted to startle the horses, especially since Audrey had been inside one of the stalls.

"How are they?" Brice asked about the animals when they reached the stables, and he put the white gelding in an empty stall.

Audrey flattened her lips. "I had a little hope when the fluids perked them up, but that didn't last. The results from my blood test were inconclusive, which puts me right back where I was. I'm going to have to send the blood samples off for more tests. I just hope we have the time for that."

"You got this," Caleb said as he motioned to the vials. "Maybe whatever the intruder left in your bag will give you answers."

Brice peered closer at the bottles. "They all look the same."

"I wouldn't have thought anything was amiss had Caleb not seen the guy," Audrey admitted.

Caleb dropped his arms to his sides. "They wanted you to use whatever is in the vial they brought."

"It could be the poison," Brice said.

Fury flashed in Audrey's eyes. "I'm going to test the contents of each vial and figure out which one is different. Then I can determine what it is they attempted to get me to use."

"How long will that take?" Caleb asked.

Her face fell. "Too damn long. I need to stay with the horses."

"You're not using any of these vials," Brice stated. "Give me a list of anything you need to replace them. I'll run to your place and pick them up for you. I need to go check on Naomi anyway."

"That would be amazing. Thank you," Audrey said. She started to turn away then stopped. "Can I text it to you? I never carry paper."

Brice laughed. "No problem."

Caleb watched as his brother put his number in Audrey's phone. A moment later, she sent a text with the info. Caleb couldn't believe that he hadn't thought of doing just that. Normally, he was thinking of multiple ways to entice a woman to his bed. What the hell was wrong with him that he had missed a prime opportunity?

He'd been too damn worried about her safety to think of getting her out of her clothes, that's what.

Brice shot him a cocky smile when Audrey turned away that felt like rubbing salt in an open wound. Not that Caleb was worried about his brother pursuing Audrey. Brice and Naomi were so sickeningly in love that Caleb couldn't be around them for very long.

It reminded him of when Abby and Clayton had first gotten together. He'd gotten used to them. He would eventually get used to Brice and his sister-in-law's love talk and kisses, as well.

Audrey turned away, covering her mouth as she yawned. She looked dead on her feet, her worry adding lines of strain around her eyes and mouth.

"Get some rest," Caleb offered. "I'll watch over the horses."

"I can't ask you to do that."

Caleb lifted his shoulders to his ears and raised his brows at the same time. "I'm going to be here. You can listen to my stories, which aren't that great. Or you can get some sleep. I promise to wake you if anything changes."

She yawned again. "I want nothing more than to sleep, but I don't think I'll be able to now."

He sat against the stall, looking toward the ill horses. Then he patted the ground. "Sit, doc. I'm not going anywhere."

Audrey only hesitated a moment before she lowered herself to the ground. She leaned her head back and sighed. "I'm going to need to check the rest of the horses to make sure they're all fine after being let out."

"Let them settle down a bit. A few have some minor scratches, but I didn't see anything worse than that. Neither did the others, or they would've told you."

"I didn't see anything either, but you're right. They need to settle down," Audrey admitted. She turned her head to him. "Thank you, by the way. I'm glad you were here and saw the intruder."

He grinned at her before looking away. "Just doing what needed to be done. I'm sorry I wasn't able to catch him."

"You would have, had the horses not been let loose. It was just bad luck."

"There's been enough of that. You and the horses needed a break, and it slipped through my fingers."

"*Our* fingers," she corrected.

His eyes slid back to her. There was something about that word that did strange things to him. "Our fingers."

She faced front. "I've been pretty lucky as a vet. I've been able to help so many animals, but I'm sitting here watching these horses slowly get worse right before my eyes, and I can't get the answers I need fast enough. If I give them the wrong medicine, it might speed up the poison, or they could have a reaction to the drug and die."

"Horses are magnificent creatures. They can do some pretty amazing things, but their bodies are delicate," Caleb said.

She straightened her legs, crossing her ankles. "That is so true. There's very little room for error."

"Why did you become an equine vet versus a regular vet?"

"My father put me on my first horse before I could walk. My mother used to show horses, and my father was a farrier. They met at an event Mom participated in and were together every day after."

Caleb shifted to get more comfortable. "So you've always been around horses."

"Yes. Perhaps that's where I got my passion for them. But I love all animals. As far back as I can remember, I was finding wounded animals and saving them. My parents indulged me, locating people who rehabilitated whatever animal I had found so I could learn. But everything always came back to the horses. I never hesitated in my pursuit to become an equine vet."

"You're certainly in a great area for it."

She lifted one shoulder in a shrug. "It pays well, I won't deny that."

"I've heard you're the top equine vet around." He watched as her lips lifted in a smile filled with pleasure that made his balls tighten with unabashed hunger.

She glanced his way, her dark eyes meeting his. "I wouldn't say that. There are others just as good as I am."

"I'm not too sure of that. I know you have your pick of who you work for. When Brice and I began our ranch, I heard nothing but good things about you. I'd planned to call and see if you wanted to be our vet, but Naomi was quick to point out that you were well and truly taken by two other ranches."

"You wanted to hire me?"

Her surprise made Caleb smile. For someone who was so good at their job, she was remarkably humble. Caleb was beginning to wonder if there was anything about Audrey he didn't like. This was something new for him, and he knew he was traversing unknown waters.

Yet he waded in eagerly.

Chapter 9

"You wanted to hire me?"

Audrey heard the words come out high-pitched and laced with surprise. Of all the things she'd thought Caleb might say, that hadn't been one of them.

He wanted to hire her. That made her ridiculously happy. And she really wished he would've called her. She might very well have taken the job.

The thought of working with Caleb, of seeing him nearly every day, made her smile inwardly. In the short time she'd been around him, she'd seen the respect others had for him. And based on what she'd heard, he was one of the most skilled horse trainers some had ever seen.

Yep. Audrey definitely would have worked for Caleb.

He grinned, confusion flashing in his brown eyes. "You say that as if you're surprised."

"I am."

"Surely, you know you're one of the most highly coveted equine vets in the county."

She shook her head. "I don't know about that. But why didn't you contact me?"

"It's pretty common knowledge that with your work at the Bremer and Hopkins farms, that they don't take kindly to you working anywhere else."

She winced. "Unfortunately, that's true. I work exclusively with both of them—though they know about each other. But that means I can't work for any other ranches. I am able to do my work at the rescue, but only because I was doing that before I went to work for either of them. However, if they knew I was here? That would cause some problems."

"Why do you work for them then? You should be able to help out friends if you want."

Audrey opened her mouth to answer, but she realized that her reasons weren't really valid. "I'll tell you what I tell Maddy. Both ranches keep me very busy. They're well known, and they never question anything I ask for in regards to the horses."

"And the reason you tell yourself?" he urged.

She licked her lips and glanced away. "Remember how I told you I saved animals?"

"Yeah."

"It's never stopped. I have a small area at the house that I share with Maddy. It's a little clinic that I use for friends and neighbors who want me to see their animals. I continue working for Bremer and Hopkins because the pay is amazing, and it allows me to work for free at the horse rescue. I'm able to purchase the medicines and supplies needed to tend to the abused and neglected animals."

Caleb removed his hat and ran his hand through his hair. Audrey's gaze was drawn to him. His light brown locks were on the longer side, feathering against his scalp with a brush of his fingers.

She knew when she wore a hat for even half an hour, she had hat head, but not Caleb. Despite being out in the heat all day and night, he didn't look dirty, tired, or fatigued in any way.

He looked . . . amazing. And downright gorgeous.

Unlike her.

Audrey could feel the dried sweat covering her. Not to mention, she didn't need to look in a mirror to know that she appeared as frazzled and exhausted as she felt. Not exactly a great showing.

"The rescue place sounds like something Brice and I would like to get involved in. And I know Clayton would, as well. We've made treks down to the Gulf when the hurricanes hit to help out with the horses and cattle left behind." His head rolled against the wood until he met her gaze.

She hadn't been looking for any help, but the idea that they were interested made her giddy. "That would be amazing."

"Get me the information whenever you can. Clayton is also really good at getting people to donate money," he added with a grin.

Audrey leaned forward and crossed her legs. He wasn't just hot, he was also generous. A man after her own heart. She needed to be careful with him. He'd not only affected her body and mind but now her heart, as well. "I'll definitely do that."

"How many ranches have you worked at?" he asked.

She stifled another yawn. "I've worked for three ranches since I started. I quit working for one horse ranch because the owner threatened to fire me if I continued sharing my time with the rescue horses. There is something to be said for knowing the ins and outs of an establishment. I'm able to know every detail about the horses and can stave off most injuries before they even happen."

"But?"

She shifted to face Caleb. "Both Bremer and Hopkins approached me not long after I quit the first ranch. I decided it might be better to split my time between two places. They grudgingly agreed with that and how I spent my spare time. It's worked for several years, but things don't always go smoothly."

"Why not have an open practice and see anyone and everyone?"

Audrey bit her lip. "It sounds bad, but it comes down to money. By working for a ranch, I have a steady position and a constant paycheck. That wouldn't be the case if I worked for myself."

"Perhaps not," Caleb said. "But you'd be your own boss. You'd get to dictate what was done when and who you work for."

"You sound like my sister," Audrey said with a laugh.

Caleb smiled and went back to looking at the horses.

Audrey nervously picked at her jeans. Finally, she got up the nerve to ask, "Who did you ultimately decide to use as a vet?"

"Mac Miller. He works with Clayton and his father, so we trust him. But he's all but retired. Brice and I are going to have to search for a new vet soon."

"I'll do it."

The words were out of her mouth before she realized what she'd said. But once uttered, Audrey didn't want to retract them.

Caleb's gaze jerked back to her. "What of Bremer and Hopkins?"

"Who cares?" she said with a shrug. Then she barked out a laugh. "Oh, my God. That felt really good to say."

"We'd love to have your services, but I won't hold you to this. You're tired and under a lot of strain right now."

She gaped at him, offended and outraged that he would question her. "I mean what I say."

"I have no doubt," he hastened to add. "I'm just giving you a way out if you need it."

She lifted her chin. "I won't."

"Good," he said with one side of his lips lifted in a grin.

Their gazes locked, held. Audrey was all too aware that they were sitting close enough to touch—and how she very much wanted to reach over and put her hand on his arm. Maybe feel the muscles beneath her palm. Perhaps even be drawn against his chest.

Audrey sighed as she imagined doing all of those things. She inwardly gave herself a shake and jumped to her feet to check on the horses. The chestnut who had been sick the longest hung his head, his eyes closed. She walked into the stall and talked to him, but the animal didn't appear to hear her.

"He doesn't look good," Caleb said from the door.

She shook her head and ran her hands over the horse's back, worry knotting her stomach. "He's cold."

"Cold?" The shock in Caleb's voice echoed her own.

Within moments, Caleb was beside her. He put his hand next to hers to feel the gelding shivering. The temperatures had dropped from the upper nineties to the mid-eighties once the sun went down, but that shouldn't have been enough to cause the horse to shake.

The chestnut let out a sigh and crumpled to the ground. He went down hard, as if his legs had given out. He rolled to his side and lay still. Audrey remained calm and checked his vitals, despite knowing that this was a very bad sign.

Caleb rushed to get a blanket. They covered the horse, both kneeling next to him.

"His breathing is shallow," she said. Her gaze swung to Caleb. "I don't know what to give him, but if I don't do something, he's going to die."

Caleb glanced over his shoulder at the vials. "You might grab the wrong one."

"Or give him something that harms him instead of helps. I hate feeling this helpless." Her heart was slamming against her chest, her stomach roiling.

Caleb covered her hand with his. His palm was large and callused and comforting. "Sometimes, things are out of our hands."

"I don't think I can accept that."

Caleb's gaze was filled with sorrow. "You don't have a choice."

She frowned at his use of words. Then she looked back at the chestnut to find that he had stopped breathing. Emotion rose up so swiftly that it choked her.

Her heart sank with realization. She was supposed to save him. She'd failed, but she'd be damned if she did the same with the others.

"I'm so sorry," she told the horse as she stroked the side of his neck.

She didn't pull away when Caleb put an arm around her and drew her against him. The longer she looked at the deceased animal, the more determined she became to figure out what poison had been used.

Because if she didn't do something soon, she might be standing over two more dead horses tomorrow.

She sniffed and wiped at her face, but she didn't pull away from Caleb. It felt good to be comforted, to have someone to share the pain with.

"What can I do?" Caleb asked softly.

She nodded, her mind working through everything. "I've taken blood, but I've found nothing. The syringe didn't have anything left in it to help, and while we have the vials, I need to test each one to figure out exactly what's inside. Until I can get to that, I need to do a necropsy."

"Tell me what you need. I'll get it."

Audrey looked around, her mind racing. "I have everything I need to do the procedure. I just need a place to do it. Somewhere more private."

"You start prepping everything, and I'll contact David. What else?" Caleb asked.

She got to her feet. "Everything I need is in my SUV."

Caleb gave a nod as he rose. "Good. Anything else?"

"Once I've done the necropsy, I'm going to need to run tests on everything."

"I have an idea about that, but first, let me call David and find a place for you to work."

He walked away, her eyes following him. Caleb wasn't just a badass, he was also kind and bighearted. He hadn't belittled her sorrow at losing the gelding or berated her for not finding the source before the animal died. And he'd comforted her.

When Caleb disappeared around a corner, Audrey turned back to the horses. "I need y'all to stay with me. Help me. We'll work together and sort this out," she told them.

Audrey reached for her phone and called Maddy. Her sister answered on the fourth ring, her sluggish voice alerting Audrey to the fact that she'd been asleep.

"I know it's early, Maddy, but one of the horses just died."

Maddy quickly asked, "What do you need?"

"Get a pen and paper. There are a few things I don't have quite enough of here to do the testing."

They went over the list several times. Audrey added a few more items, wanting to have them just in case.

"Let me get dressed and get this, and then I'll be on my way," Maddy said.

Audrey smiled into the phone. "Thanks, sis. Would it be too much to ask for you to get everyone food?"

"Don't worry. I'll take care of everything. Just tell me that the night was uneventful. Because if you'd caught the jerks, you would've called me."

Audrey almost didn't want to tell Maddy because she knew her sister would be pissed that she'd not only missed out on catching the men but also that Audrey hadn't called her before now. "Two men came. One put something in my bag. Caleb hit him, but he got away when Brice shot at the other one, who released the horses. Neither was caught."

"Well, that just . . . sucks."

Audrey laughed at her sister's outrage that resulted in such a calm reply. "Yeah, it really does."

"Hang tight. I'll be there soon."

Audrey hung up and blew out a breath as she walked back to her SUV to gather everything she'd need for the necropsy. Audrey often got irritated with Maddy for not having a career and doing more with her life, but she couldn't ask for a better sister. When the stakes were high, or Audrey needed her the most, Maddy never let her down.

That's why, when there was still no sign of her sister an hour later, Audrey knew that something was wrong.

Chapter 10

Caleb watched as Jace used the bucket loader of the tractor to lift the dead horse and take it to the back of the property where David had told him about an empty section of a building.

"I know that look on your face," Brice said as he walked up. "You think there's trouble."

Caleb's gaze swung to Audrey as she paced the parking lot behind her SUV. Every few minutes, she'd bring her cell phone to her ear as she tried her sister again.

"I don't believe in coincidences. Maddy not answering her phone isn't a good sign," he said.

Cooper drained a bottle of water as he walked to them. "I agree with Caleb. Too many things happening."

Brice leaned an arm on the metal fence of the corral. "Someone really wants to do David harm."

"Or not." Caleb looked between his brother and his friend. "After last night, those men know we're on to them. Even if we don't know why they're hurting the horses, they'll realize we've figured out the sick horses didn't get that way on their own. That puts David in the clear."

Jace grunted in confusion. "Does it? I don't see that."

"In my mind, David is their target. This is his auction house. He's responsible for the animals," Brice said.

Caleb pulled his keys from his pocket, his anxiety over finding out why Maddy wasn't there yet high. "We can debate this later. I'm going to go look for Maddy."

"Want some help?" Brice asked.

Caleb shook his head. "I'd rather everyone stay and guard Audrey as well as the rest of the horses. I expect the men to return."

Jace's smile was anything but nice. "Let the fuckers come back."

"I'll give Danny a call to fill him in. Be careful," Brice said.

Caleb gave him and Jace a nod, realizing that the sheriff should be there. "Always."

He strode to Audrey, who stopped pacing when she saw him. The apprehension in her expression made his chest tighten. Brice notifying Danny would put everyone on alert.

"Something's wrong, Caleb."

"I know. I'm going to look for her," he said.

"And I'm coming with you," she stated.

He saw the stubborn tilt of her chin. Nothing would stop him from looking for Brice. How could he ask Audrey to stay behind while he searched for her sister? "All right."

Relief filled her eyes, and she fell into step with him. Her strides were long, her back straight as they walked to where his truck was hidden behind some stacks of hay in a covered area. He didn't try to talk to her. There was nothing he could say that would make any of this better.

Once they were in his truck with the A/C cooling them, Audrey told him which way to go to her house. He lowered the volume of the radio and sped down the road.

Audrey's gaze searched for any sign of her sister's red convertible. "She was going to get us food."

"Do you know where? We can look there," he offered.

She shook her head, her frustration and worry evident. "Let's go to my place first."

He did as she asked. Audrey gripped the truck door all the way to the house. As they turned down the long gravel drive to her place, Caleb noticed the thick woods and how set apart the building was from anything else.

A perfect place for someone to sneak onto the property and break into the home. Tension filled Caleb as he heard Audrey gasp, right before his gaze landed on Maddy's car. The door was open, but there was no sign of Audrey's sister.

"Oh, God," Audrey whispered.

Caleb slammed on the brakes and threw the vehicle into park as they reached the house. Audrey was out of the truck before he could stop her. He drew his weapon and rushed to her side, grabbing her arm before she could barrel into the house.

When she parted her lips to talk, he put a finger over his mouth. He listened for any indication of Maddy in distress or pain, as well as sounds of anyone else that might be there. Audrey parted her lips to argue, but she kept silent.

Once Caleb knew Audrey would remain where she was, he looked around. The building on the side of the house must be the clinic she'd told him about. He grimaced when he saw the door hanging off its hinges. That combined with Maddy's car door being open had him scanning the trees for signs of intruders.

After several tense moments, he looked down at Audrey and pointed toward the clinic. As soon as she saw the state of the door, her face went slack. With her eyes wide, she stared up at him.

He leaned close and whispered, "There's another pistol in my glove box. Get it while I keep an eye on things."

She nodded and numbly took a step back. Caleb waited until she had the weapon before he waved her up beside him. Together, they cautiously walked toward the clinic door. There were no sounds coming from within, but that didn't mean there wasn't someone still inside.

He pressed his back against the building and carefully peeked into the window. He saw the contents of drawers and cabinets spilled out and smashed everywhere.

Caleb ducked beneath the window and came up on the other side. Creeping slowly toward the door, he glanced at Audrey to make sure she was still with him. She held the gun securely, her breathing even.

After a quick look inside to make sure no one was waiting out in the open, he spun around the entrance, pistol aimed. He stepped over broken glass and smashed containers as he made his way through to the back room with Audrey right on his heels. He spotted the blood samples smashed on the floor, but he didn't stop.

The door to the storage area was ajar. The closet was just as ransacked as the front of the clinic. Caleb walked farther inside and saw Maddy lying on the ground. Her upper body leaned against the shelving as if she had been shoved down. Maddy's lip was busted, her cheek cut and bruised from an obvious fist to the face. Her shirt was torn, and one of her shoes was missing.

Caleb hurried to her and searched for a pulse as Audrey went to Maddy's other side. Relief surged through him when he felt the steady, strong beat of her heart. He looked up and gave Audrey a nod to let her know that Maddy was alive.

Caleb got to his feet and took another look around. "Stay with Maddy while I call the sheriff and an ambulance. Then I'm going to check out the house."

Audrey nodded as he spoke, her hand gripping Maddy's tightly.

He made his way to the house and walked through every inch of it. No one was inside, and as far as he could tell, nothing had been messed with, which meant the attackers had wanted something in the clinic.

Or they wanted to stop something from happening.

Was it the blood from the horses Audrey had tested? How could they know about that? She hadn't told anyone but those at the auction house and Maddy.

And no one even knew that Audrey was going to do a necropsy on the horse. How could anyone know to stop what they didn't realize had occurred?

Unless they were aware.

Caleb briefly closed his eyes and sighed. The poisoners knew that the horses were going to die, and it would make sense that Audrey would do testing to find the reason.

Caleb sent a quick text to Brice, Clayton, Jace, and Cooper to update them. Then he sent Danny Oldman one, as well. There were many perks to having the sheriff as a friend.

He walked back to the clinic to find Maddy awake and holding her head with one hand. The woman looked worse for wear, but she was alive. That's what mattered. Audrey looked up at him. For the first time, there was fear in her eyes. Before this, she had barreled into the situation with determination and a little frustration. He didn't like seeing the distress in her gaze.

"Maddy said there were two attackers. They were wearing black ski masks."

Just like the guy Caleb had seen at the auction house. He squatted before Maddy. "What else can you tell us?"

Her face was swelling rapidly from the hits. She visibly swallowed and slowly lifted her head to him. Pain shone in every inch of her countenance, making anger churn within him. He'd begun this by helping David, but the deeper he sank into this web of intrigue, the more he found himself becoming emotionally involved.

"I got dressed and came to the clinic," Maddy said. "I unlocked the door and began to fill a box with part of Audrey's list. I took it to my car."

She looked out the door and pointed. Her eyes teared up, and she lowered her hand to her lap.

Caleb caught Maddy's gaze. "Take your time. They're long gone."

"And we're here," Audrey added with a reassuring smile.

Maddy nodded despite the tears. "I heard something behind me after I put the box in my car. I was on my way back in here to get the rest when I looked over my shoulder and saw them. I ran inside and tried to shut and lock the door, but they were too strong. They kicked it in, sending me flying backwards."

Audrey stroked Maddy's back as she talked. With each word, Audrey's anger became more palpable.

"Then what happened?" Caleb asked.

"One came at me, while the other started opening cabinets and tossing everything out," Maddy explained.

Caleb smiled at her. "You're doing great, Maddy. Can you tell me if they said anything?"

She blinked through her tears and sniffed. "They didn't say a word."

That didn't sound right. Obviously, they had come for something. "Did they take anything?"

"They could have after one of them shoved me against the shelves. I hit my head, and everything went black. They didn't want me. They wanted something here." Maddy cried harder as she looked at Audrey. "I'm so sorry."

Audrey shook her head vehemently. "This isn't your fault. You did nothing wrong. Everything here can be replaced. You can't. All that matters is that you're okay."

"The ambulance will be here soon to take a look at you. That's a nasty bump on your head," Caleb said.

Maddy instantly pulled back. "I don't need that."

"At least let them look you over," Audrey quickly said.

Maddy sighed loudly. "Fine. I'd rather be helping you."

"I need to make sure you're okay first," Audrey replied with a smile.

Caleb helped Maddy to her feet and started walking her to the truck to await the ambulance. He got to the door of the clinic and looked over his shoulder to find Audrey standing near the vials of blood he'd stepped over earlier. Something was on the floor.

"These are the ones I took from the sick horses," she said as she met his gaze. "I didn't find anything. Why would they destroy all of this if I didn't find anything?"

"That's a very good question," he said.

Audrey stood and walked to Caleb and Maddy. "I need to run the blood again."

"I'll help," Maddy said.

"First, we need to get you seen to," Audrey stated firmly.

Caleb walked out of the clinic. The crunching sound of tires on gravel filled the air. He looked up to see a patrol car. It stopped beside his truck, and Danny climbed out. The sheriff started toward the clinic. Right behind Danny was an ambulance.

Caleb relinquished Maddy to Audrey, who walked her sister to the ambulance. He watched them as he greeted Danny. "Thanks for getting here so soon."

Danny's hazel eyes swept the area. "Sure thing. I'll let the paramedics take a look at Maddy. In the meantime, want to walk the scene with me?"

Caleb nodded, and for the next fifteen minutes, he walked Danny through everything that had happened since he and Audrey had arrived.

Danny made notes in the little black notebook he carried, the expression on his face grim at what he found. "Maddy is lucky she's alive."

"And unmolested."

The sheriff gave a sad shake of his head. "That, too. I'm sure they would have done more if they'd believed they had time for it."

"Do you have any idea who might be responsible?" Caleb asked.

"I sure as shit wish I did." Danny closed the notebook for a moment. "I was on my way to the auction house when you texted me."

"There's a lot to tell." Caleb ran a hand down his face. His worry over the horses was now mixed with the possibility that Maddy and Audrey were in danger. If only he could figure out who the men were after. And why.

Danny caught his gaze as more squad cars pulled up.

"We're going to go through the crime scene to pull prints, but if the men wore masks, I doubt they'd be so kind as to leave a fingerprint."

Suddenly, Danny nodded his head and said, "Ma'am."

Caleb shifted to see Audrey walking up.

Audrey's smile was forced. "Sheriff." Then she turned her gaze to Caleb. "It doesn't look as if Maddy needs to go to the hospital. They're cleaning her up now."

"That's good to hear," Caleb replied.

Danny nodded. "Very."

"She is determined to return with us to the auction house," Audrey continued. "So, Maddy stopped the first deputy she saw and is giving her statement now."

Danny grinned. "Good."

Caleb saw the question in Audrey's eyes regarding how he had Danny's private number to get ahold of him. "I've known Danny for years. He's helped Clayton keep me and Brice in line."

Danny laughed, the lines crinkling around his eyes. "Oh, Clayton had that handled all by himself. I just stood back and watched the mayhem."

Caleb smiled in return. "As only a friend does."

Danny blew out a breath and turned to Caleb. "I'll be at the auction house as soon as I wrap this up. Then, I want to know everything."

They shook hands, and Caleb walked Audrey to the truck where Maddy already waited. The three rode in silence back to the others, just as the sun came up.

Chapter 11

Audrey couldn't stop shaking. It didn't matter the training she had with guns or the self-defense classes she had taken. Nothing could have prepared her for finding her sister lying unconscious on the floor.

It was everything she could do not to turn and look in the back seat where Maddy was huddled. Her outgoing, always-smiling sister was subdued, withdrawn. Fear was etched in every line of Maddy's face, and she had drawn herself into a ball.

It was a good thing the intruders weren't still there, because Audrey wouldn't have hesitated to pull the trigger.

She didn't know why they hadn't killed Maddy, but she was thankful for that at least. But the attackers had done enough damage to her sister. It wasn't just Maddy's face and body that were bruised, it was her spirit, as well. Her bright, shining soul was dimmed, and Audrey feared that it might never glow again.

And Audrey didn't even have her father to turn to. She would have to weather this alone. The thing was, she wasn't sure she was strong enough.

Something warm covered her hand where it rested on the center console. Her gaze locked on Caleb's long fingers curling around hers.

She lifted her eyes to his profile. He glanced at her, giving her hand a little squeeze. There were no words needed. The gesture told her that he would be there for her. A man she barely knew had risked his life for her already.

Audrey wasn't too proud to accept help. Whatever mess David had pulled her into was too deep for her to wade through on her own. She needed help.

No. She needed Caleb.

She leaned her head back against the headrest and closed her eyes. The weight of the ill horses, her sister's attack, and the time constraint of figuring out the poison felt like she was carrying the heavens upon her shoulders like Atlas.

The truck jerked as it rolled over the cattle guard at the auction house, and the movement pulled her from the sweet oblivion she had slipped into between waking and sleep. She blinked her eyes, adjusting them to the light.

To her shock, she realized that Caleb had kept a hold of her hand. She was loath to move, and apparently, she wasn't the only one. When he parked the vehicle, none of them moved to get out.

"Thank you," she said, looking out the windshield.

He nodded. "My pleasure. Are you all right?"

Audrey glanced behind her to Maddy and smiled. "Yes."

Once more, his hand squeezed hers. "That's good to hear."

She spotted Brice watching them. He studied the truck for a moment, and a look passed between the brothers. Brice then turned and said something to someone Audrey couldn't see. A moment later, the older Harper walked away.

"I don't want to see anyone," Maddy suddenly said.

Caleb didn't hesitate to say, "You don't have to. I can take you to David's office. Someone will be near, watching at all times."

There was a beat of silence, then Maddy said, "But Audrey is going to need me."

"I'll be fine," Audrey hurried to say as she shifted to look at her sister.

Maddy sat up straight. "You wouldn't hide away after an attack."

"I don't know what I'd do," Audrey admitted. "I might."

Maddy shook her head. "I know you. You wouldn't break."

"And neither have you."

Her sister blinked before a small smile played on her lips. "I didn't, did I?"

"See? You're stronger than you think."

"Maybe," Maddy mumbled and reached for the door.

It swung open, and she exited the truck. Audrey's gaze slid to Caleb, who gave her an encouraging smile.

"It's going to be all right," he promised.

And she actually believed him.

Audrey hated that she had to release his hand to get out of the truck. She found herself drawn to Caleb as they met at the front of the vehicle where Maddy waited.

But when Maddy headed toward the stables, Audrey said, "I thought you wanted to be alone."

Maddy lifted one shoulder in a shrug. "I thought I did,

but you need me. Let me help. If it gets to be too much, I'll let you know."

Audrey almost argued with her, but she realized it was pointless. She nodded, and they continued walking.

Her sister had been violently attacked and was in pain, but she kept her head high, and her shoulders back as she walked.

Audrey's bag had been taken to where the dead horse awaited her. Maddy didn't seem affected by the news and changed her course to the building. Even when the three of them saw the others waiting, Maddy didn't slow.

No one said a word about the blood on Maddy's clothes or the fact that her face looked as if it had been used as a punching bag. The men moved out of the way as Audrey led her sister to a chair as she began laying out the items she needed.

Each time Audrey looked up, Caleb's eyes were on her. She knew that no one would get near her or Maddy as long as Caleb and the others were near. And she needed that kind of reassurance.

She stilled when she heard a woman's voice. Brice rushed from the building in a hurry. It wasn't long before he returned, hand-in-hand with a blonde. Brice couldn't take his eyes from the woman who was obviously his wife.

"Y'all don't look any worse for wear," the woman said. Then her eyes landed on Audrey and Maddy. The woman released Brice's hand and made her way toward them with a plastic bag. She held it out to them. "I'm Naomi. I thought you could use more estrogen out here."

Maddy actually smiled before she winced at her cut lip. "I'm Maddy, and this is Audrey."

Audrey took the bag and looked through it. There was

some aspirin, bandages, and other assorted items to tend minor wounds.

"That's not all I brought," Naomi said.

Slim, pretty, and kind, Audrey instantly liked Naomi. By the way the men treated her, she was well loved by them all.

"Tell me there's food," one of the men said, golden blond hair peeking from beneath his hat.

Audrey guessed that the two men standing near Caleb were the friends that he and Brice had enlisted to help. In all the craziness, she had yet to actually meet them.

"There's always food for you, Jace," Naomi said with a laugh. "Abby sent over a plate full of cookies, but she said you had to share."

Jace turned to leave when Clayton cleared his throat. The next thing Audrey knew, Jace stood before her.

His hazel eyes held hers as he tipped his head. "Ma'am. I'm Jace Wilder, and the one standing over there twiddling his thumbs is Cooper Owens."

"Hey," Cooper said, a frown darkening his face. "I was going to introduce myself."

"It's nice to meet you," Audrey said. "As I'm sure you already know, I'm Audrey, and this is my sister, Maddy." Then she looked between Jace and Cooper. "Thank you for the help last night."

Cooper touched the edge of his hat with his finger as he bowed his head. "Our pleasure, ma'am." His dark green eyes landed on Maddy. "If you need anything, let me know."

"Thanks," Maddy replied.

Without another word, Jace was out the door.

"I, ah, better go help him," Cooper said. "Or else Jace might eat everything before we even know what there is."

After he was gone, Clayton walked to Maddy and squatted down before her. "I can have Naomi take you to the ranch. I know Abby would love to spoil you. And there are plenty of rooms for you to use."

Maddy's smile was easier than it had been since they found her. "Thank you, but my sister needs me. And I need to be here for her."

Clayton straightened and nodded at them. "I'll give you both a few minutes. Audrey, let us know when you're ready for the necropsy."

"I'll get started right away, actually," she said.

Brice removed his hat and held it in his hands. "Perhaps it's time we find out exactly what happened at your place first."

"There isn't much to tell," Caleb said. "We got there and found the clinic torn up. They didn't leave a single cabinet alone. Everything was pulled out and destroyed."

Audrey fished out some aspirin for her sister and gave them to Maddy, along with a bottle of water. "None of my equipment is salvageable either. I'm lucky that what was at the clinic is backup to what I have in my SUV."

Clayton exhaled loudly. "I think you should have some help."

Audrey glanced at Caleb to gauge his reaction. "I have Maddy."

"Who needs to rest," Naomi pointed out.

Audrey nodded even as Maddy tried to say that she was fine. Her sister was far from okay, but Audrey wanted Maddy close if for no other reason than to keep an eye on her.

"You're talking about Mac," Caleb said to Clayton.

Maddy frowned. "Mac?"

Naomi turned to her. "Mac is the vet for the East Ranch.

He's also worked for Brice and Caleb for the past three years."

"We trust him," Brice added.

Caleb nodded as he looked at Audrey. "And the best part is, Mac has everything to run any test for the necropsy. Two is always better than one."

Audrey licked her lips as she took in what they had told her. It would be helpful to have another set of eyes on things since she was going on two days without sleep. But she still had her reservations. "While I appreciate what you're doing, do you think it's wise to bring someone else in on this?"

"Mac trusts Clayton wouldn't put him in harm's way. Years of working together has built a bond," Caleb said.

Audrey realized that she didn't have that kind of bond with either of the ranches she worked for. Perhaps it was time she took a closer look at her employers and figured out what was more important—a big paycheck, or people she respected and trusted.

"Well?" Naomi asked, her brow raised.

Audrey blinked, aware that they were waiting to hear what she thought. "If Mac is willing to help, then yes."

"I'll make the call," Clayton said and walked out.

"Mac won't tell Clayton no," Brice said.

Audrey turned to the horse. "I've not checked on the other horses."

"I can do that," Naomi said. "I help Mac on occasion."

Audrey looked at Brice's wife and smiled in relief. "Thank you. My iPad is around here somewhere. If you could add in notes, that would really help me out."

"It's here," Maddy said as she leaned over in her chair and withdrew the tablet from the bag to hand to Naomi.

Audrey knelt by her bag and searched through the

contents. She had some of the items for a necropsy. The rest was in her SUV, which she needed to get. It wasn't everything she would've wanted, but at least she could get started. The sooner she found answers, the sooner she could help the other horses.

"What do you need?" Caleb asked her.

She didn't question how he knew she needed anything. It was nice, though. Definitely something she could get used to. She didn't know much about relationships, though. Who was she to assume what it would be like with Caleb?

"Several things from my SUV," she replied.

Brice nodded. "Tell me. I can get them for you."

She grinned. "Wonderful. It'll be easier if you drive my truck here, though."

He held out his hand, and she fished the keys from her pocket to toss his way.

Naomi scrolled through the iPad, glancing at the notes. "I'll use the same format you used. If I have any questions, I'll let you know."

Audrey looked up in time to see Naomi and Brice walk out together. Unwittingly, her gaze panned to Caleb. Once more, he stared at her.

She wished she knew what he was thinking, because his face revealed nothing. Audrey heard a forlorn sigh and rolled her eyes as she realized that her sister was there, witnessing everything.

Caleb walked to Audrey. "What more do you need from me?"

The answers that popped into Audrey's head had nothing to do with veterinarian work.

Chapter 12

Caleb knew a lot about horses. He'd fallen in love with them the moment he arrived on the East Ranch. Every chance he had, he was with the ranch hands, learning every tidbit they would share about the majestic animals.

He did the same with the farrier, the vets, the trainers, and anyone who had any kind of wisdom about horses. The years he'd spent in the Army away from the animals had left an empty ache in him that only stopped when he returned home.

But all the knowledge he had seemed insignificant as he stood with Maddy while Audrey conducted the necropsy on the dead gelding.

Caleb walked from the building when the procedure was finished and had a new appreciation for equine veterinarians—especially Audrey.

"Not what you expected, huh?" Maddy asked as she came to stand beside him beneath the shade of the overhang.

Caleb glanced at the closed door behind them. "Does one of us need to be in there with her?"

"Naw. Audrey has it covered," Maddy stated. "The one thing you'll learn about my sister is that she could rule the world if she set her mind to it. Nothing stands in her way when she wants something. She doesn't know the meaning of 'give up.'"

Caleb studied Maddy, noticing that she was moving slower and slower as the aches of her body began to make themselves known.

Maddy's black eyes met his. "Audrey never turns away help, but she's also not the first to ask for it. She will try to do whatever it is on her own first. I'll put Nair in your shampoo if you tell her, but she's usually right."

"I won't tell her," Caleb said as he chuckled.

Maddy tentatively touched her split lip. She closed her eyes and kept them shut for a few moments.

Caleb could tell that she needed to rest. "Why don't you get some sleep? There's a couch in David's office."

"Yeah. I think I will," Maddy said and started toward the metal building.

Caleb was about to go with her since she looked unsteady on her feet, but she lifted a finger and pointed it at him as she glanced his way.

"I don't think so, cowboy. Stay with Audrey. I can make it."

Caleb watched her until she reached the office and went inside, the door shutting behind her. He turned and spotted Clayton leaning against the side of the building. "What are you doing out here?"

"Waiting on you."

The ominous tone of his brother-in-law's voice didn't sit well. "Why didn't you come inside?"

"I did, but all three of you were so absorbed, you didn't see me."

"Is something wrong?"

Clayton shook his head as he pushed away from the building. "Mac is on his way, but I wanted to talk with you alone."

"About?" It was never a good sign when Clayton was so cryptic.

Clayton removed his hat and ran his hand through his dark blond hair. He sighed and turned the hat around in his hands. "Audrey and Maddy seem to be taking things in stride."

Now he knew what Clayton was getting at. Caleb nodded. "Audrey has something to focus on. So did Maddy for a bit, but I'm not sure how long that's going to last. You want to take them to the ranch, don't you?"

Clayton's pale green eyes met his. "I don't think they should be alone."

"I agree. However, Audrey won't leave while the other horses are still ill."

"True. Maddy at least needs to go."

"That I agree with," Caleb said.

"I doubt those men will be back after being shot at."

"Are you sure about that?"

Clayton put his hat back on his head. "They know we're on to them. It might be beneficial for us to take turns keeping a lookout for the next few nights, but I think they're done here."

"Here?" Caleb asked with his brows raised, considering Clayton's words. "Where do you think they'll strike next?"

"I wish I knew." Clayton looked out over the acres of land. Parts were empty, while others held horses, and still other sections cattle.

The longer Caleb looked at the animals, the more a nagging thought went round and round in his mind. He was missing something.

Clayton came to stand beside him to look out over an area with cattle. "What?"

Then it hit Caleb. "Why horses?"

"What?" Clayton repeated, his brow furrowed as he turned his head to Caleb.

"The cattle stay out there grazing until it's time for their auction. They're much easier to get to than the horses. Then, there are the goats and pigs. Why did the men poison the horses?"

Clayton's face went hard with anger. "To bring in an equine veterinarian."

"Yeah." Caleb turned to the door that led to Audrey. "Is it by chance that David called Audrey?"

Clayton shook his head. "If anyone knows David, they know he's loyal to a fault. He and Audrey's father were close friends."

"So, of course, he'd call Audrey."

They looked at each other. Unease stirred in Caleb. The last time he'd felt this way was three years ago when some men had been after Naomi and Brice.

Clayton snorted, his mouth twisting. "We had a few years without an incident."

"You make it sound as if it follows me and Brice around."

"I'm beginning to think it does," Caleb replied dryly.

Caleb took off his hat and slapped it against his leg. "It comes down to whether the poisoning of the horses was to hurt David or bring in Audrey. Or both."

"If we hadn't caught the men in the act last night, the

poisoning would've continued, and it would've ruined both David and Audrey."

Caleb wiped a hand over his mouth. He wanted out of his sweaty clothes and to have a decent meal, but neither would be happening anytime soon. "All of this could be about both of them."

"It could, indeed. We won't know until we dig deeper."

"Has anyone spoken to David?"

Clayton glanced at his watch. "About a half hour ago. He should be here soon."

"So no one went after him like they did Maddy?"

"That entire attack has me wondering why they did it. It was done too late at night for anyone to be at the clinic."

Caleb returned his hat to his head. "I agree. I think Maddy was right. They weren't after her or Audrey. I think the men wanted to make sure that Audrey couldn't do any testing on the horses to figure out the poison. Except she can with the equipment in her SUV."

Clayton crossed his arms over his chest. "Good point."

"If these people know we're involved, they'll know we'll call in Mac."

"Fuck," Clayton grumbled and yanked out his phone. A moment later, he said, "Shane, I need a favor."

Caleb grinned as he thought of the East Ranch manager. Shane had spent the majority of his life dedicated to the Easts, but three years ago, he'd found himself smitten with Beverly Barnes, the owner of the local newspaper. The two had been together since.

His thoughts halted when Clayton put away his phone.

"Shane is going to take a few men and head to Mac's," Clayton said.

"Good." The unease within Caleb didn't lessen, though.

Clayton was silent for a long minute. "Both of our ranches have excellent security. Take Audrey and her sister to the Rockin' H when this is all finished. She'll be safe with you."

Caleb knew that no place was safer than Clayton's, but his brother-in-law also had three children and a wife to think about. "When the time comes, I'll try and talk Audrey into coming with me."

"If you can't?"

Caleb shrugged. "Then I guess I'll be going wherever she goes. One way or another, we're going to figure out who these people are after and put an end to it."

"Damn straight we are," Clayton said with a grin.

The door to the building opened, and Audrey walked out. The apron, gloves, and goggles she'd worn were gone. She said nothing to the two of them as she walked to the side of the building and leaned against it. Then she slid down it until she sat on the concrete. Only then did she lift her gaze to Caleb.

"Done?" he asked.

She nodded slowly, her eyes closing briefly. "All I have to do now is the testing."

"Mac should be here soon to help out," Clayton said. "Why not take a little break?"

Caleb asked, "Hungry?"

"I'm so past hungry that the thought of food actually makes me sick," she said.

Clayton stared toward the front of the auction house. "If Jace ate all the food, I'm going to skin him. Wait here, Audrey. You'll have something to eat if Jace has to prepare it himself."

Caleb laughed as Clayton walked off. He watched his

brother-in-law for a moment before he swung his head to Audrey. "At the ranch, food isn't a big deal. My sister always has tons of it. She learned soon after Jace and Cooper began coming over that she could never have enough groceries in the house."

"Obviously, she's a good cook."

"She is, but Jace just likes food. He'll eat anything. And he never shares. Ever."

Audrey let loose a laugh that made his balls tighten. It was vibrant and earthy, just like her. His craving for her intensified to a fever pitch, and yet it still didn't make him run away. No, he remained, soaking up every inch of her beauty.

"He would never get along with Maddy then because she's always stealing food off other people's plates."

"Then I'm definitely going to have to put them together. It'd be worth everything just to watch Jace's face the first time Maddy took something from his plate."

"Oh, yes. Please. And I have to be there, as well," Audrey said with a bright smile.

"You will be."

There was still a smile on her lips when she sighed. "Thank you for the laugh. I needed that."

"I'm here for whatever you need."

"Anything?"

Was it his imagination, or had there been a glimmer of mischief in her dark eyes? His mind immediately went to the carnal aspect of things, and he nearly groaned aloud at the thought of their tangled bodies rolling around on his bed. "Anything."

"You might regret saying that."

He shook his head. "Not when it comes to you."

The line was one he'd said many times before to ease his way into a woman's life. But this time wasn't like the others. *Audrey* wasn't like the others.

She tore her gaze from his and picked at her fingernails. "Where's Maddy?"

"I sent her to David's office so she could rest. I think it's all catching up with her."

"I knew it would."

Caleb leaned against the pole that held up the metal roof of the overhang. It was nice just standing out here with Audrey. Their easy camaraderie made him comfortable. Which was at odds with the desire that burned through his veins at a fever pitch.

"I never thought anyone would go to my clinic and destroy it," Audrey said and squeezed her eyes closed.

Caleb squatted beside her in the next breath. "It's not your fault."

Her lids lifted, and she speared him with her dark brown gaze. "Isn't it? I got involved in this. I brought my sister into this. And you're entangled now, as well."

"We're here because we want to be. Same as Maddy. And trust me when I say whoever these people are, they've messed with the wrong family. We protect what's ours— as well as our friends. You and your sister are counted among those now."

Chapter 13

Phil's eyes went to the burner phone that vibrated when the text came through. He'd been waiting on the message for hours. Yet he was slow to reach for the cell.

He'd thought the job was easy money—and he was all about easy. For thirty years, he'd been on the wrong side of the law. He'd committed a variety of crimes, but he'd never killed anyone.

Even someone like him had a code they lived by. He would happily rough someone up, but he made sure to never involve children.

He was particular about the people he took jobs from, too. Never just anyone off the street. He had to have either worked for them before or been referred by a former client.

Unfortunately, sometimes, there was a client who seemed like a decent person—until Phil took another job with them and discovered just how demented they were. That's what was happening now.

The phone buzzed again.

Phil leaned up from his seat to reach for it. He glanced into the room to Zeke, whose arm was heavily bandaged thanks to a doctor Phil knew who worked off the books for people like him.

GOOD JOB.

Phil snorted as he read the text. *Good job*? Really? That's all? Phil sighed and tossed the phone aside. No sooner had it came to rest than it sounded again.

With anger churning, he snatched the cell back up and looked down.

YOU AREN'T FINISHED YET.

He hovered his fingers over the buttons for a moment. Then he sent his reply of: I'VE DONE ALL THAT I WAS PAID TO.

THEN I WILL PAY YOU MORE.

ANOTHER 10K. He laughed as he sent off the text, thinking it would never be accepted.

DONE.

Phil frowned. The fact that this client was so ready and willing to hand over that kind of cash meant that they had another plan.

He looked up, his gaze not seeing the framed replicas of some of the world's greatest paintings. Instead, he began to wonder if this job would take him down a road he'd sworn never to tread.

I WON'T KILL.

Minutes went by before the reply came. I'VE NOT ASKED THAT OF YOU.

JUST REITERATING. WHAT DO YOU NEED ME TO DO NOW?

Phil frowned as he read the text that popped up on the screen. He sent off a quick reply and rose to walk into the back room where Ricardo was lifting weights.

Ricardo's black eyes met his in the wall of mirrors as he lowered the hand weights to the floor. His thick black hair was cropped close to his scalp. "You okay, *jefe*?"

Phil no longer noticed Ricardo's heavy Spanish accent. Though he might be short of stature, Ricardo was a natural when it came to committing crimes. He moved as silently as a ghost, and could easily slip away from anyone after him.

"Boss?"

"I'm fine," Phil answered. "It looks like our current job isn't quite finished."

Ricardo smiled as he stood and faced Phil. "That's good."

"It's going to be just the two of us until Zeke is better. The bullet might have only penetrated his shoulder, but its path tore through muscle and lodged in the bone."

"He's going to be out for days," Ricardo said, his eagerness evident in the bright shine of his eyes. "When do we begin?"

Phil glanced at the various workout machines and weights that he had filled the large room with. He made use of them almost daily, keeping his body in shape so he could continue working. The moment he allowed age to catch up with him, the authorities would, as well.

He planned to retire before that happened. Matter of fact, he was beginning to think retirement might come quicker than he'd expected.

Phil blinked and realized that Ricardo was staring. Belatedly, he recalled the question. "We begin now," Phil stated and turned on his heel.

Audrey blinked several times to try and give her now dry eyes some relief. After the chaos of the past day, she was surprised that a van full of veterinarian equipment arrived at the auction house without incident.

Audrey glanced at the building where Maddy still rested. She half expected the noise of Mac's arrival to wake her sister, but Audrey was glad that it hadn't. Maddy needed the rest.

Audrey turned her attention back to the others. Her gaze immediately went to the black hat that belonged to Caleb. She let her eyes wander down his back, lingering on the tight ass that his jeans molded to before she took in his long legs.

If she hadn't been enamored with him before, she'd become so the moment he called her and Maddy part of his circle. In the short time she had spent with the East/Harper family, she'd discovered two things.

They loved each other unconditionally.

And they always looked out for one another.

While Jace and Cooper weren't blood, they were still part of the family. The two were more like brothers to Caleb and Brice than mere friends, and even Clayton treated them as such.

To know that she and Maddy were now included in that very exclusive circle made Audrey . . . well, deliriously happy.

Caleb suddenly stopped walking and looked back at her. Their eyes met, and his lips curved into a smile. She smiled back, unable to stop the reaction. He had that kind of effect on her. And she liked it.

"You're going to eat before you get started," Caleb said when she caught up with him.

She laughed. "Now you sound like Maddy."

Caleb frowned. "Do you often skip meals?"

"Not intentionally. I get to working and forget."

He shook his head, his face contorted with confusion. "Don't you get hungry?"

"Yeah. I suppose."

He faced her. "When did you eat last?"

Audrey thought about it a moment and said, "Last night. The sandwich David brought."

"And before that?"

She had to search her memory before she recalled when it was. "Dinner the night before."

"That seals it. You're definitely eating before you get back to work."

Caleb took her arm and pulled her in another direction. Her stomach growled the moment she smelled the pizza. They entered the stables, and she spotted the table where ten boxes of pizzas were set up, along with a variety of bottled drinks.

Naomi rolled her eyes when she saw them. "Just as I predicted, Jace ate nearly everything I brought. So, as punishment, I made him order these," she said with a smile and motioned to the pizzas.

Audrey's mouth watered the moment she opened the

first lid. She was suddenly ravenous. She shifted through the boxes until she found her favorite and took a slice. Her eyes closed as the first bite landed on her tongue.

When she opened her lids, Caleb was staring at her oddly. Then he said, "I'll be back."

She watched him leave, wondering what she'd missed. Audrey turned back to Naomi, who had a shrewd look on her face. "What?"

"Nothing," Naomi said with a secretive smile. Then she switched gears and reached for the iPad. "The horses are holding steady right now. I've kept them on the saline for hydration as you instructed."

"Have they tried to eat?"

Naomi wrinkled her nose and shook her head. "I did get the roan to sniff a cube of sugar. I thought the mare might take it, but she didn't."

"That's more than I've gotten since arriving yesterday."

"Has it only been one day?"

Audrey sighed and took another bite.

Naomi held out an ice-cold bottle of Coke.

"Oh, yes," Audrey said as she accepted it, drinking several gulps before returning to the pizza.

"So," Naomi said with a grin. "What do you think of Caleb?"

The question caught Audrey off guard. She choked as she swallowed, causing her to cough. The entire time, Naomi watched her carefully.

"Excuse me?" Audrey asked, her voice hoarse from coughing.

Naomi shrugged. "I saw the way you looked at him. And the way he looked at you."

"I . . ." Audrey struggled to find the words.

Naomi waved away her incoherent utterance. "I understand. The Harper boys are hard to resist. I didn't even try when it came to Brice. I got so swept up in it all. There was no point in trying to find my feet. I just went with it."

Audrey stared at Naomi, unsure of what to say.

"Maybe you should do the same."

Audrey's mouth opened, but no words came out. She wouldn't even admit to her sister that she found Caleb cute. No, he wasn't cute. He was handsome. Drop-dead gorgeous.

The kind of good-looking that made women forget there were other men on the planet.

Audrey looked down at the half-eaten piece of pizza. Was she resisting Caleb? She was pretty sure that wasn't the case. In fact, if there were any hint that he might be into her, she wouldn't hesitate to show her own interest.

Audrey absently took another bite, but she didn't taste it. Had Caleb flirted and she hadn't seen it? It was a distinct possibility. After all, when she was dealing with horses, she tended to forget about everyone and everything.

But surely she would've noticed that.

She slumped against the side of an empty stall, aware that she was fooling herself. She wouldn't have seen or noticed any kind of flirting.

It was one of the reasons she never had relationships. Maddy called her a serial dater. Her father used to say it was because she had such high expectations. Her mother once said that if she didn't open her heart, she would be reduced to one-night stands.

Audrey had seen nothing wrong with her continual rotation of dates. Until now. Why? How had one handsome cowboy changed that? And she didn't even know if he was interested in her.

She finished off the pizza and soon reached for another slice. Before she realized it, she'd eaten four. Perhaps Maddy had a point. She should make more of an effort to eat regularly. Maybe then she wouldn't gorge herself on food when she did have a meal.

Audrey finally emerged from the stables, her belly full and the caffeine from the soda doing wonders to wake her up. She was headed toward Caleb and Brice when she happened to glance toward the building where she had been doing the necropsy.

Smoke billowed from under the door. She took off running as Caleb shouted her name. She could only think about getting to the samples that she had taken from the gelding.

All she heard was the sound of her own rapid breathing as she pumped her arms faster, urging her legs to move quicker. She kept repeating *no, no, no, no* in her head.

Suddenly, she was looking at the sky as something slammed into her. Her breath rushed from her as she found herself on the ground with something on top of her. A second later, an explosion made the ground tremble.

She had no idea how long she lay there before someone moved the hair out of her face. She looked up into brown eyes she recognized.

"Caleb?"

"Are you hurt?" he asked, looking her over as if he expected to find something. "Audrey? Are you hurt?"

She shook her head and reached up to touch the blood mixed with sweat running down his face. His hat was gone, and he was covered in dust. He stilled at the touch of her fingers on his cheek.

"You're injured," she whispered, shaken and dazed to her very core.

Chapter 14

It was everything Caleb could do to sit still as Audrey cleaned his head wound. They'd set up in the sale barn because it was the closest building to the stables. He hadn't felt anything hit him in the explosion. He'd seen the concern on Audrey's face and immediately spotted the smoke.

There had been nothing in the building to catch fire. He'd known instantly that someone had been there to wipe away any trace of the horse so that Audrey couldn't finish her exam.

He'd reached her quickly enough and brought her to the ground. It had been by sheer luck alone that he'd done it right before the building blew.

Brice paced a few yards away, while Clayton stewed. Cooper was scouting the area for tracks and to see how many there were. Naomi stood guard over the remaining ill horses.

"You were damn lucky," Brice said. He speared Audrey with a dark look. "Both of you."

Audrey didn't say anything as she continued cleaning

Caleb's wound. Matter of fact, she hadn't uttered a word since telling him that he was injured.

The fact that Caleb couldn't stop thinking about being cushioned by her soft body when he should be more concerned with the obliteration of the dead horse and the evidence was worrying.

She slowly lowered her arms and then met his gaze. Caleb wanted to pull her against him, to wrap his arms around her and tell her it was going to be all right. It was a gesture he had done countless times with other women, but he wanted it to mean something this time.

His brain froze, and instead of uttering reassuring words, Caleb sat there, seized by shock—and more than a little dismayed by what had just gone through his mind. He didn't think about wanting more. With anyone.

Ever.

Caleb pulled his gaze from hers before he gave in to the hunger riding him so hard. He'd never felt anything like it before, and he wasn't sure what it meant. And right now wasn't the time to find out.

Clayton walked up then. He glanced at Caleb but focused on Audrey. "I should've told you, but I took the majority of your samples."

"That's great news. Where are they?" Audrey asked, her eyes wide.

"In David's office with Maddy. And don't worry," he continued, "I've got Jace keeping an eye on her and the office."

Audrey blew out a loud sigh of relief. "Thank you."

Clayton shot her a quick grin.

Caleb got to his feet and glanced up at the stadium seating that was bathed in light. How many times had he sat up there watching others bid on his horses?

Now, everywhere he turned, he expected there to be an enemy. It was much as his life had been as a Green Beret.

Caleb swallowed and turned to face the door, only to find Clayton watching him. Caleb had learned long ago that his brother-in-law somehow always knew when something was wrong with him and Brice.

It had been Clayton that Caleb had turned to when the nightmares from his missions threatened to rule his life. Caleb had kept it from Brice since his brother had his own issues at the time.

Clayton's advice helped, but it was really the quiet acceptance and love from the horses that had helped Caleb shift back into civilian life. Every once in a while, the past came back, but he was always able to stand against those horrible memories.

"If anything had happened to Maddy. . . ."

Audrey's words trailed off. Before he realized it, Caleb was on his feet, his arm looping around Audrey's waist to pull her back against his chest.

"But it didn't," he said. Caleb knew exactly how she felt. He'd been in her shoes over a decade earlier when Abby was shot, and again just three years ago when men were after Brice and Naomi after the pair discovered that some prominent businessmen were raping women.

Caleb knew there was no reason to keep holding her, but he couldn't seem to release her. He liked the way she fit against him. She felt . . . right.

As if she belonged in his arms.

He'd never felt that way about anyone. It scared Caleb enough that he loosened his hold and took a step back.

Audrey turned to him. She frowned as she ran her gaze over his face. "You're in pain."

She had no idea. Caleb's body physically ached to have

her against him. And, oh, to kiss those enticing lips of hers. To peel away the clothes and see that delicious body. To—

"Here you go," Audrey said as she bent and handed him some aspirin.

The naked image he had of her evaporated as he accepted the pills and tossed them into his mouth before downing them with water. When he raised his head, his gaze clashed with Brice's, but he quickly looked away. His brother and Clayton saw entirely too much, and frankly, he didn't want to see what was in their eyes.

Because it might force him to look at his feelings. And that wasn't something he could do. Not now. Maybe not ever.

Audrey turned to Clayton. "I need to see what you managed to save."

"Right this way," Clayton said as he ushered her out of the area.

"I don't like this." Brice started pacing again. "I don't like any of this."

It didn't matter that Caleb had spent years in the military away from Brice and the rest of the family while risking his life on missions. Brice would always think of him as the little brother who used to tag along behind him and need looking after.

Just as Abby would always look at both him and Brice as kids instead of adults.

"I don't either," Caleb admitted.

Brice stopped and put his hands on his hips as he dropped his chin to his chest. "You didn't see how close the metal from the building came to landing on you."

"I've been in worse situations. So have you."

Brice turned his head to him, his blue eyes locking on Caleb. "Maybe. But I wasn't with you in the Army, and you weren't with me. That was war. This is different."

"This is home."

"Damn straight."

Caleb walked to his brother. "They fucked with the Harpers. That was their first mistake."

"It's going to be their last," Brice vowed in a cold tone.

Cooper came into the area. He huffed out a breath as the cold air from the A/C blew on him. "Two sets of tracks. They're on foot and heading to the back of the property. We can catch them. There are plenty of horses here."

"No," Caleb stated.

Brice's brows snapped together. "Why the hell not?"

"Because that could be what they want us to do. We're moving about as if we think the threat is over. Day or night, we need to keep vigilant until Audrey can get this sorted. Besides, I don't think Danny will take too kindly to us treading on his turf."

Cooper removed his hat and scrubbed his hand over his sweat-soaked, golden locks. "Good point."

"I heard Clayton on the phone with Danny after the explosion. He'll be here shortly," Brice said.

Caleb's head throbbed with a dull ache, making it difficult to think clearly. "With Mac helping Audrey do the testing, we should know something soon."

"I'm going to get set up to patrol the northeast side until the deputies arrive," Cooper said before he returned his hat to his head and left.

Caleb looked at his brother. "Maybe you should take Naomi and go home."

"She can't stand to be there alone right now."

It took a moment for Caleb to remember what day it was. The results of the fertility tests that both Naomi and Brice had taken were due in that day.

Brice's face lined with worry. "How many buildings are on this property?"

"A dozen or so," Caleb said with a shrug. "What are you thinking?"

"We need to get David to check every one to make sure it's locked. If anyone is going to come at us, they'll have to do it out in the open."

Caleb hesitantly touched the tender skin near the hairline on his forehead. "Good idea. That'll leave Danny and the other deputies free to go after whoever attacked Maddy and came at us, which I believe are the same men."

Brice grunted. "No doubt. You should stick close to Audrey."

Brice was gone before Caleb could argue. Not that he wanted to bicker over it since he wanted to be with Audrey. But it was the desire to *be* with her that had Caleb so worked up.

Because while he wanted Audrey in his bed, he wasn't just thinking about sex. He was thinking of other things like holding her, talking about horses, and taking her to dinner. What really set him back on his heels was that he wasn't thinking about having sex with her. He was thinking about making love to her.

Caleb strode from the sale barn and made sure the door was locked behind him. One sweep of the area and his gaze found Audrey. She was smoothing back her hair and twisting a band around the length as she re-did her ponytail while Clayton and Brice unloaded Mac's equipment to take to David's office.

Caleb walked to the van and lifted the next item. He glanced at Audrey once more to find her making her way to her SUV. Everything she needed was already there, but since Mac wasn't a mobile vet, they had to set everything up. The microscope was heavier than Caleb expected. He entered David's office and waited for Mac to tell him where he wanted it.

Caleb bit back a smile when he spotted David hastily moving things off his desk so it could be used. Mac's booming voice was in direct conflict with his short stature. At just barely five foot four, he was used to the short jokes. Oddly enough, they never seemed to bother him.

In no time at all, the equipment was set up. Mac nodded his head to David and walked to the desk, his expression focused.

"Do you have everything?" David asked.

Mac gave another quick nod. "Audrey has already given me half the samples.

"Then we'll leave you to it," Clayton said.

Brice reached the door first. "I'll be with Naomi in the stables."

"I'll—" Clayton began when his phone rang. He pulled it from his pocket and smiled as he said, "Hey, babe. Hang on. It w—"

Caleb laughed because he and Brice knew exactly what was happening on the other end of the line. Abby must have found out about the explosion and had an earful to give Clayton.

David shook his head. "You'd think Clayton would've learned after all these years to call Abby when something happens."

Clayton shot him a look that promised retribution as he walked out, still trying to get a word in.

Caleb slipped out and went to Audrey.

"You here to help?" she asked with a grin when she saw him.

"If you need me."

Her smile faded. "Ah. You're here to guard me."

"I'm here to do both," he corrected.

After a moment, she shrugged. "I can accept that. And I can also say that I'm happy you're here. It seems like it's been one accident after another."

"Do what you need to do. Let us worry about any more attacks."

"I can do that."

She licked her lips and turned away. Caleb shifted his attention outward to scan the area, but his gaze slid back to Audrey. She looked adorable in her safety goggles. With her focus on the samples, she forgot all about him.

Not that he minded. He quite liked watching Audrey work. She was dedicated and thorough. Her passion for the horses matched her skill and knowledge as an equine veterinarian.

He'd dated successful women before. But not one of them could match Audrey's focus and fervor. When he trained the horses, he also forgot about others and anything else around him.

Maybe that's why he was drawn to Audrey. They were much alike with how they worked, despite the different fields.

Or, it could be the raw, primal craving he felt for her.

He didn't want to ignore it, but to acknowledge and act on it was something altogether different. Because it was a road Caleb had never traveled before.

A road he had intentionally avoided at all costs.

Now, it stood before him, beckoning him to give it a go. And he wanted to. He knew it would be good with Audrey. Hell, it could be great.

And that's what kept him from moving forward.

Chapter 15

Audrey stretched her neck before lifting her arms over her head and reaching to each side. Then she linked her hands behind her and arched her back. Hours hunched over were wreaking havoc with her body.

Caleb hadn't left her side the entire time. No matter what she needed, he was there to get it for her. It kept her focused and moving from one sample to the next, even when the sheriff and his deputies arrived and swarmed the area, looking for signs of the culprits.

When she finally finished, the sun was setting. She drained the bottle of water and turned, her gaze locking with Caleb's. God, he was handsome. He'd done more for her in a few days than any guy had before. He'd risked his life, protected her, Maddy, and the horses. And through it all, he remained steady and calm.

She knew she could count on him. He'd had ample opportunity to bolt and run, but he wasn't that kind of man. He was the kind who did anything for those he cared about.

Audrey became giddy recalling how he'd said that she

and Maddy were part of his circle now. For the first time in two years, she felt some of the weight lift from her shoulders.

Even with the current situation, she didn't feel as if she were drowning. Because Caleb had thrown her a life preserver.

"I'm done," she said, unable to contain the smile any longer.

"Does that smile mean you found what you were looking for?"

"It does. Mac doing half the samples and then us switching to make sure everything matched what each of us found, cut down the time significantly."

Caleb nodded. "What is the poison?"

"C. botulinum."

"Botulism?" he asked in shock.

She was just thankful that she'd discovered what it was. "Yeah. It had to be a very small dose. Otherwise, they would've died quickly."

"How do we treat it?"

She twisted her lips. "Another reason I'm thankful Mac was here. Because while I have a vaccine for botulism that I give the horses I treat, I only have a small dose of the antitoxin. Mac, however, has more. Together, we can get the three horses the antitoxin, as well as any antibiotics they'll need."

She drew in a breath and grabbed a needle from her bag as Mac walked out of the trailer with David by his side. The small group walked to the stables together. Audrey's heart sank when she saw the state of the ill horses. There was a chance the antitoxin would come too late, but she wouldn't think of that now.

Her blood rushed in her ears as she walked to the first

horse and stroked its neck. Out of the corner of her eye, Audrey spotted Caleb filling Naomi and Brice in on what was going on.

"Easy, boy," she murmured to the horse and filled the syringe. She then stuck it into the drip line and pushed the medicine through. Every prayer she had ever learned ran through her head while she waited for some sign that the remedy had worked.

One by one, she and Mac treated the three horses. Once it was finished, they stood outside the stalls, watching the animals.

Naomi leaned her arms on the stall door. "How will we know if it's working?"

"We'll have to wait and see," Mac said in a subdued tone.

Audrey looked at him. She now understood why the Easts and Harpers had trusted him for so long with their animals. Mac was amazing at his trade. He was fully invested in an animal regardless of who it belonged to.

That was the mark of a great vet, and she was honored to have worked alongside him.

"Thank you," she told him. "I couldn't have done this without your help."

Mac ducked his head in embarrassment and ran his hand over his bald head. "I think you would've managed just fine."

Brice looped an arm around Naomi. "Have faith, Audrey."

It was something her sister would say. Her head snapped up as she looked around. "Where's Maddy?"

"Clayton convinced her to go with Shane to the ranch to pick up some food Abby made," Caleb answered.

Brice chuckled. "Abby said we weren't eating more takeout. And when she worries, she cooks."

"Jace is going to be thrilled," Naomi said with a grin.

But all Audrey could think about was the fact that Clayton had somehow gotten her sister to leave. "Maddy never does what anyone wants her to do."

Caleb moved to stand beside Audrey. "Clayton is a master at getting people to do what he wants. By the time Maddy left, she believed it was her idea, and that Clayton wanted her to stay."

A bubble of relief rose up in Audrey and came out like a chuckle. "That's . . . amazing. I need to learn that trick."

"It gets even better," Brice said. "Clayton then phoned Abby and told her that Maddy was coming. Your sister has no clue what awaits her because Abby won't let her leave. She'll have Maddy in a hot bath, her belly full, and tucked in a bed within hours."

Audrey looked upward and hastily blinked at the surge of emotion. "I'm never going to be able to repay any of this kindness."

"The great thing is, you don't have to," Naomi said.

Brice smiled at his wife before he gave her a kiss. Then he looked at Audrey. "My beautiful other half is right. You owe us nothing."

"Welcome to the world of the Easts and Harpers," Mac said with a wink. "They're some of the best people in the world."

"I'll second that," Naomi replied.

Audrey swallowed, all too aware of Caleb's closeness. His nearness was exhilarating. And now that she and Mac had discovered the poison, she found she couldn't stop looking at him.

Hell. Who was she kidding? She hadn't been able to

stop looking at him since the moment she first saw him. He did something wonderfully amazing to her. It didn't matter how or why. Just that he did.

Caleb walked into the roan's stall and began talking to the horse as he gently ran his hand down the animal's back. Audrey was taken aback by how the mare instantly responded to him.

The horse's ears swiveled around to listen to Caleb. Then the beast's large head lifted and turned. Caleb praised her, constantly stroking the animal.

Audrey had seen others who had a way with horses, but Caleb's skill went beyond anything she'd ever witnessed before. It was like the horse understood him. Like Caleb was a horse whisperer.

Caleb looked up over the horse and let his wide lips slowly lift in a smile. It was the kind of grin that made a woman's legs turn to jelly. And Audrey should know because that's exactly what happened to her.

"He's looking better," she said.

"Told you to have faith," Brice said.

She couldn't remember ever being this tired. Not during finals of her senior year in college. Not during the many horse births that she had been a part of. Nor any of the surgeries she'd had to perform.

Audrey drew in a breath and slowly released it.

"Now it's time for you to rest," Caleb said.

She frowned, thinking of losing another horse. "I can't. I need to be here for—"

"For what?" Mac asked. "The others are right. You need to rest. You're dead on your feet. I'll remain and look after them."

"Sleep is not a weakness," Caleb said softly from beside her.

She hadn't even known he was there. Or maybe she had, instinctively. Perhaps she was so used to him being around that she sought him out without even knowing it.

Caleb held out his hand. She looked at it in confusion, but she took it. Without a word, he led her out of the stables and back to David's office. Audrey had no idea where anyone was, and she was too drained to care.

She didn't even have the wherewithal to argue when Caleb sat on David's couch and pulled her down beside him. He pulled out his phone and turned on some music. Audrey grinned when she recognized Dean Martin's voice. He'd been her mother's favorite singer.

They sat together as more of the Rat Pack songs played, one by one. It became nearly impossible for Audrey to keep her eyes open.

When Caleb reached up and gently tilted her head so that it rested on his shoulder, she wanted to say something witty or charming, but sleep quickly pulled her under.

Many women had been in Caleb's arms, but the only one that he had willingly led to a couch just so she could sleep was Audrey.

He shifted her so that her head rested on his lap. He played with the ends of the long, black hair of her ponytail. And before he knew it, his fingers caressed down the side of her face.

He'd known her for only two days, but in that time, they had been under extreme duress several times. That kind of pressure revealed people at their worst—but Audrey had been amazing.

She never faltered, never hesitated. She knew what had to be done, and she did it.

Caleb's head whipped to the side when the office door

opened and Brice poked his head in. Caleb put a finger to his lips to caution his brother to speak in low tones.

Brice nodded, his gaze dropping to Audrey's sleeping form. "This is a first," Brice whispered.

Caleb shot him the finger.

His brother chuckled. "It's only been thirty minutes, but the horses are recovering nicely. Why don't you take Audrey back to our place?"

There was nothing Caleb would like better, but he knew it would be the wrong thing to do. "She needs to see the horses when she wakes."

Brice gave a nod. "I like her. So does Clayton."

"She's an amazing vet."

Brice rolled his eyes. "You know what I meant."

Caleb cut him a dark look when Brice's voice rose at the end of the sentence. He pointed to Audrey and motioned for Brice to keep his voice down. "I am what I am. Don't try and change me."

"You're good at a great many things, brother. You break women's hearts every day without even trying. I've seen you look at them a million ways. But there's a different expression on your face when you look at Audrey. You might want to think about that when you try and tell yourself you'll never change."

Caleb didn't reply. A long moment later, Brice walked out. He didn't like his brother's words. Not because they weren't true.

But because they were.

The thing was, Caleb had always known he could never be in a relationship. And he'd known why. Thanks to their mother, the three of them had abandonment issues so deep, Clayton still had to reassure Abby—even after all this time.

Their mother leaving had left a profound scar upon

them. Somehow, Abby and Brice had been able to get past it. But Caleb knew that he never could.

He might have been only six at the time, but the knowledge that his mother didn't love him enough to stay wasn't something he could forget easily. He'd always known that he had been too much trouble and not sufficiently loveable to keep their mother with them.

Was it just because he'd been a child? Or were there things about him that would always be there? He'd come to believe that it was something innate about him. Some part of his DNA that made him incapable of inspiring the kind of love and affection that his siblings had found.

Caleb was okay with that. He'd found other ways to seek the closeness he so desperately needed.

Besides, there were worse things in life than living alone.

Chapter 16

Audrey opened her eyes, her gaze landing on David's desk and Mac's equipment. She thought about the horses and how they were doing, but she knew if they'd worsened, someone would've come and gotten her. Her mind then turned to Caleb. He'd seemed to occupy a large percentage of her thoughts over the last couple of days.

Though that time seemed like it should be more like weeks or months instead of just days.

She drew in a deep breath, which caused her cheek to move. Her skin rubbed against denim, and she froze. That's when she realized that she was lying on her side. She didn't remember falling asleep in such a way.

Audrey did recall sitting down next to Caleb and closing her eyes. She inwardly grimaced as she remembered putting her head on his shoulder.

She slowly sat up, careful not to move the couch cushion too much. She turned to find Caleb with his head leaning back and his hat covering his face. One of his arms lay along the back of the sofa, and the other was on the armrest.

A quick glance outside through the window showed that it was daylight. Audrey couldn't believe that Caleb had stayed with her all night. Then again, he was a gentleman. He wouldn't shove her off his leg just so he could get up.

Audrey pulled the ponytail holder from her hair and shook out the strands. She raised her hands over her head and arched her back. After hearing it crack a few times, she stretched her neck.

She glanced at Caleb and saw that his hat was shifted just enough that he watched her. His eyes were open, and there was a smile upon his face.

"Rest looks good on you, doc," he said as he lifted his head and adjusted his hat so that it sat properly.

Audrey couldn't help but grin. "I do feel better."

"Good." He got to his feet and held out his hand. "Want to see the horses?"

She took his hand, and he helped her to her feet. They walked together from the building to the stables. Audrey glanced down at their joined hands. She'd half expected him to let go, but then again, that wasn't the type of man Caleb was.

The moment she saw the animals eating, Audrey was overcome with emotion. She hurried to the roan and choked back a sob when the mare lifted her head and neighed in greeting. The horse walked to the stall door and hung her head out.

Audrey put her hands on either side of the animal's face and pressed her forehead to the roan's. They stayed like that for a moment before Audrey straightened and rubbed the horse's ears.

The next two horses weren't quite as active, but they

were moving about and eating. Audrey wasted no time in removing all three of the saline drips.

When she returned to Caleb's side, Brice and Naomi were with him. Audrey looked at the couple and smiled in gratitude. "Thank you."

"Don't think twice about it," Brice said. "This is what friends do."

Caleb jerked his chin to the animals. "They look good."

"They're recovering, but I still want to keep an eye on them. There might be prolonged damage, especially with the two that had the poison within them the longest," she said.

Caleb looked around. "Where's Clayton?"

"He should be returning any moment. He went home to Abby and the kids last night, and then stopped by the sheriff's department to talk to Danny," Naomi explained. "Once he's here, both you and Audrey can leave."

Audrey started to open her mouth to argue, but then she thought about a shower and a change of clothes. She also needed to check on Maddy. Her sister had been through an ordeal.

Brice chuckled when Clayton walked into the stables. "Speak of the devil."

"That's me," the tall cowboy said with a wink. Clayton glanced at the horses. "Great going, Audrey and Mac. We never had any doubt."

She'd had enough skepticism for everyone. Still, she exchanged a look with Mac and smiled at Clayton. "Thank you."

Mac let out a loud yawn. "It's my turn to go get a little rest on David's couch. Then I'll load up my equipment."

Audrey waved to Mac as he ambled off.

"Get Audrey out of here for a bit," Clayton told Caleb.

Brice then said, "Maddy is resting at Clayton and Abby's, so you don't need to worry about her."

"You mean she's not trying to get home?" Audrey asked in surprise.

Clayton shook his head. "Abby even came up with arguments to keep your sister there for a day or two, but she's not had to use them."

That was good, right? At least Audrey liked to think so. Normally, Maddy didn't want to be away from home. Was that because her sister enjoyed her independence?

Or was it because Maddy believed that Audrey needed someone looking out for her?

She feared the answer was the latter. Especially since it was apparent that several people were here to do just that, and Maddy didn't want to leave the East Ranch.

"Audrey?"

She swung her head to Caleb and realized the four of them were waiting on her to say something. "I'm glad Maddy is taken care of."

"Then let us take care of you," Clayton said.

Audrey took a step back and forced a smile. All she could think about was how long her sister had lived with her and why. Did everyone really believe she couldn't take care of herself?

"Thanks, I—" she began.

Caleb stepped in front of her, blocking the others. "Do you need help packing anything? I know you won't be gone long, but I also know you don't want to leave anything behind."

"I can get it," she said.

He put his hand atop hers. "But you don't have to. I'm here to help. Let me."

How silly would it be for Audrey to turn away assistance? And yet, she couldn't help thinking that perhaps they didn't believe she could take care of herself.

Horses, definitely.

Herself? She was now wondering the same thing.

"Right." She immediately turned and began picking up her things.

But she still saw the dark look Caleb shot the others. Audrey thought it better to ignore it and pretend that she hadn't seen anything. In no time, she had all her things together.

When she looked up, Brice, Clayton, and Caleb were off together, talking. Naomi walked up beside her. The two stood in silence for a long moment, watching the men from the shade of the stables.

Then Naomi said, "If you want to go home, you can. You're a grown woman, capable of making your own decisions."

"But?" Audrey asked as she turned her head to Naomi.

"These men, this family actually, have a way of surrounding someone with such warmth that it's impossible to say no. Abby didn't say no. I didn't even think of refusing."

Audrey frowned. "I'm not either of you."

"That's right," Naomi said as she smiled at her. "You're not. You're you. Someone completely different. Someone Caleb can't take his eyes off of. Just look," she said and jerked her head to the men.

Sure enough, as soon as Audrey looked over, she saw Caleb watching her.

Naomi nudged her with an elbow. "What will it hurt to go with Caleb?"

"Where, though?"

"Does it matter?" Naomi asked with a wicked gleam in her eyes.

The little flutter in Audrey's stomach wasn't something she had felt before. It spread at the thought of spending time alone with Caleb.

No horses, no threats, no other people.

Her breath hitched.

Naomi laughed. "Girl, every one of us has regretted a decision. Don't let this be yours."

"He hasn't asked."

Naomi winked at her. "He will."

Audrey watched the woman walk away. When she turned around, Caleb was making his way to her. She swallowed nervously.

"Cooper is getting some rest," he said. "When he gets back, Jace will take a few hours. They're going to keep an eye on the horses tonight. Danny has deputies in uniform and plain clothes patrolling to make sure there are no more visits. And the security system works great."

"I should be here to pull my weight."

Caleb raised a dark brow. "You've done enough. More than enough, actually. It's time for you to take a much-needed break."

Audrey licked her lips and glanced back at the horses again. "Well, I would like a shower."

Caleb grinned. "Me, too."

They shared a laugh.

Caleb drew in a breath. "My brother-in-law wasn't wrong, you know? Whoever these guys are, they could come back."

"For David or the horses?"

Caleb paused for a moment. "For you."

"Me?" Audrey hadn't expected that. "Why do you think they're after me?"

Caleb lifted one shoulder. "They could've poisoned any animal here if they were after David. Instead, they focused on the horses."

She nodded as the realization sank in. "Anyone that knows David knows we're close. Of course, he'd call me."

"Exactly."

Audrey thought of the sight of Maddy, bloody and bruised. She didn't want to end up like that.

"Do you know why someone would be after you?"

She shook her head. "I don't have a clue."

"It's all right. We'll figure it out."

"What do you suggest in the meantime?"

"I can take you to your sister. There's plenty of room there. Or. . . ."

"Or?" she urged when his voice trailed off.

Caleb shrugged. "I can take you to my ranch. I have a house on one side, and Brice has one on the other. You could stay at either."

In a snap decision, Audrey said, "I think my sister is fine with Abby. I don't need to go there. I'll come with you."

"You want to bring your truck or leave it?"

The fact that her eyes still stung made her worry about getting behind the wheel and trying to focus. "Do you mind driving?"

"Absolutely not. You ready?"

She nodded, knowing that she would've answered differently two days ago. But a lot had changed in that time. More than she was ready to admit.

And she thought there might be even more changes on the horizon. Yet that didn't scare her. She was actually excited to see what other decisions she'd make and if they went outside her norm.

Audrey didn't stop Caleb from taking her bag. He even opened the door to the truck for her. She tried to think back to the last man who had done something like that, and sadly, the only other one who had done it was her father.

He used to tell her that times could change, but manners never did. It was too bad her dad wasn't around, because she knew he'd like Caleb.

Audrey buckled her seatbelt and waved to the others as Caleb climbed into the vehicle and started the engine. And then they were off. As they were pulling out, she realized she had no other clothes.

"Do you mind if we stop off at my house to pick up some things?" she asked.

He shot her a heart-stopping grin. "Was already headed there."

When they got to her place, she waited for him to search the house to make sure no one was waiting for her. Then she stood in the middle of her room and wondered what to pack. It was suddenly very important for her to look good for Caleb.

Audrey found her favorite pieces then went into the bathroom and collected the few items she needed from there. She threw it all into an overnight bag. When she walked into the front room, she found Caleb looking at the various family pictures on the wall.

He led her from the house after she locked it. As they drove off, her heart hammered double-time in excitement.

Chapter 17

She was at his ranch. Caleb's mind raced, trying to remember if he'd left his clothes strewn about. It was a common occurrence, so there was a high probability that there were items everywhere.

Abby used to tell him that someone would come to his place one day that he wished he would've picked up for.

And wouldn't you know it, that time had finally come.

Caleb's palms sweated as he gripped the steering wheel and drove slowly down the long drive. There were two ways to get to his place. He could take the shorter route from the back road that led straight to his house.

Or, he could take the longer path that took them past Brice and Naomi's house as well as two of the barns and several corrals.

The last time Caleb had been this nervous was at prom when he wasn't sure how the night would end. He'd fumbled with Tammy Germane's zipper to the point where he thought he'd broken it.

He and Audrey hadn't spoken much since they left her

place. The music had filled the silence while she stared out
her window, watching the passing scenery.

Her fingers tapped to the beat. She seemed at ease,
while Caleb thought his heart might burst from his chest
at any moment. The A/C was on full-blast, but sweat was
running down his back, perspiration that had nothing to
do with the heat, and everything to do with the beautiful
vet sitting next to him.

The road took him straight to his garage. Caleb slowed
the truck as he punched a button to open the door. He'd
never noticed how agonizingly slow his garage door was
before that moment.

Finally, he was able to drive forward and park. He
turned off the ignition. His gaze was drawn to Audrey.

"Are you all right?" she asked.

He was anxious about her entering his house.

He was tense about her seeing what an absolute slob he
was.

He was on the verge of panicking about finally being
alone with her.

"I'm fine. You?" He managed to say the lie without
missing a beat.

She grinned. He loved how easily she smiled. And when
she spoke, she looked directly at him, making eye contact.
Whether it was intentional or not, it made it so that he was
focused solely on her. No one else existed for him.

"I'm good," she answered.

There was nothing else for it. Caleb had to take her inside. For a second, he wondered about asking her to stay
out here while he did a quick fluff-and-stuff just to pick
up the worst of his mess.

But she had worked her cute ass off for far too long. She

needed a break, and he didn't have the heart to make her wait another minute for her shower.

"Come on in," he said as he opened his door and got out of the vehicle.

She was out and following him to the entrance of the house.

Caleb paused and looked at her over his shoulder. "Be prepared. It's a mess."

"I don't care."

That's what most people said, but for once, he actually cared what she thought. Maybe he could get her in the shower and then spend the time picking up.

He unlocked the door and stepped into the house. There was an area for him to take off his muddy boots and hang up his jacket before a short hallway led them into the kitchen.

"This is beautiful," Audrey said, letting her hands run along the black and gray granite. "I love the dark wood cabinets."

"I'll take you for a tour after your shower," he offered.

She laughed and met his gaze. "Deal."

Caleb motioned for her to follow as he took her to the second bathroom. It was never used, which meant it was clean. One relief, at least.

"Take as much time as you want," he told her as she walked inside the room.

She turned to him and smiled. "I'm going to take you up on that offer. But I'll be sure to leave you some hot water."

"Don't worry about that." He pulled the door shut and waited for a heartbeat.

Then he ran around the house, picking up all his clothes

and tossing them into the basket in the laundry room. As soon as he finished that, he filled the dishwasher with dirty dishes—only to realize halfway through that it had clean dishes inside.

"Fuck it," he murmured.

After a quick wipe-down of the cabinets, he ran to his room and made the bed. Just when he thought he was finished, he took a peek into his bathroom and winced.

Years in the military hadn't erased his slob gene. Moving as fast as he could, he cleaned the toilet, sink, and countertop. Despite the quickness of it all, Caleb was quite impressed with his handiwork.

He blew out a breath and walked to the mudroom where he took off his boots and hung up his hat. Then he shuffled to the kitchen and opened the fridge.

It had taken some getting used to once he moved off the East Ranch. Abby always kept the pantry and refrigerator stocked. It was a chore he hated.

Thankfully, he and Brice had a system. One of them went each week and bought groceries for both houses. But all of that would change when his brother and sister-in-law had kids. They'd been trying for about a year now. Caleb expected news any day that a baby was on the way.

He heard the water cut off. Caleb glanced at his watch and grinned. Audrey had heeded his suggestion and had taken a long, hot shower.

It wasn't long before she walked from the bathroom with her black tresses wet and tousled. She looked so damn hot, that for a moment Caleb forgot to breathe.

"I feel like a new person," Audrey said with a chuckle.

He swallowed hard, his gaze dropping to the thin gray sweatpants that stopped just below her knees and the black tee that hugged her breasts.

"Thirsty?" he asked.

She nodded and shoved her hair out of her face before she sat on the barstool on the opposite side of the island from him. "Sure."

"I've got milk, water, soda, and beer. Oh, and wine," Caleb added as his gaze landed on the wine holder on the counter.

Audrey pressed her lips together as she considered the options. "I'll take a beer."

Caleb took out two and removed the cap from hers before handing it over.

She lifted her beer and waited for him to clink his against hers. "Thank you for this."

"It's my pleasure."

After she took a long drink, she turned and looked at the open floor plan that had the living and dining area behind her. "Wow. This is gorgeous."

"It's my favorite part of the house," Caleb said as he walked around the island to stare out the wall of windows that looked over the rolling hills. "I knew I wanted this view. I brought the architect out here and showed him. We designed the house around it."

"Are there always horses out there grazing?" she asked.

"Always. Sometimes, I see them playing. I never tire of watching them."

She glanced at him and smiled. "They are magnificent."

"If you like this view, you should see the one at the East Ranch. It's where I got the idea."

Audrey shrugged. "I think this one is pretty perfect. You should have made sure you have the same view from your bedroom."

"I do."

Their eyes met and held. God, he wanted her. The kind

of craving that wouldn't be satisfied until he had her. The type of need that intensified until it consumed him.

It wasn't the lust he normally felt. The kind that disappeared after sex. This was something more. Something much deeper.

Caleb wasn't at all sure he wanted to go down this road. There were too many bumps and holes to navigate.

Still, he knew he could stop it. The fact that he hadn't meant. . . . What did it mean? That he wanted this? The confirmed bachelor?

"You wake up to Heaven every morning."

Caleb nodded. He knew that Audrey meant the horses and view, but all he could think about was waking up next to her. *That* would be Heaven.

She faced the windows again and took another drink of the beer. "This is seriously making me rethink my house," she said with a laugh.

"How long have you lived there?" Finally, something he could ask that didn't make him think of sex.

With her.

Naked and sweating.

And moaning in pleasure.

Fuck. He needed to get himself under control.

"Seven years," she answered, oblivious to his internal dialogue.

Caleb needed to be a gentleman. Audrey wasn't just any woman. She wasn't the regular kind that he hit on and had sex with. She was a friend of the family now, which meant that if he slept with her, he couldn't walk away like he normally did.

Otherwise, his entire family would be on his ass about it.

"I don't have much in the house to cook, but I think we

can scrounge something up. And I can order pizza," he offered.

She lifted a shoulder. "I'm up for anything."

"How about a tour first?"

"Please," she said, her dark eyes shining.

Caleb took her down the hallway where the bathroom
was. He showed her the room he used as his office, which,
oddly enough, was always kept perfectly neat and orderly.

Next were the two guest bedrooms, and then the back
room, which served as his theatre. With all the windows
in the living area, it made it hard to watch TV sometimes.

They retraced their steps to the kitchen where he took
her past it to another hallway that led to the master bedroom and bathroom.

No sooner were they inside his room than she walked
to the windows. And all he could see in his head was him
taking her, naked, right there.

Chapter 18

The view. Audrey kept telling herself to look at the magnificent rolling hills and the horses grazing, but she couldn't stop thinking about Caleb.

She even walked to the windows in his bedroom to put some distance between them. But all that did was remind her that they were in *his* room.

With a very large bed.

Caleb had been kind to her. He'd held her hand, yes, but did that mean he liked her? All he'd done was use that gesture to take her from one place to another. It wasn't like they were on a date or anything.

And as for her falling asleep on his leg, most likely, he was just being kind and didn't want to disturb her. He could've gotten up at any time and walked away. But that wasn't who Caleb was.

In fact, now that she thought about it, he hadn't done anything to suggest that he was interested. She'd gotten herself all worked up simply because Naomi had said something about the way Caleb was looking at her.

Perhaps all the little things—like the long looks and the sexy smiles—were just that. Looks and smiles. Maybe Caleb did that to everyone.

Audrey usually never hesitated to make the first move on a guy. For some reason, it made it easier when she wanted them out of her life. As if by her going to them, she then had the first right of refusal.

It was silly, but it had become quite a habit.

So it was crazy when she couldn't even bring herself to flirt with Caleb. He and his family had done so much for not only her and Maddy but also for the horses.

And to be honest, she wasn't in the mood to be rebuffed in any way.

The condensation from the beer wetted her fingers, turning the digits icy, so much that she had to switch hands. She wiped her damp fingers on her sweats. She'd chosen them because they flattered her figure, contouring her legs and clinging to her hips, but they weren't as tight as yoga pants.

Audrey fidgeted, trying to find something to say. Normally, she didn't mind silence, but going in circles over whether or not Caleb might find her attractive was causing the quiet to drive her batty.

"It's a beautiful house," she said.

Caleb came up to stand beside her, one hand in his front pocket and his gaze out the window. "Abby says I'm a minimalist. I hate clutter, so I only put things in the house that I love."

"I think I'm more like you. I bought maybe three pictures," Audrey said, thinking back. "Then Maddy moved in. The day after, she brought in all kinds of knickknacks."

Caleb's head swung to her. "Did you like the items?"

Audrey looked at him as she shrugged. "Some, yes. The

majority, no. But I didn't have the heart to tell her. She feels it's her duty to act like a parent."

"She did mention something about making sure you eat," he teased.

Audrey rolled her eyes. "I tell her I eat, but in her eyes, if she doesn't see me with food in my mouth, then I'm lying."

"Siblings, huh?"

"Yeah," she replied with a nod. "But I don't know what I'd do without her."

Caleb took a long drink of beer. When he lowered the bottle, his attention was once more out the window. "Abby still mothers me and Brice. It's not her fault. For years, she was sister, mother, and father to us. It's how I knew she'd be a great mom."

"How many kids do she and Clayton have?"

"Three," Caleb said with a grin full of love. "They're the best."

Audrey couldn't tear her eyes from him. He shared small details of his life, but just enough to make her hungry for more.

"Do you want kids?" As soon as the words were out, Audrey wanted to take them back.

"I don't think so." Then he looked at her. "You?"

"I've never really considered it. I don't hate kids."

He threw back his head and laughed. "Well, that's a good start."

She smiled and chuckled. "I suppose. I've just been so involved with work. My friends know better than to mention anything like that around me. For the longest time, they were on me and Maddy both, wanting to know who we were dating and if we were going to settle down."

Caleb nodded as he listened.

Audrey frowned as she thought about those conversations. "Why is it that in this day and age, so many people still consider getting married and having children the only option? Look at the divorce rate. Has anyone pondered that perhaps everyone getting married is doing it with the wrong people?"

"So you don't want to get married?"

His eyes were piercing as they carefully watched her. Audrey wasn't sure if his inquiry was a trick question or not, but either way, the only option she had was to answer with the truth. If Caleb didn't like it, he didn't like it.

"My parents had an amazing marriage. The kind you see in the movies, you know? I always said that if I decide to settle down, it'll be with someone that I truly, madly love. I won't take less than that."

Caleb lifted his bottle in salute. "Good for you."

"What about you?" Since she'd spilled her guts, she wanted him to do the same.

He pressed his lips together and let out a long breath. "My parents never should have gotten married. Had my father not died, I'm not sure they would've stayed together. Or maybe that's because I'm biased against my mother."

"As anyone in your shoes would be," Audrey added quickly.

"Abby wasn't looking for love. Neither was Brice, and yet both my siblings found it. And I believe it's the kind of love that's real. The kind that lasts. The kind that people fight for every day and work to keep going."

"They're so lucky," Audrey said in a whisper.

"Yeah. I suppose they are."

She pulled her eyes from Caleb and looked out the window. There were depths to Caleb that he didn't let many people see, but she thought that maybe she'd gotten a brief glimpse. His smile and easygoing nature hid much. That was obvious.

Then again, she hid a lot, too. She rarely told anyone much about herself. It was just easier to keep people at arm's length if they didn't know her.

"Do you get lonely?" Caleb asked.

"Yes. You?"

"Yeah."

She switched the beer to her other hand and took a sip of it. "It always hits me when I least expect it."

"When you're surrounded by others."

"Or late at night when I can't sleep."

Caleb cleared his throat and shifted his feet as if he were uncomfortable with where the conversation was headed. "What about Maddy? Does she have someone?"

"Maddy floats through life to the beat of her own drum. She does what makes her happy, and while I don't always agree with it, it's hard to argue the outcome when she's always smiling. There was a guy a few months back. It got pretty serious, but one day, everything he'd given her was packed in a box, taped shut, and put in the garage."

One of Caleb's brows lifted. "Did you ask?"

"Of course," Audrey said. "I wanted to know if I needed to go kick some sense into him or whether she left on her own. The fact she wouldn't discuss it says that it was something bad. I keep hoping that, eventually, she'll tell me, but I already know the truth. The guy broke her heart. Maddy is the most sensitive person I know. She let him in, gave him her love, and she was left to pick up the pieces."

"She seems to be doing all right."

Audrey lifted a shoulder in a shrug. "Don't we all do things to mask how we really feel?"

"Good point. Most people do." He turned to her. "You hungry?"

"Sure." Anything to turn the topic to something lighter or happier.

They'd managed to traverse into deep waters, and while she hadn't minded sharing with him—which was odd enough—she wasn't sure why she hadn't quickly changed the topic.

Perhaps it was because there was a possibility that Caleb understood some of the things she had experienced. To reveal even a hint of pain was something she *never* did. Not even to her sister.

Audrey told anyone who asked that she wasn't lonely. How could she be when surrounded by people and horses all day?

But it was a bald-faced lie. The loneliness went so deep that, at times, her heart physically ached. Not even that could stop her from discarding men as she did.

Partly because, deep in her soul, she knew that they weren't right for her. They were Mr. Right Now. But even that was getting old. She was tired of making up excuses not to see them again. She opted for lies rather than the truth because she didn't want to be mean.

Once in the kitchen, Audrey was surprised when Caleb pointed to a stool and told her to sit. She sat back and watched as he pulled out sausage and a box of pasta. As he worked, he began talking about the horse he was about to start working with.

She knew what he was doing. Like her, he wanted out of the deep pool of thought they had been in. This conversation was light and easy. His smile was back as he glanced her way in between chopping onions and bell peppers.

Audrey laughed and asked questions to keep the dialogue going. She was impressed by his skills as a cook. Obviously, the years spent with Abby had taught him not only how to be responsible, but also how to handle himself in the kitchen.

He was no novice. Caleb moved as if he had been cooking for years. The expert way he chopped, to the ingredients that he threw together without ever looking at a recipe.

Audrey could cook as long as she had something to guide her. Without a recipe, she wouldn't know the first thing about what to put with what. It would be a disaster if she tried.

As the aromas of the meal filled the kitchen, her stomach rumbled in anticipation.

When Caleb turned to dish the meal into a bowl, it looked like something she would get in a restaurant. The spiral pasta and veggies were lightly coated with a Parmesan-garlic flavored sauce that made her mouth water.

Caleb set aside the pots and grabbed his bowl to come around and sit beside her at the island. "During the cooler nights, I eat outside."

"You cook every night?"

He laughed and shook his head. "It's difficult to cook for one, but I do sometimes. We have Sunday lunch with Abby, Clayton, and the kids. The rest of the time, Brice, Naomi, and I trade off cooking."

"That sounds nice."

Caleb jerked his chin to the food. "Careful, it's hot. And it is nice. Naomi is a photographer, so she's not sitting in the house by any means. Her business has become so successful that she's having a difficult time keeping up with demand."

"Is it hard working with your brother every day?" Audrey asked. "I'm sure there are fights and such. While Maddy doesn't work for me, she's almost like an assistant. She does little things to help me out."

"And do y'all fight?"

Audrey grinned. "We're sisters. What do you think?"

"Exactly," he said with a chuckle. "Brice and I argue. It comes with the territory. But at the end of the day, we're brothers. We work it out."

"So did you mind when he and Naomi got together?"

Caleb paused as he stirred the food and slowly shook his head. "Not even a little. She's good for him. Naomi is exactly what Brice needed, just as he is what she needed."

"I love happy endings," Audrey said and took a bite of the pasta.

She closed her eyes and moaned at the explosion of flavor in her mouth. It was the most delicious meal she'd ever had.

When she lifted her lids, she found Caleb staring at her, his expression unreadable.

Chapter 19

"Well?"

Brice straightened from leaning against the stall and looked at his wife. He couldn't, for the life of him, figure out what she wanted. "Well, what?"

"It's been hours since Caleb and Audrey left."

Brice lifted his brows and nodded. "That's right."

Naomi sighed dramatically and rolled her eyes. "Brice Harper, you can't tell me you didn't see how your brother looked at her."

Brice adjusted his hat atop his head and rested his arm along the stall door. He'd spent the last hour and a half brushing down each of the horses. "Darlin', you know I did, but you also know Caleb. There is nothing on God's green Earth that would get him to commit to a woman. Not even someone like Audrey."

"What does that mean?" Naomi asked, crossing her arms over her chest. "Someone like Audrey?"

He shook his head. "Oh, no you don't. I'm not falling into that trap again."

Naomi laughed as she walked up to him and wrapped her arms around his neck. "I do love messing with you."

"Don't I know it?" He gave her a quick kiss.

"Seriously, though. You don't think there might be something between them?"

Brice pulled her against him so that her head rested on his chest. He kissed the top of her head. "I know you want Caleb to find someone."

"No," she interjected. "I want him to be as happy as us."

"That doesn't always happen, sweetheart."

"It could."

Brice looked at the stable roof. "I want nothing more for my brother, but I'm not sure it can happen. Even if the love of his life stopped him in his tracks, I still don't think Caleb could get past his issues."

"You did," Naomi said after a moment.

He rubbed his hand up and down her back. "You helped me do that. And I was willing. There's a difference. Caleb told me years ago that he would spend his life alone. He won't ever put his heart into a situation where a woman could leave him."

"That's so sad."

"He'll be okay. We'll make sure of it."

What Brice hadn't even told his beautiful wife was that he'd long been worried about Caleb. His brother went through women faster and faster as the years went on. None lasted longer than a night. The only good thing was that Caleb had never brought them to his house.

It was one of his brother's rules. He went back to the woman's place so he could leave when he wanted. Much easier than asking them to go when he grew tired of them. Which was almost as soon as he'd taken his pleasure.

Brice tried to tell Caleb that he was filling his life with

nights of sex to make up for his loneliness, but his brother didn't want to hear any of it. Caleb went back to joking and laughing as if the conversation had never happened.

But Brice got the message.

All these years later, Caleb still bore the sting of their mother's abandonment. In fact, he felt it deeper and harder than either Brice or Abby. And Abby used to think that Brice had gotten the brunt of it because Caleb was too young to remember.

She was wrong. So wrong.

Naomi lifted her head. "What is it?"

"As an outsider looking into my family, who would you think got hurt the worst from our mother leaving?"

Naomi studied him, a frown marring her brow. "It scarred Abby certainly. She was just starting her life, but she put that on hold to raise you and Caleb. But she was also older. While it hurt and obviously left her with the same abandonment issues as you and Caleb, I think she handled it better."

"Okay."

"You," Naomi continued, "found the note your mother left first. You read it and realized what had happened."

To this day, Brice remembered that sinking feeling as if someone had a hold of his ankles and was pulling him down into . . . nothing. He'd curled up on the floor, rocking back and forth as he wondered what he'd done to make his mother leave.

Naomi touched his cheek. "Your wounds are healing, my love, but I know you still battle them. For a long time, you didn't realize that your mother leaving had done such damage. But when you did, you faced it head-on."

He turned his head and kissed her palm before pulling her down to his chest. "And Caleb?"

"He didn't react to what had happened right away. All he wanted as a six-year-old was breakfast. So, he woke Abby. She found the note and then you, and she did her best to get the world right for both of you again. But because Caleb didn't respond the way you did, both you and Abby believed that he wasn't affected."

Brice swallowed. "I can't remember if Caleb was still in bed when I got up or not. We shared a room, so I should know."

"You never asked him?"

"It's not something we three talk about."

Naomi shot Brice a flat look. "Perhaps you should. Because I think there's a real possibility that Caleb wasn't just up, but that he saw your mother leaving."

It felt as if Brice had been kicked in the chest. He shook his head, wanting to deny it, but it made sense. Of the three of them, Caleb was the only one adamant about being alone, about never trusting anyone enough to allow them close to hurt him.

"Oh, God," Brice murmured.

Naomi hurried to say, "It's pure speculation on my part."

"Why else would he be so averse to relationships?"

"He's not against it, love. Look at what he has with you, Jace, Cooper, Clayton, Abby, and the kids. Even Shane, for that matter."

Brice ran a hand down his face. "It's women."

She nodded. "Yeah."

"What do I do?"

"Be there for him. Whether it's tomorrow or twenty years from now, he's going to meet someone that makes him want to get close. If he doesn't run away, he's going to need his family to help steady him."

Brice smiled down at her. "You're part of that family as well, darlin'."

"I love you, Brice."

"I love you, too, Naomi."

Dinner had been excruciating. Not because Caleb was with Audrey, but because the longer he was around her, the more he wanted her.

When she moaned at the taste of the food, he'd gone instantly, achingly hard. It was all he could do not to yank her against him and kiss her.

He slowly walked through the stables. He'd had to get out of the house for a minute. She'd insisted on cleaning the dishes, so he used the excuse of checking on his horses to leave.

"Coward," he mumbled to himself.

Caleb had always been able to steer conversations in whatever direction he wanted—even if it was to get the woman he was with away from him. It was a skill he'd honed years ago and used ruthlessly.

One of the kids from the high school who worked part-time around the ranch had already fed the horses. With both Brice and Caleb having equal shares of the business and splitting the land, there were several barns, corrals, and pastures to maintain.

Luckily, there was never a shortage of kids who wanted to see how a ranch ran, though both he and Brice screened them diligently. You could always tell a bad apple when the horses wanted nothing to do with them. There had been a few cases that had slipped through, but they'd caught it early on and fired the kid.

The funny thing was that both of them had assumed it would take years to build their horse ranch, which would leave all the duties split between them. But they had grown so quickly, that now Caleb was toying with the idea of asking Brice what he thought about hiring a ranch manager like the East Ranch employed Shane.

That would free up Caleb and Brice to do what they did best. With Brice traveling all over to buy the horses, and Caleb spending so much time training them, Naomi was trying to pick up the slack while doing some of their office work, but that wasn't fair to her.

Caleb walked from the barn to the fence to look out over the land. A black-and-white-paint stallion pranced back and forth as he looked into another pasture where the mares were.

Caleb always loved a challenge, and the stallion would certainly be that. The paint was feisty and stubborn. Caleb didn't want to break him. The last thing he wanted was to take away what made the stallion so beautiful. His approach to training horses was much different than most.

He'd left the stallion alone for the past couple of weeks, only getting close enough to bring him feed each day. The horse wouldn't let Caleb get within twenty feet of him. Building the trust was the hardest and longest part of the process, but it was one that solidified the next step in the training.

Caleb walked to the gate and let himself in. As soon as the stallion heard the click of the gate latch, his ears swiveled to Caleb.

Caleb chuckled. So far, the mares were more interesting to the horse. Caleb wanted to see how close he could get before the paint looked his way. He'd yet to touch the stallion since releasing him into the pasture.

Halfway to the horse, the animal's great head swung

around. Caleb slowed his steps as he stared into the horse's dark eyes.

"Easy boy," Caleb murmured. "You remember me. I know you do because you're that smart. Besides, I'm the one who brings you food. But I don't have any now, do I?"

The horse flicked its tail.

Caleb grinned. "You want to know what I'm doing here, don't you? Well, I think it's high time you and I got to know each other without food coming between us."

The stallion pawed the ground with one hoof and snorted.

"Not a fan of that suggestion, huh? Well, too bad, because I'm going to stand my ground. I swore when you got here that I wouldn't hurt you, and I won't. Just ask any of the other horses here. They'll tell you."

The horse grew still, his body twitching only when a gnat landed on him.

Caleb kept his steps slow and held the animal's gaze. "You know how handsome you are, don't you? Those mares can't take their eyes off you. Who knows? You might get cozy with one yet. But not until I give the all-clear. You see, you and I need to be friends first."

Caleb was about twenty feet from the stallion. This was as close as he'd gotten for weeks. He stopped for just a heartbeat. Then he took another step.

The stallion's shrill neigh sounded a second before he charged. Caleb held his ground, despite adrenaline pumping through his veins.

Suddenly, the horse slid to a halt and reared, his front hooves pawing at the air. When he landed, he was only two feet away. Caleb knew better than anyone that if the horse had wanted to kill him, he could have. It wouldn't have mattered if Caleb ran or not.

The stallion blew out a breath and blinked, his sides heaving.

Caleb smiled. "Are we going to be friends now?"

He held out his hand and waited for the horse to sniff it. Once the paint did, Caleb moved closer and rubbed his palm down the animal's forehead, brushing aside the black and white mane.

"We're going to be good friends, you and I," Caleb said. "And we need to come up with a name for you."

The stallion bobbed his head up and down as if in answer, then spun around and ran off. Caleb was smiling as he watched the animal.

When he turned toward the house, Audrey stood at the fence, her face white.

"You scared the hell out of me," she stated. "He could have killed you."

"One of us had to bend. It wasn't going to be me."

Just as he wouldn't bend and give in to the longing within him that he felt for Audrey.

Chapter 20

Audrey hated reckless behavior. Why then did Caleb's actions excite her?

He walked toward her, never moving his gaze from her face. The closer Caleb got, the faster her breathing came. Her blood ran hot in her veins.

Caleb didn't go to the gate. He came straight to her. With ease, he climbed the wooden fence and jumped down beside her. He was so close, she could reach out and touch him. Muscles strained his button-down, the sleeves rolled up to his elbows.

With his hat gone, Audrey got to see the thick, light brown locks that he kept trimmed short on the sides and longer on top. He absently shoved the hair that had fallen into his eyes back with a hand. It was such a simple gesture, but it did something strange to her. She swallowed hard, her body achy and . . . needy.

"I'm going to take a shower."

Audrey blinked, taken aback by his words. Of all the

things she hoped he might say, of all the things she thought he could've said, that wasn't one of them.

"Oh. Okay," she mumbled.

He gave her a nod. "Stay out here as long as you like."

Then, he was gone. Audrey felt like such an idiot. At least she hadn't said or done anything to let him know that she was attracted to him.

She snorted loudly. "Attracted, my ass. I want to climb his hot body, licking my way over his skin as I go," she said to herself.

It had been a long time since she'd been so wrong about a man before. Was it because she had nearly worked herself to death over the past few days? Or was it because she was around someone so damn gorgeous and kind and generous?

Abby turned to the fence and rested her arms on it before she placed her forehead against the top rail. It was all her sister's and Naomi's fault. If they hadn't said anything about Caleb, she wouldn't be feeling these . . . *things*.

Liar.

She really hated her conscience sometimes. Especially when it was right. And this time, it was dead on.

It was a wonder that Caleb hadn't already been snatched up by some lucky woman. He was a catch for sure. Not because of his connection to the East Ranch, but because of all his other amazing qualities.

Audrey lifted her head and looked at the paint stallion. He was an utterly magnificent animal. One that she wouldn't be able to part with. The way he held his head as if he knew that he was special was something to see. The stallion pranced and neighed, showing off to the mares. And they responded with an answering neigh.

Several of the horses ran to the fence to greet the stallion, touching noses and sniffing each other. Thankfully, none of the mares were in heat. Otherwise, the paint might break through the fence to get to them.

That's what Audrey wanted. A man who would break through fences or anything else that stood in his way to get to her. She had yet to encounter anyone like that.

Her thoughts immediately went to Caleb. He would do that for the woman he wanted. He wouldn't let anything or anyone prevent him from getting to the one he loved.

And for just a split second, Audrey allowed herself to wonder how that might feel if she were the one Caleb desired.

It was such a heady sensation that she had to stop the thoughts before they went on too long. Audrey knew better than to allow herself to drift into fantasies. Because real life never measured up.

She'd learned that the hard way. All the wonderful fairy tales her parents had told her as a child had made her into quite the romantic. She dreamed—as most little girls did—of a man coming to her rescue and sweeping her off her feet.

He didn't have to be a knight. She wasn't picky. But she'd fully expected something like that to happen to her. Besides, every story had a grain of truth in it.

Then she started dating. In all fairness, she didn't expect much from the boys in high school. They were boys, after all.

Her romantic nature had led her straight to romance novels. And all her dreams multiplied a hundredfold. She was the heroine in every book be it medieval, a woman in WWII, or a story set in modern day, the future, or even something of fantasy.

She'd learned to flirt and kiss in high school, which she knew had prepared her for the future. So, her attention was fixated on college. She'd known it would happen then.

Every day she woke with a bright smile, waiting for the man/prince/knight/warrior from the fairy tales and romance books. Maddy used to tell her that the books were ruining her for real life.

But when did she stop looking for her man? When did she stop expecting love to find her? For the life of her, Audrey couldn't figure it out. She still considered herself a romantic, but why then had she shunned relationships?

It wasn't because of her parents. She'd had a wonderful life as a child and still did as an adult. The tragedy that'd struck her family was just that. A tragedy. Others dealt with such things all the time.

That's not what made her keep men at arm's-length, though.

So, what was it? Did she get tired of waiting? Or was it that the men she encountered were nothing like what she was looking for? She'd given quite a few a fighting chance, but each of them was lacking in some way. No one ever measured up.

An image of Caleb filled her mind.

He could. Audrey had recognized that from the first moment she saw him.

But she was so used to being on her own, making her own decisions and doing whatever she wanted, that she now worried she would never be able to make room for anyone else in her life.

She looked over her shoulder toward the house. The sun made it impossible to see in the windows and tell where Caleb was. She'd just been with him for a few hours and was already tied in knots. The rest of the day and night were still ahead.

Maybe she should return to the auction house. It was safer there.

You don't want safe. You want him.

She squeezed her eyes closed and faced forward. God help her, but she did. She wanted to feel Caleb's arms around her, to have him pull her against his hard chest and hold her tightly as he slowly lowered his face to hers and kissed her.

Then she wanted him to yank off her clothes and—

"No," she said aloud.

She wouldn't go down that road. That would be too much to bear and make finding any kind of sleep impossible. She was already hot from being around Caleb. Letting her imagination go to how it might be with them together would keep her tossing and turning all night with desire.

Audrey shoved her hair to one side and tried to turn her thoughts to something else. If she had her phone, she would have checked in with her sister, but her cell was in the house, and she didn't want to go back in yet.

She walked along the fence toward the stables, then veered inside to take a look at the horses within. Audrey wasn't surprised to see that it was a state-of-the-art building with an A-frame ceiling to give plenty of airflow.

As she made her way through, she noticed the small lights that shed just enough glow so as not to be harsh. Added to the skylights spaced every twenty feet, it lightened the inside just enough. There were twenty large stalls. Along with a feed room, and a tack room, she was also surprised to find an on-site veterinarian clinic, outfitted with everything.

Audrey paused to pet a black horse who stuck her head out. She spotted a brush and grabbed it before opening the door and giving the mare a little push to back her up. The animal immediately took several steps back and blinked at Audrey with dark eyes.

"You are quite beautiful, but you know that, don't you?" Audrey said as she let the horse sniff her.

Then she began brushing the animal, starting at the neck and working her way down to the shoulders and across the mare's back. Though Audrey expected nothing less, it was obvious that the horses at the Rockin' H Ranch were well cared for.

Once Audrey had finished brushing the horse, she gave the mare a light pat and ducked under her head to leave. There was something about spending even a little time with a horse that settled Audrey.

Her mind was no longer jumbled. She had a smile on her face as she walked back to the house and entered. No sooner had she come through the door than she caught a glimpse of a shirtless Caleb as he walked from the laundry room.

Audrey couldn't move, couldn't even breathe. She watched him return to his bedroom without noticing her.

Hard muscles gleamed just beneath skin kissed by the sun. His shoulders were wide and thick. His chest bulged with muscles, and his stomach. . . . She had to close her eyes and reach for the door to steady herself.

So much for being centered. Perhaps she should spend the night with the horses. Slowly, she closed the door behind her and let out a long breath.

"What did you think?"

Her eyes snapped open. Her mind was still on his hard body. Thankfully, she didn't blurt out that he was sinfully hot. At least he had on a white tee with his jeans now. "About?"

"The stables. I saw you head that way before I jumped in the shower," he said as he stopped beside the island.

He was giving her a peculiar look. Audrey forced a smile and happily grasped onto something she could talk about. "It's beautiful. Where did you get the design?"

One side of Caleb's lips lifted in a proud grin. "Thanks to working with Clayton, we got to go all over the country and sometimes even abroad to check out horses and cattle. There was something about each stable that I liked, and I made sure to incorporate it into my design."

"You did a great job."

He gave her a nod. "Thanks. Any horses strike your fancy?"

She laughed and made her way toward him, more at ease now since he was clothed. "All of them, of course. But I did show some attention to the black mare."

"Ah. We bought her from a sheikh. She's an Arabian."

"I've not had a chance to spend much time with Arabians. Most of the horses I handle are Quarter Horses or thoroughbreds."

"Spend as much time as you want with her."

"So, a sheikh, huh?" Audrey asked, wanting to know more.

Caleb laughed loudly. "It was quite by accident. We were in upper New York, looking at a mare when I saw her. She was fighting the men trying to load her into the trailer. I immediately walked over to her and took the leads from the men. She calmed instantly. I walked her around for a bit. I had no idea her owner was there. He had flown her from Saudi Arabia to breed her, but she hadn't taken to the flight well."

"Most don't," Audrey added.

Caleb nodded in agreement. "This sheikh found Brice and asked if we'd be interested in buying her since I was the only one who had been able to calm her in over two weeks. No one else could even get near her."

"I'm glad you were there. Right time and place, apparently."

He smiled. "She walked right into the trailer for me, and we brought her here. I've had offers from others to buy her, but she's not going anywhere."

Audrey knew at that moment that the man she had been looking for was none other than the hot cowboy in front of her.

Chapter 21

"I'm glad."

Caleb loved the sound of Audrey's voice. It was soft and husky. And it did crazy things to his already hard cock. At this rate, he was going to have to take another shower. A cold one this time.

He cleared his throat and shifted his weight from one foot to the other. "Are you tired? Do you want to rest?"

"I'm fine."

"I don't want you to think you have to stay up. You were awake a long time."

"So were you."

Caleb shrugged. "I've had many years of such nights. It doesn't bother me."

"I can see that." She grinned and looked up at him through her lashes. "I'm a bit envious."

He laughed. "Don't be. If I closed my eyes right now, I could be asleep in a second, but then I'd throw off my entire schedule. It's better if I stay up until it's time to go to bed. But that's me. You don't have to do the same."

"You sound like you want to get me into bed."

Caleb stilled. His arousal twitched, eager to be buried deep inside her. How in the hell would he get through the night? As it was, he had to keep distance between them. Now, with her statement, he didn't know whether to laugh, run from the house, or launch himself over the island and drag her into his arms.

Neither said a word as they stared at each other. So many things to say went through Caleb's head. But none of the words made it past his lips.

The shrill sound of a cell phone ringing broke the silence—and their stand-off.

"That's me," Audrey said.

Caleb leaned his hands on the quartz countertop and dropped his chin to his chest. "What the fuck?" he asked himself.

Normally, he was suave and so smooth, Jace and Cooper often called him "Butter" as a joke. It was like he could no longer find north.

As soon as he heard Audrey approaching, he straightened. "Everything all right?"

"Yes," she said with surprise in her voice. "Can you believe it?"

"I can."

She set her cell on the island and sat on a stool. "I can't."

He frowned at her, realizing that there was more to her thought. "But?"

"These people," she said, waving her hands, "whoever they are. They went to extremes to poison the horses, wreck my equipment, and then set fire to the dead horse just so I wouldn't be able to find the cure."

Caleb leaned back against the counter behind him and

crossed his arms over his chest. "You don't think they're finished."

"Not by a long shot. Do you?"

"No."

She drew in a deep breath before she released it. "It's why none of you wanted me home alone."

"Yeah."

She pressed her lips together as her gaze moved to the quartz for a moment. "Do you think they'll try to poison more horses?"

Caleb crossed one ankle over the other. "There's a distinct possibility. That's why Jace and Cooper are staying at the auction house on guard with the police without showing themselves."

"But I have the antidote now. It'd be stupid for them to poison any more animals."

"I agree, but it's better to be cautious."

"What aren't you telling me?" she demanded, eyeing him skeptically.

Caleb studied her for a long moment. Audrey was strong mentally. She faced things head-on and didn't skirt around any issues.

He dropped his arms and put his hands on the counter beside him. "Who do you think these people are after?"

Audrey didn't have a quick response. In fact, a full minute went by before she said, "Most people would believe David since it's his auction house. I was one of those people."

"But you don't anymore?"

"I don't know. It seems obvious that it's him, but I asked myself why. David doesn't have enemies. He's one of the kindest people I know. My next guess would be the owners of the horses, but one of them was a rescue, so that couldn't possibly be it."

"Besides," Caleb said, "only David and the owners know which horse is which once it's unloaded at the auction."

Audrey nodded. "Good point."

"So. . . ." he pressed.

"You want me to keep going?" she asked, wide-eyed.

"Yeah."

She licked her lips and leaned her forearms on the island. "Okay. Well, if those two options are eliminated, then you have to look at who David would send for if the animals got sick."

Caleb stared at her, waiting for her to grasp the situation.

Audrey cocked her head to the side. "You still think it's me. David has two or three vets he calls out for such things."

"Not for something like this," Caleb pointed out.

"But . . . they haven't hurt me."

"Not physically, no, but there are other ways to come at someone."

Audrey gaped at him. "You mean professionally?"

"You are one of the most sought-after equine vets in the area."

"But I work for two ranches. That effectively takes me off the market."

"Yet you helped David," Caleb stated.

Audrey rose from the stool and walked toward the living area before hastily turning back around. She took another two steps before she halted. "By keeping my attention on the horses at David's, I have neglected my duties at the other two farms. They've called numerous times, and I've asked for personal time, but neither owner is particularly happy with me. If they want to fire me, let them. I think I can find work again."

"Easily."

The soft smile that tilted her lips at his compliment made his balls tighten.

"Thank you," she said. "Tell me how any of this hurts me."

"You have your reputation, and that's what they could be after."

Audrey swallowed hard. "It's the one thing I've worked hard to build. I kept thinking this was about David or someone wanting to hurt horses."

"They could've put that poison into any animal at the auction house. Matter of fact, it would've been a hell of a lot easier to go to other places than the auction house to do this. No, I think this is all tied to you somehow."

Audrey pivoted and walked to the window. For long moments, she stood there silently, unmoving. Caleb knew it was foolish, but he still walked to her. He stopped behind and just to the side of her.

He put a hand on her shoulder and lightly squeezed. "It's going to be all right, you know."

Audrey reached up and covered his hand with hers. Then she faced him. "Are you always so confident?"

"No."

"I think you are," she said in a soft whisper. "I'm not scared with you."

It would be so easy to touch her face, caress her cheek, and then close the distance to put his lips to hers. He'd done it a million times with other women.

He let his arm fall from her shoulder because he wasn't

strong enough to resist her pull. But to his shock, she grabbed the hand before it could return to his side.

Caleb frowned at her. Didn't she know he was hanging on by a thread? Couldn't she see that he was fighting with everything he had not to give in to the desire that raged like a storm within him? Surely, she saw some of it.

Then she released him. Caleb felt such loss, such a void within him that a bellow rose inside his head. When Audrey turned to leave, he didn't stop her, just watched her walk toward the hallway.

She got another two steps before he went after her. He was moving before he even realized it. When he reached her, he whirled her around to face him.

"Caleb?" she asked.

He clenched his jaw, telling himself to go to his room. Instead, he said, "Tell me to leave you alone."

She blinked, her brows furrowing. "What?"

"Tell me to walk away. Tell me you aren't interested."

There was a beat of silence. "What if I am?"

She was killing him. He glanced away and clenched his fists at his sides. "Dammit, Audrey. Tell me to walk away!"

"No."

With that one word, he was lost. Utterly.

Completely.

They reached for each other at the same time, their bodies colliding in a frenzy of longing and hunger. He pressed her against the wall, rocking his aching cock against her softness as their tongues dueled.

Her hands were moving over his back and shoulders as he plundered her mouth. She kissed him with abandon, holding nothing back.

And he wanted more, *needed* more.

She pushed him away and gave him a come-hither look

as she backed toward his bedroom. His blood ran hotter at her teasing.

He smiled at her swollen lips and the desire that filled her dark gaze. Caleb rushed after her, finally grabbing her when they reached his room.

Their lips met again, the kisses fiery and hot as they yanked at each other's clothes until they were skin-to-skin. Finally.

He leaned back and looked at her. She was breathless, her lips parted. He wanted to etch this memory into his mind forever. The blatant desire on her face, the carnal cravings that drove both of them.

Caleb tightened his arms around her and lifted her to walk to the bed. As they fell back onto the mattress, the only thing that mattered in the entire world at that moment was Audrey.

Chapter 22

She burned.

For him.

Audrey couldn't stop touching Caleb. His skin was warm, his muscles firm beneath her palms. And his weight felt amazing on top of her.

Their limbs twined as she tried to get closer to him, and he to her. She hadn't gotten to look her fill, but she was learning every amazing inch of him with her hands.

Her breath hitched when his fingers tangled in her hair, and he gently tugged her head to the side. His lips left an intoxicating warmth in their wake as they trailed down her neck. Chills raced over her skin when he paused and dipped his tongue into the hollow of her throat.

Audrey pressed her lips against his shoulder, but she forgot what she'd intended to do after, when he cupped one of her breasts and massaged it. The feel of his callused hands on her skin made desire tighten low in her belly.

She gasped when he pinched her nipple, rolling the

turgid bud between his fingers. Her blood ran hot, scalding her with the force of her desire.

Of her longing.

Caleb shifted, and his mouth wrapped around the peak. The soft rasp of his tongue against her sensitive nipple had her moaning. Her head fell back as she struggled for breath while pleasure swarmed her as he mercilessly teased her.

She could feel his arousal pressed against her leg. She wanted to move, to rub against it to help with the ache building at the juncture of her thighs, but his weight held her still.

Another moan, this one louder, fell from her lips when he shifted his focus to her other breast. The pleasure was so intense, so powerful, that there was no turning away from it.

No running.

Suddenly, Caleb rolled onto his back, taking her with him. He held a breast in each hand, gently massaging the globes. She stared down at him, watching the way he seemed enthralled with her chest. Then his gaze lifted to meet hers.

His desire was no longer hidden. It blazed hot and bright. And it made Audrey's stomach quiver in excitement and anticipation.

Audrey shifted her hips so she rubbed against his arousal. All she needed to do was move slightly, and he could be inside her. But she didn't get the chance as he sat up. His arms came around her while his mouth claimed her lips for another scorching kiss that left her breathless and needier than ever.

Somehow, Audrey ended up sitting on the edge of the bed as Caleb knelt before her. She blinked, her mind trying to sort through the haze of pleasure to figure out what had happened. Then it didn't matter as he rested his hands on her thighs.

She widened her legs. The sight of Caleb's chest rising faster had her clenching the covers in need. She leaned back on her hands and looked her fill at his magnificent chest once again.

His hair was tousled, and she loved it. That, combined with his rapid breathing and his heated gaze only heightened her hunger. Desire tightened again, stronger. Needier. He smiled as he caught her gaze.

Slowly, he moved his big hands down to her knees and then caressed upward. She bit her lip, waiting impatiently for him to touch her where she needed him. But he didn't.

Instead, the pads of his fingers softly skimmed down the inside of her thighs. Once more, chills raced over her body. As good as his touch was, the moment his fingers trekked back to her sex, she stilled.

Waiting. Hoping.

She couldn't look away from him. He held her entranced. Kept her suspended between pleasure and torture.

With agonizing slowness, his fingers crept closer to her throbbing sex. His thumbs brushed against her vulva. She forgot to breathe as she waited for more.

Three heartbeats later, his fingers moved upward, spreading her. Her lids closed and her head fell back. The moment he found her clit and swirled his finger around it, she was lost, tumbling into the abyss of ecstasy.

The strength in her arms gave out, and she collapsed onto the bed fully. Then his mouth was on her, his tongue taking the place of his finger as he expertly gave her pleasure.

Caleb had never seen a more gorgeous sight. Audrey's body was perfection—from her full breasts to the indent of her waist to her slightly flared hips. He couldn't get enough of her long, lean legs either.

But the way she was laid out on the bed, her legs open, and her body displayed for him, was mesmerizing. She wasn't shy or embarrassed. She knew what she liked, and it showed in the way she reacted to him.

He glanced at her breasts to see them moving as she breathed. Her hips rolled in time with his tongue. She embraced her sexiness, and it turned him on even more.

"Please," she begged. "I can't wait. I need to feel you inside me."

Caleb lifted his head to look at her. He'd planned to continue his assault on her sex for much longer, but who was he to deny both of them when she obviously couldn't wait.

He stood and put a knee on the bed. When her eyes lowered to his straining cock, he paused to let her look her fill. To his surprise, she sat up and wrapped her fingers around him firmly. She moved her hand up and down his length several times before she slowly lay back.

Unable to resist, he bent with her. She then guided his rod to her entrance. Caleb slid inside her with one thrust. The sight of her eyes closing in bliss made his heart skip a beat.

Her black locks were spread around her, and wanton desire etched every facet of her face. She lifted her lids. The moment Caleb looked into her dark depths, he was lost.

He'd crossed some invisible line that he hadn't known was there. One that he'd avoided before at all costs. But now that he was past it, he didn't care. He wanted to be with Audrey. He wanted her in his arms and in his bed.

Whatever came next was anyone's guess.

Caleb pulled out slightly and then began pumping his hips, slowly at first and then building speed as her sounds of pleasure became louder. She clung to him, her nails digging into his skin, but it only pushed him to give her more.

Moans weren't enough. He wanted her screaming. He wanted her completely and utterly at his mercy.

The faster he slid inside her tight, wet sheath, the quicker her hips rose to meet his. But it still wasn't enough.

He couldn't touch her like he wanted, like he needed. Caleb looped his leg around hers and rolled, pulling her with him as he flipped onto his back.

Audrey didn't miss a beat. She straddled his hips, a soft smile curving her mouth. Their breathing was harsh and loud, their bodies coated with a light sheen of sweat.

She pushed against his chest and sat up. He was buried deep within her, and every movement of her hips caused him to tighten his grip on her.

With a twist of her head, she flipped her hair over her shoulder. Then, she started riding him. Her hips shifted back and forth as she ground against him.

The sight of her with her lips parted and her face flushed as she rocked her body was the most sensual, wanton thing he had ever witnessed.

Right up until she dropped her head back, exposing her neck. Caleb was absolutely enthralled. He watched her breasts swaying before he reached up and cupped them. The mounds filled his hands, but it was the hard nipples poking against his palms that he loved.

She moved faster, her hips rocking quickly as her breathing grew shallower. He bucked his hips. Her answering cry was all he needed to hear.

He was close now, so close to climax, but he didn't want to give in. Not yet. Not until Audrey had taken her pleasure.

Caleb watched Audrey's face and the emotions that showed there. He knew she was about to orgasm by the way she bit her lip and dug her nails into his chest.

Suddenly, she stiffened and cried out. He gripped her hips and held her as he thrust hard and fast. Her body jerked as she clenched around him. Caleb gave in to his own pleasure then. He'd never climaxed with a partner before, and he found that it deepened the connection between them.

This was more than just sex. More than just sharing pleasure and each other's bodies.

This was. . . .

He refused to think about it. Instead, he basked in the afterglow of their ecstasy.

Audrey lifted her leg and rolled onto her back. He turned his head toward her, unable to look away. And when she looked at him, there was a smile upon his face.

"Wow," she murmured.

He shifted to face her and moved her hair from her forehead. "I'm not finished with you, doc."

Her grin widened. "Good, because that's exactly what I was hoping you'd say."

Phil stared into the twilight from his seat on the back porch. He knew what was coming, and he wasn't looking forward to it.

The burner phone was quiet. It was how he liked it, but he knew it wouldn't last. As soon as he'd set fire to the building with the dead horse inside, he'd known it was a bad idea.

He'd run as fast as he could from the quickly accelerating blaze, but he could feel the heat of it on his skin even now. The explosion had been a surprise. He should have factored in all the chemicals the vet had used, but he hadn't cared.

His orders had been to get rid of all traces of the animal, and that's what he'd done.

There had been nothing in any of the newspapers or on the police scanner about the sick horses at the auction house. Surely, if the next two animals had died, there would have been reports.

That's what his employer wanted. At least, that's what he thought they wanted. The truth was, they had kept their real intentions to themselves.

And that's how he liked things.

It wasn't unusual, but he'd begun to have his doubts about this job. At the rate his employer wanted things done, Phil was afraid that their next request would be murder— one thing he refused to do.

Everyone had a limit, and that was his.

The phone buzzed behind him. It fell from the arm of the rocking chair to the deck. He wanted to ignore it. The contract he had with his employer was, in fact, finished. He could throw the burner away and forget that it ever existed if he wanted to.

Except he knew his employer's identity. And he knew they would go to extremes to ensure that no one discovered who they were. Including killing Phil.

As long as Phil worked for them, he was safe. At least, he *hoped* that was true.

Phil picked up the burner and read:

YOU FAILED. THE VET DISCOVERED THE POISON AND SAVED THE HORSES.

He closed his eyes, sighed, then he sent his reply. I DID WHAT YOU ASKED. EVERYTHING WAS DESTROYED.

OBVIOUSLY NOT.

Phil waited for the message to continue but it didn't. Did this mean that he was finished? He really hoped so because he had a bad feeling that this was going to be the case that got him caught by the law.

After decades of autonomy, he wasn't about to give that up. No matter how much money was offered. Because you couldn't put a price on freedom.

Phil started to set aside the phone when it buzzed again. A sinking feeling filled him.

THERE'S SOMETHING ELSE I NEED.

Chapter 23

Audrey stared at the wall. She was on her side nestled against Caleb. This was usually the time when she made her excuses and left. But, oddly enough, she was quite content just lying there.

Caleb's hand lay on her hip. Some might think it was done casually, but she knew differently. He had tightened his fingers on her before loosening them. Almost as if to let her know that her body wasn't just a resting place for his arm.

She smiled. Neither had said anything since they rolled to their sides. She wasn't sure what to say. It wasn't like she had been in this position before. The fact that she was staying the night pretty much relieved that issue of if she should stay or not.

But it brought another: where would she sleep?

Audrey's mind flashed back to when they'd made love. Her stomach trembled when she recalled how Caleb had touched her, kissed her.

Held her.

She replayed the events over and over in her head, and each time, her heart raced, and it felt as if a thousand butterflies had taken flight inside her stomach. No one—not one single person—had ever made her feel even a tenth of what Caleb did.

"You're supposed to be resting," Caleb mumbled near her ear.

She tried to bite back her smile. God, what was wrong with her?

Oh, that's right. She knew. Caleb.

"I, ah, I am," she said.

He kissed the top of her ear. "Your definition of resting is quite different than mine."

She couldn't stop smiling. "Is that right?"

"Uh-huh. Definitely. You need to reevaluate things. Follow my lead," Caleb replied drowsily. Then he pulled her against him and snuggled her even tighter.

Another five minutes passed before Caleb sighed loudly. "You're not going to sleep, are you?"

"No, but I like lying here. With you."

That was a first for Audrey. Damn. There seemed to be several firsts that included Caleb. What did that mean? Did she want to know? Did she dare to find out? Because all of this felt so easy. That meant it was good. At least, she hoped so. She didn't have much experience to fall back on.

He rose up on his elbow, causing her to fall to her back. She looked up at him as he gazed at her curiously. Had she said too much? Everything she'd voiced was true, and she wanted him to know that. But maybe she *had* said too much.

"There was a hint of surprise in your voice at that confession," he said.

She blinked. Confession? Yeah, she supposed it was an admission of sorts. "Was there?"

"Audrey, if you regre—"

"No," she said hastily before he could even finish the sentence. The one thing she had no compunction about was being with him. "I don't. Not at all."

He nodded once. "Good. Because neither do I."

She had to touch him again. She sifted her fingers through the sides of his hair, letting the cool, short strands caress her skin. "I don't have to stay tonight, though."

"Do you want to leave?"

Audrey took in a deep breath as she ran through all the possible answers. Once more, she decided on the truth. Her eyes lifted to his. "No."

"I want you in this bed with me, but that's going to be your decision. No pressure. Okay?"

"Okay," she replied.

"Just know that I'll be joining you in yours if you leave."

She busted out laughing as he grinned. As the laughter died, they lost themselves in each other's eyes. Caleb's head lowered slowly. Right before his lips touched hers, Audrey's eyes shut.

Their kisses before had been full of lust and passion and fire. This one was soft, gentle. And, somehow, it held even a deeper hunger.

Audrey liked it. Perhaps too much, because she suddenly started thinking about being with Caleb tomorrow, and the day after. And the day after that. A woman who shied away from relationships was now thinking about being in one.

And it made her smile.

Her arms wrapped around his neck as his tongue slid

past her lips. He kissed her deeply, thoroughly. When he finally lifted his head, she felt as if he had touched the deepest parts of her that she hadn't even known were there.

He ran his knuckles down the side of her face. "I want nothing more than to have my way with you all night."

"Sounds good to me."

Caleb chuckled. "I'm thinking I should feed you first."

"I can wait."

"Your stomach can't. It's been rumbling."

Audrey covered her eyes with a hand. "Well, that's embarrassing. I didn't even realize it."

He pulled her hand away. "Consider it fuel for later."

"I can do that."

She got another glimpse of him when he rose from the bed to grab his clothes. There wasn't a part of him that she didn't find sexy and altogether alluring. She was in dangerous territory, but even realizing that couldn't get her to backpedal.

He grabbed her feet and yanked her towards the end of the mattress. Soon, they were laughing again as she tried to bat his hands away and stay in bed. In the end, he won by sheer strength alone. He lifted her and set her on her feet.

How was it that Caleb was a man she could have a passionate exchange with one minute, tell him private things another, and then laugh with a heartbeat later?

Once dressed, they made their way into the kitchen. He rummaged in the pantry as she got out some water. When she turned, Caleb stood in the pantry doorway, holding up a box of crackers and a can of spray cheese.

"I've not had that in forever," she said, reaching for the cheese.

He held the can out of her reach. "Oh, no. This is only for pros. You'll have to earn your right to use the can."

"And how do I do that?"

His sexy grin made her heart skip a beat. "A kiss will work."

She cocked a brow at him, but the stern look didn't last long as she walked to him, rose up on her tiptoes, and placed her lips on his mouth.

Strong arms came around her and dipped her backward. Caleb looked down at her and winked. "Sweetheart, you are now crowned a pro. Would you like to do the honors first?"

"Please," she said and reached behind her to grab the can.

They straightened and walked to the living area where they sat in the middle of the room. Audrey got a cracker and eagerly popped off the cap, pressing the nozzle and watching the cheese come out of the container. She put the snack into her mouth and sighed in contentment.

She chewed and swallowed while Caleb took his turn.

"I used to beg my mother for this every time we went to the store," she said.

Caleb laughed, nodding. Around his food, he said, "We never had money for it, so once, when I was about nine, I stole a can. Abby was furious when she caught me and Brice eating it."

"Did she make you return it or pay for it?"

He shook his head. "She lectured us for all of a minute about stealing before she took the cheese and had some herself."

"I can't wait to meet your sister. She sounds amazing."

"She is."

Audrey chuckled and made herself another cracker.

For several minutes, they ate and looked out the windows, simply enjoying each other's company. Audrey was having the best day. To have something so wonderful come from something so horrendous was mind-blowing, but she wasn't going to question it.

"You look content," he said.

She gazed into his brown eyes and nodded. "Very. I like the simple things in life."

"I'm as simple as they come."

"Oh, no. I sincerely doubt that," she said with a laugh.

He put his hand over his heart and gave her a fake wounded expression. "What? You don't believe me?"

Audrey shook her head, grinning. "Not one bit."

"Good, because it was a damn lie," he said with a chuckle.

"High-maintenance, huh?"

"The highest," he confirmed with a teasing wink. "And you?"

She squeezed the cheese onto another cracker. "I think I'm somewhere in the middle."

He leaned on one hand while he bent his leg, propping his foot up and resting his other arm on his knee. "So you like simplicity, but you also want someone to treat you like you're the most special woman on Earth."

"Yes," she said with a nod.

Caleb reached over and took the can from her and used the last of it to make a design on the cracker he held. Then he extended it to her. "That's not too much to ask, you know."

Audrey turned her palm upward and watched as he set the cracker in her hand. She didn't know if it was a meaningful gesture or not. This was what she got for only casually dating. And it wasn't like she could just come out and ask what it meant.

Her mind cautioned her about reading too much into things.

But her heart . . . oh, her heart was bursting with happiness.

It was ridiculous, but she couldn't seem to help herself. The gesture had to be one of the sweetest things ever. Audrey took the cracker and brought it to her mouth. Just before it passed her lips, she met Caleb's gaze.

The shield she usually saw around him was lowered. The man sitting before her now was the real Caleb. Kind, charming, funny, and absolutely delightful. All of that combined with a face and body that made everyone ogle him and come to a standstill was almost too much.

And he was with her.

Her!

She put the cracker into her mouth. Caleb's lips crooked into that sexy half-smile that always made her knees weak. She couldn't remember the last time she'd had so much fun—or passion—with a man.

It didn't matter that she'd planned to stay the night. She didn't think she'd want to leave anyway. And that was huge.

"So," she said. "What are your plans for the ranch?"

Caleb glanced outside. "Just what you see. We could continue to grow, and I suppose we will, but I don't want us to become so big that Brice and I can't handle things ourselves. If we hire others to help us do our jobs, then we're too big."

"Are you worried that others won't train the horses as you do?"

He snorted, but nodded. "That's exactly it."

"Then train them."

"That still means I have to trust the people we hire to ensure that they're doing what they're supposed to."

She couldn't help but smile at him. "That's called running a business."

He gave her a flat look. "I know that. Don't forget, I was part of the East Ranch for many years. I worked on it from the time I was fourteen until three years ago. I know every facet of that ranch."

"I don't understand why you wouldn't want to be as well known."

"Oh, I didn't say I didn't want to be well known. I want people to seek us out to either buy horses or train them. I want people to know that when they come to us, it's ensured they'll get a well-trained horse that hasn't been abused."

Audrey brought her knees to her chest as she licked the remnants of the food from her lips. "Now I see. It takes years to build that kind of reputation. Hiring others to help could damage it with one bad incident."

"Exactly. Clayton raises, breeds, and sells cattle. His stock is highly sought after by other ranchers, but there is no training involved with them. You have to take care of the animals, but they stay out to pasture."

"You'll succeed."

Caleb gave her a peculiar look. "Why do you say that?"

"It isn't in your nature to fail."

Chapter 24

Something had to go wrong. Caleb needed it to.

By this time, Caleb could usually point out at least three things about a woman that he didn't like. Whether it was that she wore too much perfume, chewed with her mouth open, or had an annoying laugh. Hell, he'd gotten so picky that he sometimes refused to see a woman again because she was rude to a waiter.

It didn't take much for him to find reasons not to be around a woman again. Why the hell wasn't that happening with Audrey?

He liked the way she tucked her hair behind her ears. And the way she laughed. She gave in to the action, joy erupting over her face and flashing in her eyes. He liked that she could take a joke and quickly turn it around on him. She was thoughtful and compassionate and just so damn sexy that he couldn't get enough of her.

Had he changed? Or was there nothing to dislike about Audrey?

He feared it was the former, for sure.

They were drifting into territory he wasn't familiar with. And he needed to get his feet under him again. Quickly. Before he did something stupid.

"What?" she asked when she caught him staring.

Caleb shrugged and shook his head. "Just looking at you."

"It's the way you're looking," she said softly.

He brushed his fingers down her cheek. "How?"

"Like you're seeing me."

"I do see you."

She lowered her eyes to the floor and moved her head back and forth. "No. *Really* seeing me." Then her gaze lifted to him.

"I want to see you."

He held out his hand and waited for her to link her fingers with his. When she did, he brought their joined hands to his lips and kissed the back of her hand.

"What are your plans?" he asked. "Do you intend to work for the two horse farms forever?"

She wrinkled her nose. "I don't think so. They've both kept me busy, and it's been easy to focus on the horses at each place. Maybe that's why I've not thought ahead."

"And?" Caleb pressed.

"I was late getting to Bremer's the day before, and he wasn't at all pleased. He's livid that I didn't come by today. Worse, I didn't show up at Hopkins' yesterday. I did call them. Do you think they'll fire me?"

Caleb laughed and shot her a look. "You can't be serious. They're not going to fire you. They'll give you hell, for sure, but they won't release you."

"You certainly sound sure of it."

"Because I am. As I told you before, good equine vets are hard to come by. Ones like you are even rarer."

"I hope you're right."

He shrugged and sat straight, still keeping their hands joined. "Go see both tomorrow. You can explain that there was an emergency."

Her eyes widened. "I won't tell them who or what, and that's exactly what they'll want to know. It's why I told them I had an emergency."

"What do you like about working for them?"

"Both trust me fully and rarely question anything I tell them is needed for the horses. I like Ted Hopkins the best. He's a decent fellow and good to his other employees. Robert?" She shrugged, twisting her lips. "I already told you how he keeps the vet clinic at the stables well equipped with all the latest and greatest. He spends hundreds of thousands on purchasing horses and maintaining them."

"But?"

She tried to hide her smile. "He's a bit of a douche."

Caleb threw back his head and laughed. "I could've told you that. I've known Robert for some time. We often show up at the same sells. He likes to throw his money around. He has a big ego."

"You've interacted with him?"

"Let's just say that when we're in a bidding war over a horse, he only wins when I allow him to."

Her smile widened. "I'll never be able to look at him the same."

"Then don't. You know you'll find another job quickly. Hell, I'd hire you on the spot."

Caleb hadn't meant to say that, but the words just flew from his mouth as if his mind had no control over things. Which, obviously, when it came to Audrey, was true. His mind was mush.

She studied him for a long moment. "If we hadn't

already talked about this, I'd think you were offering me that because we slept together."

"I'm offering you the position because I wanted you to begin with, but you were taken. If you're considering other options, I'm throwing my hat into the ring first." He shot her a grin. "And I'm hoping the fact we slept together gives me a slight advantage."

Her gaze dropped to their hands. "I've already said I'd work with you."

His smile died. Somehow, he'd said the wrong thing. If he'd been looking for an out with Audrey, he'd just found it. It was there, waiting for him to grab it and run. But he didn't.

He couldn't.

Caleb went over his words again, trying to determine which had been the culprits to remedy the situation, because somehow, it was very important that he did. But he couldn't figure out what it was.

"Audrey, I'm sorry if I said something that offended you."

She jerked her head up and quickly said, "No, no. It's fine. I'm just thinking."

His heart thumped in what he could only imagine was fear. He wanted Audrey smiling and laughing again, not contemplative and quiet.

She suddenly rose to her feet and pulled her hand from his. After briefly meeting his gaze, she turned and walked toward his room. She took three steps before pulling her shirt over her head.

Caleb stood in the next heartbeat. He walked to the shirt and picked it up. Looking down the hall, he saw another item of clothing on the floor. He went to it and picked up the sweatpants.

His gaze slid to his bedroom where he found the lacy, dark green bra that he hadn't paid attention to earlier. When he reached it, his attention was diverted by the sound of the shower turning on.

Caleb's fingers went numb, and the clothes he held tumbled from his hand when he caught a glimpse of Audrey stepping into the shower with her hair piled atop her head.

His eyes locked on her gorgeous body through the clear doors as she stood beneath the spray of water. He'd never undressed so quickly in his life. Then he was in the stall with her.

He came up behind her, sliding his hands around her waist. She leaned back against him and sighed, tilting her head to the side. The sight of her slim neck was too good to pass up. Caleb kissed down the column of her throat as his hands came up to knead her breasts.

His eyes were locked on the water that ran over her hard nipples before falling to the shower floor. He pinched one of the peaks and heard Audrey's audible moan.

Before he could begin anything, she pulled out of his arms and reached for the soap. She lathered it in her hands and then turned to him. There was a smile on her face as she began soaping up his body.

Caleb was so surprised that he just stood there watching her bathe him. She began at his shoulders before working her way down his arms and then back up again. Her hands smoothed over his chest and stomach before she shifted behind him and scrubbed his back.

He closed his eyes at the sensation of her touching him. It was innocent but sexual at the same time. And he couldn't wait until it was his turn to wash her.

His eyes snapped open when her hands moved over his butt and then to his legs. Once she reached his ankles, she shoved at him to get him to turn around. Caleb did as commanded to find her on her knees before him. She kept her eyes on his legs as she meticulously bathed the front of his limbs.

The closer she came to his aching cock, the more it strained, yearning for her touch. And then her hands were on him.

Caleb ground his teeth together as she pumped her soapy fists up and down his length. She then ran her fingers around the sensitive head of his rod several times, bringing him such pleasure that he was about to lift her and take her right then.

Just as he was about to reach for her, Audrey stood and turned him toward the water to rinse. But Caleb grinned as he reached behind him and dragged her toward the spray.

He took the soap from her hands. "My turn."

It was his first time giving someone a bath, but if he had his way, this was the only way he'd take a shower with Audrey from now on.

He noted that her chest was rising and falling quickly—even before he'd touched her. Finally, he'd soaped up his hands, but he kept the bar in one palm. Then, he took one of her hands in his. Finger by finger, he washed her, moving up to her wrist then her elbow and finally her shoulder. Only to switch to the other arm.

With both of her arms washed, he moved to her neck and down to her chest. His mouth watered at the sight of her breasts. He took his time washing each globe, paying special attention to her nipples.

He made himself move to her stomach then to her hips and farther down her legs. Caleb then shifted behind her and washed her back. He repositioned her just enough so the water was already rinsing her.

Her head was back against him, her lips parted. He put aside the soap and rinsed his hand before he slid it to her sex. Slowly, he stroked her, dipping his finger inside.

Their passion had swept through them swiftly the first time. This time, he planned to go slower and give Audrey the pleasure she deserved.

Without a word, he shut off the water. Audrey blinked as he opened the shower door. When she turned to him, he took her hand and led her out. There, he quickly dried her off before doing the same to himself. Then he led her to the bed.

She released her hair, letting the damp ends tumble down her back. Caleb slid his fingers into the thick length and wound the strands around his digits, tugging her head back to expose her neck.

Their gazes met, held.

He didn't understand his hunger for her, but it didn't matter. Not now, at least. Not when he had her in his arms. He kissed her, letting their tongues slide against each other. He could kiss her for eternity, but there were other parts of her he wanted to taste and touch.

Releasing her hair, he gave her a little push to sit. She lay back. Caleb spread her legs and knelt between them. His fingers slid over her sex to find her clit. Then he could deny himself no longer.

He lay between her thighs and ran his tongue over her gradually, softly. Then he concentrated on her sensitive bundle of nerves, swirling around the tiny, swollen nub.

Her hips rose slightly as she fisted the covers and moaned. That only spurred him on. Caleb licked and laved, ruthlessly enveloping her in pleasure. Soon, her moans turned to cries, and the louder she became, the more he gave her.

Audrey's head thrashed from side to side, her body trembling as he brought her to the verge of release. Then he pulled back. Her breathing was harsh in the silence of the room, but he gave her little time to compose herself as he pushed a finger inside her.

Her head lifted to look at him. He slowly moved his finger in and out of her. Then he added a second. She moaned, her head falling back onto the mattress.

Once she was focused on his fingers, he returned his tongue to her clit. Her back arched off the bed as she called out his name. A moment later, her body stiffened as the climax swept through her.

Caleb didn't relent until her body stopped moving. Only then did he flip her onto her stomach and raise her up to her knees.

Their night was just getting started. There were so many things he wanted to do to her body, and he wasn't going to waste another second.

Chapter 25

Her body still pulsed from the astonishing, incredible orgasm Caleb had given her. Audrey blinked, only belatedly realizing that she was on her hands and knees.

The French said that an orgasm was a little death, and she could attest to that. All she'd known was bliss so intense, so deep that she had lost consciousness. For a few seconds, or minutes, she didn't know.

She looked over her shoulder to see Caleb on his knees behind her. He gave her a questioning look, and she moved back, rubbing her butt against him.

His smile was sexy, but it was the promise of pleasure in his gaze that made her sex clench. He put his hands on her hips and entered her in one smooth motion.

Audrey bit her lip and looked forward as he began to push and pull her along his length. She moaned as he thrust harder, deeper inside her until she couldn't tell where she ended and he began.

To her surprise, she found herself on the verge of another

climax. Caleb quickened his pace, giving her no option but to tumble over the edge into pleasure once more.

"Audrey," he said. "I feel you."

She couldn't answer as her body spasmed from another intense orgasm. Her arms buckled as he continued to pound into her. Then he buried himself deep and stilled, his fingers digging into her hips.

After a moment, he pulled out of her and fell to his back. Audrey slid her legs out from under her and lay on her stomach, thoroughly worn out.

He slapped her lightly on the ass and kissed her cheek. She smiled at him because she wouldn't have been able to form words if she tried.

Her eyes closed, and she found herself drifting off to sleep. She didn't know how long she was in that in-between stage of wakefulness and sleep when she heard her name. She raised her lids to find Caleb looking at her.

"I'm sorry," he said.

She frowned, wondering what he was talking about. He'd been fabulous. What did he have to apologize for?

"I know better. And this is something I never do. Never. But I got so caught up in you that I forgot. Twice."

Now she was really confused. She couldn't figure out what Caleb was talking about, and she was too tired to even care. She closed her eyes, thinking that they could discuss it when she woke up.

The crinkling of a wrapper brought her back to the present. It took her a moment to realize what the small square Caleb held up in front of her was. A condom.

"Oh, shit," she said as she pushed herself up on her arms. "I never forget."

Caleb looked ashamed. "Me either. I have no excuse."

Audrey felt a little sick to her stomach as she comprehended what they had done—twice—and the implications. She even carried the prophylactics in her purse in case a guy claimed to not have one. She always made sure that she never had unprotected sex.

She looked at Caleb to find him watching her. "We're both to blame. It's not just on you. I didn't say anything either."

That was because she seemed to forget the entire world when she was with him. It was just the two of them, without any of the normal worries or intrusions. It had been nice.

But now, reality reared its head.

"I should regret it, but, oddly enough, I don't."

She'd had unprotected sex twice. She could be carrying his child. Caleb's baby. As she evaluated the situation, she found that she felt the same as he did. There was no panic or fear or even anger. "I don't either."

They smiled at each other.

She might feel differently if she came up pregnant. No sooner did she think that than an image of a little boy who looked like Caleb flashed in her mind. Her heart swelled at the thought.

For someone who never thought about children, talking about them twice in one day was out of the ordinary.

"Come here," Caleb urged as he moved to his back.

She shifted and rested her head on his chest. The moment his arm came around her, everything felt right. As if this were where she was supposed to be. As if everything had led her right to Caleb so she could find the happiness that currently filled her.

Maddy would say it was Karma.

"You're not going to sleep now, are you?" he asked.

Audrey grinned. "I'm actually thinking about my sister. She believes in Karma and Fate and all that."

"You don't?"

"I didn't."

There was a pause. "Meaning, you do now?"

"I don't know."

"What changed?"

She shrugged. "I don't really know. It's like, over the past three days, my world has been shaken about, and I didn't grasp it until just now."

"Are you upset by it?"

"That's just it," she said with a little laugh. "I'm not. Which, I'll be the first to admit, is odd. I'm okay with change, but when I want it. Not when it just happens."

Caleb chuckled and kissed her head. "That's pretty much everyone."

"There are some who hate change of any kind."

"True," he relented. "What changed for you?"

She wasn't sure she wanted to go into specifics, especially since it involved him, her feelings on relationships, and the hope that this might develop into something more. So, instead, she said, "Everything."

"That encompasses a lot of things."

"Mm-hmm. I'm reconsidering a lot of things. Who I work for and if I want to continue with either of them. Then there's my sister."

She could hear the frown in Caleb's voice when he asked, "Maddy?"

"I think she stays with me because she doesn't believe I can look out for myself."

"Have you ever thought that maybe it's because she doesn't want to be alone?"

Audrey considered that for a moment. "That's a possibility. I want her to be happy."

"Then tell her that. Give her the option. Don't just make a decision for her, because you wouldn't like it if she did that with you."

"So true."

Caleb kissed the top of her head again. "You said everything. What else is there?"

"The future," she finally said after a lengthy pause. She would never know anything if she didn't put it out there. "I've kept myself focused on my career. I did that because it was easy. I didn't have to think about my father disappearing or what I wanted. I could lose myself in the horses and whatever needs they had at the time. I forgot about myself and what I might want."

Caleb's hand caressed up and down her back. "What do you want?"

She was beginning to think that she wanted him. But was that exhaustion talking? Was it because of everything she'd been through over the past couple of days and the fact that Caleb had been there to get her through it all?

Or was it because of something else? Something deeper that she was too afraid to admit, even in her mind? Was it the peace and joy she found in Caleb's arms—and the future she could see just out of reach?

If only she had the courage to take it and see where it might lead.

"Something different than I have now."

His chest lifted and expanded as he drew in a deep breath. "Yeah."

She shifted her head to see his face. He wore a contemplative look that made her wish she could read his thoughts. "What is it?"

"Just thinking about what you said."

"Which part?" she asked with a grin.

He put his free hand behind his head. "Wanting something different."

"Do you want something different?"

"Maybe."

Audrey got more comfortable and closed her eyes. She waited for him to say more, but he didn't. And she was too tired to think of something to move the conversation along. Her mind drifted as she thought again of a little boy running in front of her and straight into Caleb's arms.

She must have drifted off to sleep, but she woke up long enough to roll over as Caleb pulled the covers over them.

"Go back to sleep, beautiful," he murmured.

She sighed as he snuggled against her, looping his arm around her.

Clayton stared into the growing darkness. His instincts told him that the culprits wouldn't be returning to the auction house that night. There were too many sheriff's deputies around for anyone to dare such a thing.

The sound of a vehicle pulling up drew his attention from the pastures. He wasn't surprised to find Danny there. The sheriff was out of uniform as he strolled up.

"It's gonna be a hot one tonight," Danny said.

Clayton grinned. "Couldn't resist, could you?"

Danny didn't even try to hide his smile. "Nope. All the good stuff happens with you."

"Good stuff?" Clayton asked with a roll of his eyes. "Tell that to Abby."

"I'll pass. So, anything?"

Clayton shook his head and blew out a breath. "Nothing, but I don't expect it."

"You still think this is about Audrey?"

"It's the only thing that makes sense. Every other angle can be forgotten because of facts or reasoning."

Danny pushed his cowboy hat back on his head. "I looked into the vet like you asked me to. Audrey, as well as her sister, Maddy, is clean, Clayton. Maddy has a couple of speeding tickets, but that's the extent of their brush with the law. And I looked deeper, as well. Asked the right people the right kinds of questions. Audrey is not only well-liked but also respected."

Clayton squeezed the bridge of his nose with his thumb and forefinger. "I'd hoped you'd find something so we could bring this ordeal to a close."

"Where is the doc?" Danny asked, looking around.

"With Caleb, back at his house."

Danny's brows shot up. "You sent her off with him? Alone?"

"They're adults. Consenting adults, I might add."

The sheriff threw up his hands. "Hey, I'm well aware of that fact. It's just that we all know how Caleb is with women. He sleeps with them once and then forgets they exist."

"He took her back to the ranch."

"You lost me there. What is the significance?"

Clayton met Danny's hazel eyes. "Caleb never takes women to his place."

"Ah. You think he'll keep his hands off?"

"Not a chance in hell," Clayton said with a laugh. But it died swiftly. "I'm hoping that if those two do come together, Caleb will see that he can find happiness just like his sister and brother."

"Oh, I see." Danny nodded and looked at the ground. "I tend to forget about the past with both Abby and Brice being married."

"Caleb told Brice that he thinks he'll remain single forever."

"That's a mighty long time."

Clayton snorted. "It certainly is."

"Why do you think Audrey could change things?"

"The way he acts around her. Caleb has always been generous with people. He's got one of the kindest hearts I've ever seen, but he never lets women who could be romantic with him close enough to see the real him. I think if anyone has a shot, it's Audrey."

Danny twisted his lips. "That's if she wants it."

"I think she does. I watched them for two days. Caleb has never been more in tune with a woman before. He worried about her and cared for her because he wanted to, not because he thought it was his duty."

"Then this is probably not the best time to deliver the news I have."

Clayton's brows furrowed as he waited for Danny to continue. Irritation filled his voice when he said, "Well? What is it?"

"Helen is back in town."

Anger rose swiftly in Clayton, but as he thought about the repercussions for his wife and two brothers-in-law, that fury gave way to concern and unease. "Fuck."

"That's exactly what I said."

"How do you know it's her?"

Danny swatted at a mosquito. "One of my deputies pulled her over for a busted tail light. I've had her name flagged from the moment I took office. I wanted to be notified if she ever returned to the area."

"Shit. I've got to get home to Abby. I have to tell her before she runs into her mother unprepared."

Danny stopped him. "What about Brice and Caleb?"

Clayton looked at the stables where Brice and Naomi were. He'd tell them first. This wasn't the kind of news you delivered over the phone. Then he was headed home to Abby. Clayton slapped Danny on the arm. "Thanks for the heads-up."

"Don't worry about things here. I've got you covered," his friend said.

Clayton waved as he hurried toward the stables.

Chapter 26

When Caleb finally opened his eyes and looked out the windows, orange and red streaked across the sky. Lying against him was none other than Audrey.

Her back was to him, and her body curled slightly away as she squished one of his pillows between her arms and used the top part to cushion her head. Her long hair was spread behind her and lay partially on his arm.

He slowly rolled over and rose from the bed. Caleb grabbed some clothes and took them into the kitchen to dress. But he kept looking toward his room. He didn't want to get up, but chores had to be done.

After he'd buckled his pants, he looped his arms through the sleeves of his tee and turned toward the kitchen. His gaze landed on Brice sipping coffee as Caleb pulled his shirt over his head.

"Morning," his brother said.

Caleb gave him a hard look and put his finger to his lips. "Shhh. Audrey is still sleeping."

Brice set down the mug as he shifted on the bar stool and rested his arms on the top of the island. "In your bed?"

"Yeah." Caleb didn't mean to get defensive, but he knew where his brother was going with the questioning, and he wasn't in the mood.

Instead of some smart-ass retort or snort or whatever, Brice merely took another sip of coffee.

"That's all you have to say?" Caleb asked, concerned. It wasn't like Brice to pass up an opportunity to give Caleb hell.

His brother shrugged. "I just asked a simple question."

"I know you too well for you to pull that bullshit."

Brice jerked his chin to the coffee pot as he got to his feet. "Grab some java and let's get going."

Caleb leaned back against the counter and crossed his arms over his chest. Brice only got four steps before he glanced over his shoulder to see that Caleb wasn't budging.

His brother let out a long-suffering sigh and made his way back to Caleb. "What is it?"

"What are you doing here?"

"I often show up at your house in the mornings. Just as you show up at mine."

Caleb shook his head. "What are you doing here *this* morning? If something had happened at the auction house, you would've called. Now, you waltz in here and act like it's just another day."

"I never waltz."

"I'm going to punch you in the throat," Caleb stated.

Brice glanced away. "You're right. Everything is fine with the horses and the auction house. No one made an attempt to do anything last night. Danny is going to take a few plain-clothes officers to rotate shifts for a few nights."

"Audrey will be pleased. But this also means our theory was right. This is about her, isn't it?"

"It certainly looks that way."

Brice had a habit of looking away from someone when he had something to tell them that he didn't want to. The kind of thing that his brother was doing right now.

Caleb waited until he caught Brice's gaze before he said, "Whatever you need to say, just spit it out."

"Get your boots on."

"Tell me now."

"Caleb," Brice began.

He cocked his head and glared at his brother. "Tell. Me. Now."

Brice stared at him for a long time, a frown marring his brow. Then he said in a loud whisper, "You said you didn't want to wake Audrey. Get your fucking boots on and meet me outside."

After Brice had left, Caleb waited several minutes then dropped his arms and pushed away from the counter. He paused by the fridge and grabbed the orange juice for a quick drink.

He glanced toward his room again, wishing he'd stayed in bed. But whatever was about to happen would have happened either way. It was better to deal with it now rather than later.

Caleb walked to the mudroom and put on his work boots and cowboy hat. He softly closed the door behind him as he made his way from the house. He didn't need to look far for Brice. His brother stood at the fence, watching the paint stallion graze.

Brice stiffened slightly when Caleb came to stand beside him. Whatever his brother had to tell him couldn't be good. Caleb hated bad news of any sort. Nobody liked it, but when that kind of news came to the Harpers, it was always the worst kind.

"Is it about you and Naomi trying to have a baby?" Caleb asked. "Did the results come in?"

Brice shook his head. "Still no news. But no, it's not about that."

Caleb rested his arms on the fence and let his gaze slide to the stallion. Last night was an improvement he hadn't counted on happening so soon. Perhaps he could get the animal trained sooner than he'd hoped.

"Mom is back."

Caleb's thoughts ground to a screeching halt. Surely, he'd misheard Brice. Because it simply couldn't be true. Not now. Not after the three of them had made lives for themselves.

He felt his brother's gaze on him, but Caleb couldn't look at Brice yet. He was barely holding things together as it was with the news. The last thing he wanted was to talk about it.

"I'm here if you need me," Brice said.

The moment Brice's hand came to rest on him, Caleb jerked away. He spun around and stalked to the stables. As soon as he saw his saddle, he knew what he needed. Thankfully, Brice didn't try to follow.

Caleb saddled one of the males and led the gelding from the stables. Then he put his foot in the stirrup and looped his leg over the animal. Once seated, he clicked to the buckskin, setting the horse off at a run.

The sound of arguing woke Audrey. The moment she saw the view, she remembered where she was. There was a smile on her face when she rolled over to snuggle with Caleb.

Only, he was gone.

She glanced at the clock beside the bed and saw the time. It was well past eight in the morning. She never slept this late. She wished he would have woken her, but she understood that he had a ranch to run.

The sound of a car door slamming made her frown. She sat up, clutching the sheet to her bare chest. Since she didn't want anyone to find her naked, she hurriedly jumped up to get her clothes. Only to realize that she just had her sweats and shirt from the previous night. Everything else was in the other room.

Audrey put on the clothes and peeked out of Caleb's room. The house appeared empty as she tiptoed down the hallway into the kitchen. She looked around, and when she saw no one, she ran to the other corridor and the spare bedroom where her things were.

She pulled out another pair of jeans and a tee shirt that she exchanged for the casual wear. Using her fingers as a comb, she pulled her hair back behind her head and twisted the length into a bun, using an elastic band to hold it.

Just as she was about to walk out, she realized that she'd forgotten socks. Audrey rolled her eyes at herself and quickly pulled them out. She took her time walking through the house this time. The closer she came to the kitchen, the more she could hear the arguing again.

It was Brice and a woman, but Audrey would bet a thousand bucks that it wasn't Naomi. The woman's voice sounded older, more gravelly. The kind a smoker had.

Audrey paused long enough to pull on her boots before she walked out of the house. She came up short when she saw an old beige Pontiac vehicle sitting beside Caleb's truck. A woman with very short dark hair liberally laced with gray slammed her hand on the car in irritation as she walked closer to Brice.

She was so thin, a strong wind would probably break her in two. Her flesh was stretched tightly over her bones, but it was the paleness of the woman's skin that told Audrey she wasn't well.

"Get the fuck off my land," Brice stated angrily.

The tone was so cold, so enraged that Audrey was taken aback. Whoever this woman was, Brice wanted no part of her—and he didn't mind showing the world that.

"Brice, honey, please," the woman pled.

He pointed a finger inches from the woman's face. "Your mistake was coming back. There's nothing for you here. Leave."

"Not until I see Caleb and Abby. I am your mother. You can't deny me."

Audrey's knees nearly buckled. No wonder Brice was so livid. She would be, as well. And where was Caleb? Had he left before his mother got here? Or was he avoiding her?

Brice laughed, the sound mirthless and as cold as the Arctic. "You gave up those rights when you walked out on us."

"It was the best thing for you."

"Save your bullshit for someone who'll actually listen, because it won't be your children. I'm not going to tell you again to leave my land. If I have to, I'll call the sheriff and have him escort you off."

The woman lifted her chin defiantly. "I'll be back."

"The hell you will."

She didn't argue. Simply turned and made her way to the car. Audrey hadn't moved a muscle, but still, the woman's gaze landed on her. She looked Audrey up and down until she reached her vehicle. Then the woman opened the door and stared at Brice for a long minute. Her movements were slow as she sank into the driver's seat.

Brice remained there, watching until his mother started the engine and drove away. Then his head swung to Audrey.

"I'm so sorry," she said. "I had no idea, or I never would have come outside."

Brice looked down as if to compose himself. Then he yanked off his hat long enough to rake a hand through his dark hair. "Caleb rode off. I don't know how long he'll be gone. Or what kind of mood he'll be in when he returns."

Audrey nodded. "I understand."

Brice drew in a deep breath and released it. "You should know that he was smiling when I saw him this morning. Before . . . well, before I told him she was back."

"Thank you." She walked to the edge of the porch and leaned a hand on one of the thick pillars holding up the roof. "Is there anything I can do for you?"

"No. Thank you." Brice cleared his throat. "You should also know that no one came to the auction house last night. Danny and some of his men will stay on guard for the next few nights to see if anyone comes back."

Audrey scanned the horizon, wondering which way Caleb had gone. "That's good news."

"Stay here as long as you want. The ranch might be big, but we have a powerful security system. You'll be safe here. If you follow the drive east, it'll bring you to my house. Naomi is there developing some pictures if you want company."

Audrey smiled at him. "Thanks."

With a tip of his hat, he was gone. Audrey didn't have her own vehicle, and even if she did, she wouldn't have left.

Especially not with what she'd just seen with Caleb's mother.

Audrey reached around and felt in her back pockets for her cell phone. That's when she remembered that it was still inside. She retrieved it and scrolled through the texts. There was a couple from Maddy, letting her know that all was good at the East Ranch. As well as one that urged Audrey to "get it on" with the "hot cowboy."

Audrey laughed out loud at that, then sent a response so her sister would know that she was fine. Audrey also made sure to note how often she'd eaten. No sooner had that text gone through than her sister sent back a gif with a girl clapping and nodding emphatically.

That left Audrey with only one other thing to do—call the ranches she worked for. She pressed dial on the first number and brought the phone up to her ear.

"Hey, Ted," she said. "I'm sorry, but my family emergency still isn't resolved. I'm going to need another couple of days."

Chapter 27

The ground was a blur, and no amount of wind brushing against his cheek could temper the rising temperatures as the sun rose.

But no matter how far he rode the horse, Caleb couldn't outrun or escape his past. It would always be there, waiting like a dark cloud ready to blot out the brightest of days.

Just like this morning.

Caleb straightened and drew up on the reins. "Whoa," he said. The gelding slowed to a stop.

Caleb dismounted, dropping the reins so the horse could graze. Caleb walked to the thick branches of an old oak. Last night had been the best one of his life—hands down.

Why did his mother have to ruin it? It once more reminded him why he'd kept his heart safely guarded against any woman who could hurt him. Caleb fisted his hands wanting—needing—something to hit to relieve some of the anger within him. Instead, he paced.

Part of him wanted to never see the woman who'd given

birth to him again. Another side wanted to confront her, to demand that she tell him why she'd left them so long ago. But he knew no matter what answer she gave, it wouldn't be what he wanted to hear.

Because there was no excuse for her actions.

Caleb was certain that Abby would talk to their mother simply because that was his sister's way. She didn't hold grudges. Besides, she'd say it was a learning experience for the kids.

But if she were smart, she'd never let her offspring anywhere near Helen Harper.

As for Brice, Caleb wasn't sure what his brother would do if he came face-to-face with their mother. Brice might welcome her, or he might look right through her. For many years, the hatred Brice had for her nearly surpassed Caleb's. A few years ago, however, Brice had said that it might be a good idea to forgive her so they could all move on.

"I've moved on," Caleb said. He looked around, fury swelling in his chest. "I've fucking moved on!"

Even as the words echoed around him, he knew them for the lie they were. If he had gotten past it, then he wouldn't have any problems opening himself up to women. Instead, he continued to push them away, keeping himself closed off to anyone but family and friends.

Well . . . until Audrey.

Every instinct he had cautioned him to push her away, to get clear of her before things got too . . . deep. He closed his eyes, anguished. Not once had he thought of her when he rode from the house. Hopefully, she was still asleep, but what if she wasn't? What if she woke up looking for him? Surely, Brice would see to her.

Yes, his brother would take care of everything. That's one thing the Harper siblings always made sure to do—have each other's backs. For so long, it had just been the three of them.

Then Clayton was there, expanding their family. And Clayton's parents, Ben and Justine. Next came Clayton and Abby's children. And just when Caleb didn't think things could get any better, Naomi and Brice fell in love.

The small Harper family now seemed ever-expanding with Jace, Cooper, Danny, Shane, and now Audrey and Maddy.

The thing was, Caleb had known from the very beginning that each of those people would leave him one day. Not because they didn't love him, but because they moved on with their lives. He accepted that as life.

But when it came to his heart, that was another matter entirely.

He lowered himself to the ground and leaned back against the trunk of the tree. The air was filled with the songs of birds. He even heard the cry of a hawk, his favorite. But he couldn't bring himself to look up to find it, he was sunk too deep in the mire of his past.

Caleb didn't know how long he sat there before he was pulled from his thoughts by the horse, who nudged him on the shoulder with his great head.

"Hey, boy," Caleb said and rubbed the animal's forehead. He climbed to his feet and gathered the reins in his hand. "We Harpers don't run from things. We face them head-on. Together."

And that's exactly what he was going to do. He climbed back on the horse and turned the animal around. With a nudge from Caleb's knee, the gelding began galloping back to the stables.

All too soon, the buildings came into view. Whether Caleb was ready or not, he would have to face his mother and the past that wouldn't loosen its grip on him.

There was no sign of Brice when he reached the stables. Caleb removed the saddle and bridle to brush the horse down before releasing it into the pasture. He went to put the tack up when he saw the door to the vet clinic slightly ajar.

He took his time putting the saddle and other equipment away as he tried to think of what to say to Audrey. There had to be a way to explain where he'd gone without telling her of his family drama. It wasn't that he was embarrassed. . . .

Oh, hell. Who was he kidding? He was ashamed and pissed and just mortified that this was even happening. The fact that he wasn't trying to think of ways to keep Audrey away from him was overshadowed by the morning's news.

He closed the tack room door and made his way to the clinic. When he looked inside, Audrey was entering something into the computer. It seemed right that she was there. All the thoughts he had about pushing her away dimmed. The sound of music softly playing reached him. He grinned when he heard Toto.

Audrey turned to put something away and looked up, their eyes meeting. She gave him a warm smile. "Morning, handsome."

Caleb opened the door wider and stepped inside the room. "Good morning, beautiful."

"I couldn't resist," she said as she held out her arms, indicating the room.

He laughed and shook his head. "Hey, whatever it takes to bring you on board." He swallowed and glanced away.

"I'm sorry I wasn't here when you woke. I had some things to take care of."

"You can make it up to me later."

The band he hadn't known was around his chest loosened when he heard her words. "I'll make sure of that."

"Good," she said with a wink. "I've already called both of my employers and taken some vacation time. They aren't pleased, but I think I need it."

"You do."

"And I have some thinking to do about my future."

Caleb leaned a shoulder against the doorframe. "Really?"

"Yep," she said with a nod. "I've been busy this morning. I texted with my sister, and I checked in with David, who is thrilled that everything turned out well after the poisoning. Then I came to the stables just to be with the horses. But . . . I found myself in here. I hope you don't mind, but I looked over the charts."

"I don't mind at all."

She crossed her arms over her chest then nervously let them fall to her sides. "Good."

"What's wrong?" he asked.

Audrey shook her head of dark hair. "Nothing. I. . . ." She swallowed. "That's a lie. I know why you rode off. I'm worried about you, is all."

"Brice told you," he said, not at all upset about the fact. Actually, he was glad that he didn't have to explain anything because he wasn't sure the words would come. When she hesitated, Caleb pushed away from the door, a frown developing. "What?"

She briefly looked up and shifted on her feet. "It's really none of my business."

"We shared our bodies several times last night. Twice

without using protection. For all we know, you're carrying my child. Please. Just tell me."

"I woke to the sound of someone arguing with Brice. I couldn't tell who it was until I went outside." She licked her lips, her anxiety clearly growing. "Turns out, it was your mother."

Caleb turned away to pace through the barn. His mother had been here. He was glad that he hadn't seen her, but he hated that Brice had had to deal with her on his own. After a few steps, Caleb halted and spun to Audrey. "Did she talk to you?"

"No," Audrey hurried to say. "I came out as Brice told her to leave."

"How did he say it? Was he nice?" Caleb needed to know.

Audrey's brows shot up in her forehead. "Not at all. He yelled at her. Then he threatened to call the authorities to escort her off the land."

Again, Caleb was grateful that he hadn't been there when Helen showed up. He wasn't sure what he would have said to her. There were so many years of hurt and anger built up, he might not be able to do anything at all.

Suddenly, Audrey's hands were on his arm. "I'm sorry. I can't begin to imagine what you're going through."

"I never want to see her. For the past decade, I've just assumed she's dead."

Audrey pressed her lips together. "By the look of things, she isn't well at all."

"Good."

"You don't mean that, surely," Audrey said, shock in her voice.

Caleb studied her as he took a step back. "You grew up

with two loving parents. You don't know what it means to wake up in the middle of the night and watch your mother pack up her clothes and sneak out, thinking no one saw her. You don't know what it feels like to call out to her, to beg her to stay, to tell her that you love her—and have her shut the door in your face. To know you weren't enough, that your love wasn't enough to make her stay."

"Oh, God, Caleb, I had no idea."

He snorted. "No, you really don't."

Audrey wished she could take back the words. It didn't matter if Caleb hadn't seen his mom leave or not, she had no right to tell him that he shouldn't wish her dead.

She felt like an utter fool. And she wasn't sure she could take it back.

The pain in his eyes was unbearable, just as it was excruciating to hear the agony in his words as he related what had happened that night so long ago. It had left a wound that never healed.

It had scabbed over, and maybe even attempted to mend, but it never had.

Audrey reached for Caleb, but he turned on his heel and walked away. Audrey dropped her head into her hands, wishing she could turn back time. Of all the ways she'd wanted this day to go, this was not it. The entire time Caleb had been gone, she'd thought about what she would say to him to avoid just this situation. And what did she do? Ended up right where she hadn't wanted to be.

"Just fantastic," she mumbled as she dropped her hands to her sides.

Now, what was she supposed to do? She hadn't had a relationship that lasted longer than a month—and even that had been back in high school when she'd had no choice but to see her boyfriend in class. This was entirely different.

Did she go after Caleb and try to talk to him? Did she let him cool off before they spoke again? Or was whatever had been blossoming between them over?

She didn't know him well enough to discern which option to take. She'd already messed up once. She really didn't want to further the damage. But she also didn't want to leave things the way they were.

Audrey squared her shoulders and went after him. She found him lifting hundred-pound bags of feed from a flatbed trailer into the feed room.

He walked right past her, ignoring her as he moved bag after bag. Audrey saw his pain through the mask of anger he wore. All she wanted to do was hug him, wrap her arms around him and try to take some of the heartache away.

After he'd dropped a bag, she finally stepped in front of him, blocking his way. When he tried to go around her, she wrapped an arm around his neck and held him tightly.

"I'm sorry. I'm so sorry," Audrey murmured.

A full minute passed before his hands slowly came up to rest on her back. Then he splayed his fingers and held her tighter before winding his arms around her. Tears filled her eyes when he buried his face in her neck.

Chapter 28

Despite being intimate the night before—several times, in fact—there was something different, special even, about the way he held her now.

And Audrey liked it.

A lot.

He'd allowed her to see his vulnerability, his pain. And there was so much of it. She hadn't realized that Caleb held such heartache within him. He masked it beautifully, but then again, so did most people who dealt with such things.

The sound of a vehicle approaching didn't pull them apart, though Audrey felt Caleb tense slightly. Then Maddy called her name.

Audrey didn't want anyone disturbing her and Caleb, but there was no getting around life intruding. It saddened her that Caleb was the first to release her. He stepped back even as she let her hands linger upon him.

He quickly turned away and went to retrieve another bag of feed. Audrey licked her lips and pivoted to walk from the stables as Maddy continued calling out to her.

"I'm here," Audrey said when she saw Maddy at the door of the house.

Her sister hurried to her. "Why didn't you answer your phone?"

Audrey reached into her back pocket for it and found it gone. "I must have left it in the clinic," she said.

Maddy rolled her eyes. "You need to hurry and come with me."

"What is it?"

"Two horses have just been saved from deplorable conditions and were taken to the horse rescue. It's a mare and her foal. There's a chance neither will make it."

Audrey looked back and spotted Caleb watching her. "Give me a second," she told her sister and hurried to Caleb. "There are two horses I need to save."

He nodded. "Of course."

She wanted him to come with her, but when he didn't offer, she found the words to invite him stuck in her throat. Audrey hated the fear that welled liked a geyser within her. Why couldn't she just ask him to come?

Because she knew he might say no, and that would be far worse than never asking him at all.

"Audrey!"

She inwardly winced at her sister's call. She wasn't finished with Caleb, and she feared that by leaving, whatever had begun between them would wither to nothing.

"Um . . . I—" Audrey began.

"Audrey, come on!" Maddy hollered.

Caleb nodded toward the truck Maddy had started. "We're good. Go. Because if those horses die, you'll never forgive yourself."

He was right, but that didn't make leaving any easier.

She shot him a smile when she couldn't think of something to say. So, she turned on her heel and walked to her sister.

Once inside the truck, Audrey's gaze locked on Caleb. He watched them for a few seconds as Maddy turned the vehicle around. Before they'd even finished the maneuver, he had grabbed another bag and disappeared into the stables.

"I'm sorry," Maddy said. "It looks like I interrupted something."

Audrey shrugged. "It's probably for the best. I screw these things up anyway."

"Don't bullshit me, sis. I've seen you around plenty of men. You're finished with them before things even begin. You have a certain look in your eyes. You might flirt with guys. Hell, you might even sleep with them, but that's as far as it ever goes. You never let them see *you*."

Audrey swallowed, hating the words she was hearing. Maddy's description of her made her sound so callous. That's not who she wanted to be.

"I never saw that look with Caleb," her sister added.

Audrey turned her head to look out the passenger window. She squeezed her eyes closed until she was sure the surge of tears that threatened was once more in check. Then she opened her eyes and asked, "Tell me about the horses."

For the next ten minutes, Maddy described the state of the mare and the newborn foal when a neighbor had finally called the authorities, and someone went to check on the animals.

Audrey was sickened to hear that the mare and filly were in such bad shape they couldn't even stand. Mentally, Audrey thought of all the things she could do to save the horses. The foal would be the trickiest. Already weak, if it didn't get milk quickly, there wasn't much she could do.

She spotted her bag and wondered when Maddy had gotten it. Then she looked at the truck. "Whose vehicle are we driving?"

"Abby's," Maddy said as she took a turn too fast, causing Audrey to slam against the door.

Still, Audrey didn't say anything about the driving. Maddy's love of animals rivaled her own. The sight of any of them suffering could make Maddy do amazing things. Perhaps that's why it worked so well that she acted as Audrey's assistant.

Maybe Maddy stuck around because she enjoyed helping, and not because she was floundering in life or thought Audrey couldn't take care of herself. That made Audrey take a deeper look at her sister and reconsider many things.

"Did you just take Abby's truck?" Audrey asked with a frown.

Maddy rolled her eyes as she increased the speed. "Abby wanted to come, but one of the kids wasn't feeling well. Caleb, however, was one step ahead of all of us. Apparently, there's an undercover sheriff's deputy already at the rescue to keep an eye on you."

Audrey didn't know what to say.

Her sister shot her a grin. "Actually, there's someone at Ted's and Robert's farms, as well."

Caleb had done that? For her? He hadn't said anything, but then again, that's the type of person he was. It made her feel even worse for the things she'd said.

And for leaving when he obviously needed her.

She wanted to go to him, but she couldn't leave the horses on their own. Once they were seen to, however, she was heading right back to Caleb.

Audrey wasn't surprised when they pulled up to the rescue. But they weren't the only ones who had been called in.

"Damn," Maddy said. "She beat us here."

"You knew they called Patty in?"

Maddy's lips flattened in answer.

Audrey shook her head. She didn't know why her sister had taken an instant disliking to Patty. And while Audrey and Patty did compete for jobs once, that was no longer an issue.

Patty had found her footing in the community and had built a good business. Since Audrey couldn't always get to the rescue every time, other equine vets volunteered their time there, and Patty was one who was there nearly as much as Audrey was.

"Patty is a friend. You need to remember that," Audrey reminded her sister.

"Friend? You sure about that?"

The glance her sister gave her made Audrey frown. "Of course, I'm sure. We graduated high school together, and both finished college within a semester of each other."

"You finished before her," Maddy said with a grin.

Audrey rolled her eyes. No matter what Audrey said, her sister would never agree that Patty was not only a good equine vet but also a good person.

Maddy drew the truck to a stop beside Patty's. When they got out, the petite redhead was coming from the stables, her face lined with concern.

"Ugh," Maddy mumbled.

Audrey ignored her sister. She'd always envied the petite figure Patty had. Men panted after her everywhere she went. Her shoulder-length waves were pulled back away from her face to show her pale skin and the spattering of freckles across her nose.

"It's not good," Patty said when Audrey reached her.

Audrey looked into the stables. "Tell me what you've done so far."

Maybe it was because she'd been through so much over the last few days. Perhaps it was because she knew that someone might very well be trying to ruin her reputation. Or maybe it was because of the things her sister had said that made Audrey second-guess everything.

But she could've sworn Patty tensed as if irritated.

Audrey inwardly shook herself. That was ridiculous. She was simply looking for things that weren't there.

Caleb stood in the doorway of the room where Audrey's clothes lay scattered about. She had forgotten her things. Not that he minded. It meant that she had to come back for them.

At least he hoped that's what it meant.

Or maybe she'd just forgotten about them.

He ran a hand down his face. Women were complicated. He wanted to take Audrey's words and actions at face value, but he also knew from his sister and sister-in-law, that women had layers upon layers of meanings to the things they said.

He'd left the stables because he saw Audrey everywhere. The house wasn't any better. Caleb had gone to great pains never to bring a woman to his home or into his bed. Once, he'd thought it was because he'd have to kick them out. And while that was a part of it, it wasn't the only reason.

No, the truth was that he'd always secretly known that

if a woman ever did find her way into his bed, he would've crossed into territory he wasn't at all familiar with.

And sure enough, that's exactly where he was now.

He didn't backpedal or look for a way out, though. No, he found he wanted to explore this new territory.

Not only had he had the most incredible sex with Audrey, he'd also been stupid and forgotten to use protection. Though it might have been too little, too late, they had rectified the situation the three other times they'd made love during the night.

Then they'd had their first fight. Caleb had handled that very poorly, but when it came to his mother, he couldn't deal with anything properly.

When Audrey had stood before him, refusing to allow him to pass her, he'd wanted to toss her aside and get on with his day. Then, her arms had come around him, and everything within him had cracked.

The only way he'd survived was by hanging onto her.

But he hadn't been able to say anything after that because Maddy had arrived and took Audrey away. Not that he blamed Audrey for going. It was her job—vacation or not. She had a skill that animals needed. Who was he to be angry that she had been taken from him?

He walked into the room and picked up her clothes. Once they were collected, he folded each piece and put it into the bag that sat upon the bed.

There was nothing else for him to do. Yet he found himself walking to his bedroom. The sight of the bed that they'd slept in and had sex on loomed large in the room. He thought about making it up, but he didn't move from the spot inside the door.

If only he'd stayed in bed that morning, things might be different. He might have had a run-in with his mother, but he would've been there when Audrey opened her eyes.

Why hadn't he stayed? Why had he left? The chores could've waited an hour or two.

Had he left because he wasn't ready for . . . whatever the next step was with Audrey? He'd never woken with a woman in his arms before. And he'd never looked into a female's eyes first thing in the morning because he'd never allowed himself to get that close. He'd had that—and missed out.

He recalled the feeling of Audrey in his arms when they fell asleep. Waking up next to her had been absolutely amazing. He wanted another chance to gaze into her eyes in the morning light and make love to her before they started their day.

But would he get that chance?

Caleb couldn't look at the bed anymore. He turned but halted immediately when he saw Brice. He didn't know how long his brother had been standing there, but it didn't matter.

"I saw Maddy and Audrey leave."

Caleb glanced at the floor and nodded. "Two horses need Audrey's help."

"You good?"

"I'll be fine. I didn't have to see Helen."

Brice drew in a quick breath. "I was referring to Audrey."

"She told me that you threatened to call the cops on Helen. I wish I'd have been there to see that." Caleb didn't want to talk about Audrey, and he hoped his brother would take the hint.

For several long moments, Brice stared at him. "Helen wants to see you. She wants to see all of us."

"Not going to happen."

"She'll be back. You know that, right?"

Caleb shrugged. "Perhaps it's time I put up the gate and use a code to get in. That'll keep her out."

"Not on my side."

"Then put your own damn gate up."

Brice shook his head slowly. "I don't want to see our mother either, but she's here."

"So?"

"You won't be able to dodge her for long."

Caleb's brow shot up. "Are you telling me you're going to talk to her?"

"I don't know."

"Well, I'm not. There's nothing you can say to me that will make me change my mind."

"I'm not going to force you to do anything. Neither is Abby."

"Damn straight," Caleb stated. "I wiped my hands of that woman when she left."

Brice's lips flattened briefly. "We both know that statement is a lie."

"If I see her on my property, I'll consider it trespassing and call Danny to arrest her. You tell her that when you see her."

"Caleb," Brice called.

But he was done listening. He turned and stormed from the house.

Chapter 29

Audrey winced when she got to her feet and straightened her back after hours of being bent over. She and Patty, along with Maddy and some other volunteers at the rescue center, had worked tirelessly to try and save the dehydrated and starving horses.

As Audrey had feared, the little filly hadn't made it. Once the foal was gone, everyone put all their efforts into the mother. Audrey hadn't realized how much time had passed since her arrival until she put her hands on her lower back and pushed out her chest to stretch it. That's when she looked outside and saw that it was dark.

"Good job," someone said as they walked past her, slapping her on the arm.

She nodded absently, her mind on Caleb. Audrey had half expected him to show up and check on her. It was silly really. It wasn't as if he could text or call since she didn't have her phone.

It was at the ranch, along with her clothes. A perfect

excuse to return and see Caleb. Why then did her stomach tie itself into such knots at the prospect?

"Hey," Maddy said as she walked up. She took one look at Audrey, and her face contorted into a deep frown. "What is it?"

"Nothing."

"You're a good liar to everyone else. Don't forget, I'm your sister. I know you better than you know yourself." Maddy moved in front of her and crossed her arms over her chest.

Audrey glanced around her to make sure no one else was near to overhear. "I'm just thinking about . . . you know."

Maddy's lips turned into a smile. "Ah. *Him*. That's good. Isn't it?" she asked, frowning again.

"I don't know. I left under odd circumstances."

"Want to tell me what happened?"

Audrey motioned for her to follow, and they walked to the truck Maddy had driven. There, Audrey filled her in on what had occurred that morning at the ranch.

She paused. That morning? It felt like a week ago.

"Wow," Maddy whispered. "That's some situation."

"Right?" Audrey said, nodding her head. "And I just made it worse."

Maddy shrugged. "I think you made up for it in the end."

"I think I screwed it all up."

"The fact that you're worried about it hours later is a change for you. Usually, you've forgotten the man's name by now."

Audrey shoved her sister away and rolled her eyes. "You make me sound like some . . ." she hesitated, not wanting to say the word.

"Like someone who likes sex? There's nothing wrong with that."

"Yeah, well, that's not how others think of it."

Maddy rolled her eyes dramatically. "Who cares what they think. It's your life. You get to live it."

"Thanks."

"No problem. Now, tell me. How was the hot cowboy?" Maddy asked with a knowing smile.

Audrey looked askance at her sister. "What? Just because I stayed the night, you think we slept together?"

"Honey, let me put it to you this way. The looks passing between you two were hot enough to start a forest fire. So, yeah. I know the flames erupted once the two of you were alone. He looks like he knows his way around a woman's body. He does, doesn't he?"

Audrey really tried not to smile, but she couldn't hold it back. She nodded eagerly, little butterflies dancing in her stomach. "Oh, yeah. He really does."

"Made your toes curl, did he?" Maddy asked knowingly.

"I'd have to say that's an accurate assessment."

Maddy pumped her fist in the air and wiggled her hips. "Damn, I'm good. I knew the two of you together would be something spectacular."

"*We* aren't anything."

"You don't know that."

Audrey blew out a breath. "One night of amazing sex doesn't make two people a couple."

"I wish I had an argument, but I don't. You're right. Do you want something more with him?"

Though Audrey hadn't asked Maddy not to say Caleb's name, her sister was perceptive of such things. Audrey didn't like the question, and what's more, she didn't like the answer that popped into her mind.

"Audrey," Maddy pressed. "Why haven't you answered me? Maybe because the reply is a bit scary?"

"Why did you ask that?" The longer Audrey thought about it, the angrier she became.

Maddy smiled sadly. "Because, honey, someone needed to, and you weren't going to do it."

"I think I hate you."

"I love you, too. So, what's the answer?"

Audrey looked out over a field drenched in moonlight. "You know what it is."

"Say it. Out loud."

"Fine. I . . . might . . . want something more."

Maddy took her hand and gave it a squeeze. "About damn time."

"Funny. Look, I'm going to stay with the mare, but there's no need for you to. I'm being guarded, remember? Take the truck and go back to the East Ranch."

Maddy was shaking her head before she finished. "Not happening. I'm staying with you."

Audrey wasn't fooled. She crossed her arms over her chest and glared at her sister. "You said yourself that someone is watching over me. You don't need to worry."

Maddy shoved her thick hair out of her face. "For all your book smarts, sometimes, you can be pretty dense."

"That's harsh."

"That's what sisters are for."

"Riiiiiight."

Maddy moved closer, all teasing gone from her face, the expression replaced by something serious that made chills run down Audrey's spine.

"You don't see it," Maddy said. "You don't understand that you're so good at your job that others are jealous. They may not say or show it to your face, but trust me, they are."

Audrey wasn't sure how to respond to such a statement. "There are enough horses in the area to keep everyone busy."

"That might be true, but how would you feel if you went for a job and were told that you were either their second or third choice? That they were only settling on you because the one they really wanted was already taken?"

Audrey had to admit that it might make working difficult. "I see your point."

Maddy parted her lips to reply but paused.

"Oh, no you don't," Audrey stated angrily. "You began this. You're going to finish it. Tell me."

"Fine," Maddy mumbled. "You want the truth. I'll tell you what I overheard at the grocery store once. I didn't see who it was. They were an aisle over from me, but the women were pissed. One of them knew an equine vet who had a job lined up, and then they were fired so the ranch could get you."

Audrey jerked back as if hit. "Which ranch?"

"It doesn't matter," Maddy said.

Audrey lifted a brow and stared down at her sister until she finally relented with a loud sigh.

"Fine. It's Bremer."

Somehow, Audrey had known it would be Robert. "He told me that he'd been without a vet for weeks. I can't believe he lied to me."

"You're the best vet."

"Stop saying that. I wish everyone would stop saying that," Audrey said and turned around to walk away.

Maddy followed her. "It's the truth. Half of it is your skill, but the other half is your absolute love of the horses. You combine those two, and you're fabulous."

"Others have those same skills."

"Not with your flare. And this is coming from me. You know I don't pull any punches. If you sucked, I'd be the first to tell you."

Audrey gave a snort of laughter as she cut her eyes to Maddy. "Yes, you would."

"You need to be careful. Whoever is after you isn't finished yet."

"The only way to stop me from working is to kill me."

Maddy's lips twisted ruefully. "There are other ways to stop you."

The simple fact that Audrey was scared just proved how correct her sister was. She turned to go back into the stables to check on the mare. All Audrey could think about was Caleb and how she wished he were there. She wouldn't be scared if he were beside her. If he were there, she knew that no one would get near her.

"You're thinking of him, aren't you?" Maddy asked.

Audrey nodded, not even bothering to try and lie.

"Let's go by there. Patty can watch the mare," Maddy offered.

Audrey didn't reply until they reached the stall where the mare was. She was no longer lying down, but she wasn't on her feet yet. The simple fact that she'd sat up was a huge achievement, but the worst part was that she kept neighing for her baby. She didn't know yet that the foal had died.

Maddy jerked her chin to the horse. "See? She's doing better."

"If you need to go, I've got this," Patty offered as she walked up.

Audrey met the woman's hazel eyes. Was Patty Audrey's friend, or was she the frenemy her sister suggested? Regardless, Audrey knew Patty wouldn't let the mare die. "I'll be back. I just have something I need to do."

"I can handle this," Patty said and flashed a smile.

Audrey returned it, but now she was looking at everyone as a potential enemy. That wasn't a good way to live. While she tried to work out the mechanics of this new problem, Maddy was all smiles as they went to the truck.

"We need to get my vehicle and yours," Audrey said.

Maddy wrinkled her nose. "You're right. Let's head to the auction house first and get mine. We'll take this back to Abby and Clayton and then go see Caleb."

"After we drop this truck off with Abby and Clayton, you'll drive me to get mine, and then *I'll* go see Caleb."

Maddy shot her a hurt look as she started the truck. "You don't want me there?"

"Absolutely not."

"I'm hurt. You've actually ripped my heart out."

Audrey issued a bark of laughter. "Nice try. Not going to work."

Maddy was silent as they drove back to the road. After a few minutes, she asked, "Are you really okay with going back to the house after what happened?"

Audrey felt like such an idiot for not thinking of what her sister had gone through. "I wasn't there for it. You were. If you're not ready, we can stay somewhere else."

"I like the idea of Caleb's ranch."

Maddy's smile was too bright, her voice too high-pitched. Audrey knew that she was putting on a brave face because she wouldn't mention that going back to the house was the last thing she wanted to do. So Audrey would say it for her.

"Honestly, I don't think I can go back to the house yet. It's too isolated from the road and the neighbors." She used to like that, but now, all she could think about was someone closing in on her without anyone near to help.

"I think that's a good idea."

They turned up the radio, singing at the top of their lungs to their favorite Michael Bublé playlist until they reached the auction house. Audrey went in long enough to look over the horses just to make sure everything was indeed fine.

Then she got into her SUV instead of Maddy's car. She glanced at her sister to see Maddy's angry expression. Audrey just laughed and started the engine. Immediately, she saw the screen say that the Bluetooth was connected to her phone.

She looked over at the passenger seat and spotted not only her phone but the bag of clothes she'd brought to Caleb's. If that didn't tell her not to go back, nothing would.

Audrey's smile faded, replaced by a feeling of dread so deep and profound that she could barely breathe. She jumped when Maddy honked the horn at her.

Audrey's hand shook as she lifted her cell phone and dialed her sister's number because she wasn't sure she could walk.

"Audrey? What the hell? I thought you said your cell phone was at Caleb's."

She swallowed, the sound as loud as a gunshot. "It was. Along with my bag. Both are in my truck."

"Ohhhhhh, shit."

"I . . . um . . . I'm going back to the rescue center."

Maddy quickly said, "Of course. I'll have someone else bring me to get my car. I'll be there as soon as I can."

"Okay." Audrey hung up, trying her best not to feel as if someone had yanked out her heart and stomped all over it.

Chapter 30

Caleb couldn't remember a time that he'd been so exhausted. Everything hurt. He hadn't worked so long or hard in years, but it had been done in an effort to not only forget that his mother was in town but also to help him stop thinking about Audrey.

He shuffled into his house and stopped long enough to hang up his hat and peel his dirty clothes from his body before tossing the items into the laundry room as he made his way to his room and into the longest, hottest shower he could handle.

For long minutes, he just stood beneath the spray, letting the water run over him. It didn't matter if his eyes were shut or open, Audrey was always at the forefront of his thoughts. Even when he was working.

But especially in the shower.

He recalled every detail of their time together. Audrey's smile, her laughter . . . her sighs of pleasure. The fact that he wished she were still there was a serious wake-up call.

It would be easy for him to question his motives. Or

even come up with reasons why he shouldn't be with her—and there were many. Namely, his abandonment issues.

Caleb leaned forward and braced his hands on the tile. His chin dropped to his chest, and the water ran down his back. All the ways he'd run away from women poured through his mind. How did he—someone who loved 'em and left 'em—ever have a hope of having a woman like Audrey in his life?

And how would he even know what to do if he had her?

"Fuck," he mumbled and straightened, running a hand down his face.

If he even had a remote chance, then he had to face his fears. How could he think about a future with Audrey if he was still terrified of people leaving him?

He thought of Brice and Abby and, for the first time, realized that family never really left—at least not the family that counted. His brother and sister had always been by his side. And they always would be.

Why had it taken Caleb so long to see that? To understand such a crucial part of his life?

But he did now.

Caleb scrubbed the dirt and sweat from his body and hair. Finally, he turned off the water and reached for a towel. He didn't bother with clothes as he walked from the bathroom while drying off.

He glanced at the bed and briefly saw an image of Audrey lying on her side, showcasing her beautiful curves. But it disappeared as soon as it came into his head.

Without realizing where he was headed, he made his way to the spare bedroom once more. She wasn't there, but at least her clothes were. She'd have to come back for those. All he had to do was wait.

And make sure he was there when she did.

When he found the bag gone, Caleb jerked to a halt, his stomach tightening. He anxiously searched the room, thinking that he might have moved it and forgotten. Next, he went room by room in the house, looking for the bag until he finally realized that it was indeed gone.

There was only one person who would have done that.

Caleb stalked to grab his cell from the kitchen island. Except it wasn't there. He glanced into the laundry and remembered that he hadn't removed it from his jeans. After he retrieved it, he called his brother.

"What the fuck?" Caleb said when Brice answered.

There was a brief pause. "Am I supposed to know why you're upset?"

"Where is Audrey's bag?"

"Ah."

When Brice didn't continue, Caleb squeezed the phone. "An answer would be nice."

"I took care of it so you didn't have to."

"I didn't ask you to do that."

Brice snorted. "Of course, you didn't. I saw that you were upset about Mom—"

"Helen," Caleb interrupted.

"—and I knew you wouldn't want to deal with Audrey," Brice continued.

Caleb squeezed his eyes shut. There were so many things he wanted to say. Some to Brice, some to himself, but he didn't dare let any of them pass his lips.

"Oh, fuck," Brice said, shock and surprise in his voice. "You wanted her stuff there. Naomi *was* right."

Caleb sighed and opened his eyes as he walked to the sofa and sank down. "Yeah. I wanted her things here."

"I'll go get them right now. She'll never know they were gone. I just figured—"

"I know." Caleb leaned back and stared at the ceiling. "You were trying to do me a favor."

Brice mumbled something away from the phone. Then he told Caleb, "Naomi just reminded me that the bag wouldn't have been a big deal if I hadn't also found her cell phone in the stables."

If this wasn't the universe telling Caleb that they didn't belong together, he didn't know what would.

"I'll be right back," Brice said and disconnected the line.

Caleb knew it would be pointless to tell his brother not to bother getting the bag and phone back. Brice was doing what Brice always did—fixing things. Caleb couldn't even be mad at him for taking Audrey's things because his brother had only been looking out for him.

Another ten minutes went by before Caleb rose and put on some clothes. He was in the middle of buttoning his jeans when there was a knock at the door. A moment later, he heard Naomi's voice.

He walked into the kitchen and found his sister-in-law setting down a dish on the counter. She turned and looked at him, her gaze sweeping over his face.

"I told Brice to leave things as they were," she said.

Caleb shrugged. "Maybe it's for the best."

"Do you like her?"

"Yes." He didn't even have to consider the question.

Naomi smiled sadly and leaned against the island. "Then what's the problem?"

"I don't know. I've not been in this situation before. I mean . . ." He looked around and shrugged. "What do I do?"

Naomi shook her head and rolled her eyes. "Men. I swear."

"What?" Caleb asked, more confused than ever. "I mean it. I don't know—"

"What to do. Yes, I heard you," she said over him. "You watch movies, right? TV? Everything you need to know is right there for you to get. See how a couple holds hands. How they kiss, how they have their arms around each other."

Now he was offended. "I know how to do that bit."

"All the other things you want to know are in there, as well. What the next step is, how to talk about the next step, how to treat her, and everything else."

"You make it sound as if the bible to figuring out women has been right in front of us all this time."

Naomi cocked her hip and gave him an icy glare. "Honey, it has been. Pick up a romance book. Watch one of the chick-flicks that men always roll their eyes at. You'll find all you need to know."

"You want to be wined and dined. You want someone romantic."

Naomi sighed loudly. "Yes and no. Being romantic isn't always about flowers and gifts. It's about something that's meaningful to the one you care about. Follow your heart, Caleb. If you like Audrey, then don't let her slip through your fingers."

"I've never met anyone like her before. She's . . ." He shrugged and crossed his arms over his chest. "She's everything."

"Brice will bring her things back, and when she comes to get them, you need to tell her how you feel."

Caleb took a step back, appalled at the idea. "What? You're crazy. We just . . . what I mean to say is we're just getting to know each other."

Naomi pushed away from the island and walked even with him. "Can you stop thinking about her?"

"No."

"Do you wish she was with you or you with her?"

"Yes."

"Do memories of the last time you were with each other run through your mind? Conversations, touches, smiles?"

He nodded, an odd feeling developing in his gut.

Naomi touched his arm. "You might not want to hear this, but it sounds like you've got it bad for her. After all this time, finally, a woman who can get your attention in a big way."

Before Caleb could respond, the back door opened, and Brice walked in. Unfortunately, his hands were empty. And by the look of regret on his face, he didn't bring good news.

"Her truck was gone," Brice said.

Caleb snorted, feeling as if a herd of horses was standing on his lungs. "Of course, it was. After the way I've treated women for years, this is my punishment. This is Fate having a laugh at me."

"It isn't the end," Naomi said.

Brice nodded as he came to stand beside his wife. "She's right. It isn't. Find Audrey and talk to her. It's not like you two said you wouldn't see each other again."

"Our last conversation didn't exactly go well," Caleb said.

Brice made a face at him. "So? It comes down to if you want her or not. If I'd known you felt this way, I never would have interfered."

"You were looking out for me."

"You never bring a woman here, and you were so upset,"

Brice said as he scrubbed a hand over his jaw. "I can go talk to Audrey."

Caleb pointed a finger at his brother. "No. Do you hear me? You stay out of it." He then looked at Naomi. "Both of you. I know you mean well, but this is my problem to work out."

Naomi winked at him. "We hear you loud and clear. Food is waiting. Eat it before it gets cold. Come on, my love," she said as she took Brice's hand and led him to the door.

Caleb watched as they left and got into Brice's truck to drive away. He waited until the taillights faded before he grabbed the dish and uncovered it to find Naomi's famous spaghetti. He grabbed a beer and went to the theatre room. After he got comfortable in the recliner and opened his beverage, he turned on the TV and did a search for romantic movies.

If—and that was a big *if*—he were going after Audrey, he wanted to be sure he had several ideas and moves in his arsenal just in case he had to use every one of them to win her over.

He searched through the entire romance section on Netflix before he grabbed his phone and looked up the greatest romantic movies of all time.

After reading through the very long list a couple of times, he narrowed it down to a few. Surely, he'd get all he needed to know from one or two movies. At least that was his plan.

He knew how much his sister loved the old shows. One of her favorites was *An Affair to Remember* with Cary Grant, so that was the first one he picked.

Caleb took a bite of spaghetti as the movie opened.

Chapter 31

"Damn, damn, damn." No matter how many times Audrey told herself not to look at her phone to see if Caleb had texted, she still did it.

She shoved the device into the back pocket of her jeans and continued cleaning up the mess in her clinic. Caleb had Maddy's number, which meant that he could have gotten hers from her sister.

Audrey knew that he hadn't, though, because Maddy would have told her immediately. Still, that didn't stop Audrey from hoping that every ding of her phone was from Caleb.

"This is the fourth day of your moping," Maddy said from behind her.

Audrey paused in tossing the larger chunks of glass into the garbage to look at her sister over her shoulder. "What are you talking about now?"

"You, being stupid. Why don't you just go see him?"

It was the question Audrey asked herself about once an hour, but with every day that passed without hearing from him, it became harder and harder to decide to go to Caleb.

Yet she couldn't stop thinking about him. It didn't matter if she was in the middle of a movie, talking with someone, or checking on the horses, he was always on her mind. From the look in his eyes right before he kissed her, to the way he held her, to the pleasure he gave.

Bedtime was the worst. Her dreams were filled with Caleb, reliving their night of passion over and over again. She woke needy and reaching for him, only to realize that she was alone.

The night before, she'd drunk half a bottle of wine in the hopes that she could sleep the entire night. It hadn't worked. Not only was she exhausted, but she had a splitting headache, as well.

Audrey went back to work, deciding that ignoring her sister was the best option. They'd had this argument the day before. And the day before that.

It was getting old.

"I didn't come by to give you a hard time about Caleb," Maddy said.

"That's good to know." Audrey waited for her sister to continue, but she didn't. Finally, Audrey asked, "You could help me while you tell me whatever it is you need to say."

"I need you to look at me."

There was something in Maddy's voice that Audrey had never heard before. It was fear and anger mixed with worry. It got her attention. Audrey dusted off her hands and got to her feet as she turned.

Maddy swallowed and licked her lips, her gaze darting away. The one thing her sister hated was delivering bad news. In fact, Maddy despised it so much, she never did it unless she didn't have another choice.

"What is it?" Audrey asked.

"One of the horses at the Hopkins' stables is sick."

Audrey's gut clenched. "Why didn't you tell me sooner? They should have called me. I don't care if I took vacation time or not. They know I care about the horses."

Maddy blocked the door when Audrey tried to pass. It was the way her sister blinked rapidly that let Audrey know there was something more.

"Spit it out," Audrey demanded.

Maddy pressed her lips together. "It's poison."

Audrey knew without being told that it was the same people who had gone after the horses at the auction house. Her chest tightened with worry for the animal. "Why are you stopping me from going to do my job?"

"You've been fired."

Audrey blinked, unsure if she'd heard her sister right. "What?"

"Ted called the house phone and talked to me."

Audrey looked at her phone and checked. Sure enough, there was a missed call from Ted. That's when she discovered that the ringer was off. "I . . . I don't understand. Why wouldn't they want me to help? I figured out the antidote with the others."

Maddy dropped her gaze to the ground. "They . . . um . . . they're saying that you're the one who poisoned the horse."

It was like the world had flipped on its axis, tossing her head over heels. Audrey was being sucked into a vortex and unable to find her way back. She was so shocked by the allegations that she didn't know how to respond.

"I know you didn't do it," Maddy said.

Audrey reached out for the table to keep her feet. Her

hand missed it, sending her tumbling forward. Maddy caught her and wrapped an arm around her to steady her.

"It's going to be okay. Do you hear me?" Maddy asked.

But Audrey knew that it wasn't. Her reputation was on the line. It didn't matter how good a vet was if their character came into question.

Caleb had said that someone was out to get her. Audrey had foolishly thought someone wanted to hurt her. And they did, just not physically. They wanted to destroy her career.

"I've got to fix this," Audrey said.

Maddy nodded. "Yes, we do. How?"

"We find out who is after me."

"How the heck do we do that?"

Audrey took in a steadying breath. Now that she had something to focus on, she felt as if she had an anchor of sorts."

"Where do we start?"

"This is about my job." Audrey pulled away from her sister and paced around the clinic, her boots crunching on the shards of glass still on the floor. "That narrows down the field considerably."

Maddy crossed her arms over her chest as she snorted. "Then we start with Patty."

"You really think she's my enemy?" Audrey asked as she came to a stop.

"She's not your friend."

"She's nice to me."

Maddy rolled her dark eyes dramatically. "I know you've heard the saying 'keep your friends close, but keep your enemies closer.'"

"Of course."

"Well, there you go," Maddy said as if that explained everything.

Audrey opened her mouth to reply but decided against it. Maybe her sister was right. Perhaps it was Patty. But why? Patty certainly wasn't hurting for business.

"I need a pen and some paper," Audrey said.

They walked back to the house and sat at the breakfast table. While Audrey listed out the equine veterinarians in the area, Maddy set two steaming mugs of coffee on the table.

One by one, they went through each of the names until they had narrowed it down to four suspects. Unfortunately, Patty was one of them. Audrey really wanted to mark her off, but everything Maddy said kept coming back to Patty. Which is why she was a suspect.

"Should we call the police?" Maddy asked.

Audrey shook her head. "We don't know anyone well enough."

"There's the sheriff."

At the mention of Danny, Audrey thought of Caleb. She wanted to reach out to him, to ask for his help. But it wasn't just his help she wanted. She wanted him. If she called now, he would think that she wished to use his contacts to get information.

Now she really wished she'd gone to see him the day before.

"We do this on our own," Audrey said.

Maddy gave her a dubious look. "I don't think that's a good idea. Whoever is doing this has gone to extremes. They've killed one horse and poisoned five. They set fire to the building that contained the dead animal you did the necropsy on, and let's not forget what happened here at the clinic. They're not stopping."

"I'm aware of that, but what would you have me do?"

"Use the friends we have. You're not alone in this."

"That's right. I have you."

Maddy sat back and blew out a breath. "Your stubbornness might very well accomplish what the person after you is trying to do."

As much as Audrey hated to admit it, her sister had a point. "You're right."

Maddy's eyes widened. Then she slowly sat up, her gaze never leaving Audrey's face. "I'm sorry. I didn't hear that. Can you say it again?"

"I said you're right."

"I need to get that on record," Maddy said, reaching for her phone.

Audrey glared at her. "Too late. I'm not saying it again."

Maddy smiled, but it was gone in the next instant. "You know if you don't go to Caleb first, he's going to be upset. Regardless of why the two of you are apart, he'll help. And this is your career, sis."

"I don't want him to think I'm using him."

"You aren't. That's what friends do. And I remember quite clearly that we were called their friends."

Audrey shook her head. "I won't change my mind on this. We will go to friends, but it'll be Clayton."

"Bad mistake," Maddy mumbled.

They rose together and walked out to Maddy's car. Neither spoke again as they drove out to the East Ranch. Everyone knew the place. It was the largest cattle ranch in over five hundred miles.

The ranch was so large that they reached the edge of the property long before the spectacular entrance even came into view. Audrey didn't pay attention to the large structure as they drove beneath it. Instead, her gaze was on the Spanish-style house in the distance that drew ever closer as they made their way down the drive.

Before Maddy had even stopped the car, a woman with long, brunette hair pulled back in a high ponytail stood with a toddler on one hip and a smile on her face.

"Maddy," the woman called when they opened the car doors.

Audrey saw the resemblance between the woman and Caleb and Brice. Without needing an introduction, Audrey knew that she was looking at Abby.

"Hey, Abby," Maddy said and motioned to Audrey. "This is my sister, Audrey."

Abby's blue eyes came to land on Audrey. "I've heard an awful lot about you. Welcome to the ranch. Y'all come inside."

As soon as they were inside, the beautiful little girl Abby carried around held out her arms. Audrey only hesitated a moment before reaching for the child.

"Oh, Hope," Abby said with a laugh as she handed the child over. "She loves to be held. If she gets to be too much, put her down."

"It's fine," Audrey said, looking into Hope's green eyes.

Abby led them into the living room, which was glorious. So many windows. Audrey tried to take in as much as she could through them without seeming disinterested in Abby.

"As much as I'd like this to be a social call, it isn't."

Audrey jerked her head to her sister. "Maddy," she admonished.

Abby pointed to the sofa. "Sit, please. Would either of you care for something to drink? Tea? Coffee?"

"Bourbon," Maddy said.

Abby's dark brows knitted together as her gaze swung from Maddy to Audrey. "Perhaps the two of you can tell me what's going on."

Audrey lowered herself to the sofa and shifted Hope so that the child rested on her lap. "I apologize for not coming by sooner and thanking you in person for all you did with what happened at the auction house."

"Oh, I did nothing," Abby said with a wave of her hand. "I was here with the kids. I would've liked to have been there. Still, I heard so much about it from the others, as well as your sister."

Audrey glanced at Maddy. "The thing is, that . . . mess . . . isn't finished."

"How so?" Abby asked, her expression becoming intense.

Maddy leaned against a pillow next to the arm of the couch. "Remember when me, you, and Clayton had that discussion about who would want to poison the horses and why?"

"I do. We thought it might involve Audrey."

Audrey glanced at the ceiling. "Y'all were right."

Abby held up a finger and got to her feet. "I think I better call Clayton. He should hear this."

Within minutes, Clayton strode through the door and sat with his wife on the sofa. As the couple stared at Audrey, waiting for her to get on with the story, all Audrey could think about was how good it would feel to have Caleb beside her.

"I've been fired from the Hopkins' stables. One of the horses there was poisoned," she told them.

Clayton slowly sat back. "They're blaming you."

"I didn't do it," she said.

"We know that," Abby stated.

Audrey looked between them. "But how could you know that?"

"My husband has good instincts about people. And so does Caleb," Abby said.

Just the mention of Caleb's name made Audrey want to smile. She licked her lips. "I hope I'm not overstepping, but I didn't know where else to turn."

Clayton nodded his head. "You came to the right place. Tell us everything."

Chapter 32

Caleb wiped the sweat from his forehead with the back of his arm and replaced his cowboy hat as he tied off the sorrel he'd ridden to Brice and Naomi's.

The past few days, one major issue after another had kept him immersed neck-deep in matters at the ranch. Every time he thought he could break away to try and locate Audrey, something else happened.

Then, late at night, he'd hold his phone and debate calling her. He'd gotten her number from Naomi, and he'd even entered it into his cell. But he had yet to call or send a text.

He'd written what felt like several hundred different messages and deleted every one of them before he could hit send. Nothing seemed right. Not via some device. He wanted to see Audrey, to look into her eyes and gauge her reaction. Something that couldn't be done through a cell phone.

Caleb knocked lightly on the back door as he opened it and stuck his head in. The house was strangely quiet.

When he got the odd voicemail from his brother before dawn, Caleb had realized that something was wrong. A newly arrived mare that lashed out at everyone had kept Caleb busy. He was just now getting around to seeing his brother and sister-in-law.

"Brice?" he called out.

Caleb closed the door behind him and slowly walked into the kitchen. There were dirty dishes and food left out from the night before, something that was completely out of character for both Brice and Naomi.

Concern grew as Caleb made his way out of the kitchen and into the living area. That's where he found his brother sitting on the sofa with his elbows on his knees and his hands covering his face.

"Brice?" he said softly.

With a jerk, his brother turned around. Brice was unshaven, his eyes red, and his face haggard. "I didn't hear you come in."

"What's going on?" Not even in the years when Brice had been getting in trouble with the law had Caleb ever been so worried.

"We got a call from Dr. Foster last evening."

Caleb removed his hat when he recognized the name of the fertility doctor they'd been going to in order to find out why they had yet to conceive a child. "About time. What happened?"

"We can't have children."

"What? No, that can't be. Isn't there some kind of operation they can do? What about injections? What are they called? IVF or something like that?"

Brice shook his head. "We've had the same conversation with the doctor. It's not only Naomi. I . . . my sperm count is low."

Caleb didn't know what to say to that. He shook his head. "I'm sorry."

"We'll be okay. We just need some time."

"Yeah, anything." Caleb looked around. "Where is Naomi?"

Brice's gaze moved to the stairs. "She's in her darkroom."

"You two will get past this. I know it."

Brice ran a hand down his face. "I sure the hell hope so. I don't have a life without her."

"What about adoption?"

"Maybe. We're not to that point yet."

Shit. Caleb replaced his hat. "I've got everything taken care of around here. Don't worry about anything. And don't hesitate to ask if you need something."

But Brice wasn't listening. Of all the couples for this to happen to, it had never entered Caleb's mind that it would befall his brother and Naomi. From the moment they'd met, it was right out of a movie.

Though it wasn't a storybook love like Abby and Clayton's, it was still amazing. And now, to have this.

Caleb turned and silently left the house. He put his foot in the stirrup and mounted the horse. As he turned the animal around, Caleb took out his cell and called Abby. She and Clayton needed to know what was going on.

"Where are you?" Abby asked.

Caleb blinked as he nudged the horse into a walk. "Hey, sis. Good afternoon to you, too."

"Caleb, where are you?" Abby asked more firmly.

"What the fuck is going on? First Brice, and now you?"

There was a pause, then his sister asked, "What's going on with Brice?"

"He and Naomi heard from the fertility doctor. That's why I called. It's not good. They can't have children."

Abby gasped. "Oh, no. I just knew it would be something easily fixed. I even told Naomi that."

Caleb glanced at the horizon and the thick, dark clouds approaching. "I didn't see Naomi, but Brice is a wreck. Apparently, both of them have issues. I didn't ask what Naomi's was, but Brice said he has a low sperm count."

"Damn. Not today. I need to be with them."

"Not right now. They need time." Caleb frowned. "And what do you mean not today?"

Abby blew out a breath. "I'll tell you everything when you get here."

"Here?"

"Your house. Now."

The line went dead. Caleb shoved the phone into his pocket and leaned low over the horse. The mare instantly jumped into a run when he clicked to her. They raced across the land. Caleb didn't need to know what was wrong. His sister needed him, and that's all that mattered.

When his house finally came into view, he spotted Clayton's truck parked at the front. Caleb sat up, slowing the mare as they reached the stables. Luckily, one of the kids he'd hired for the summer was there, waiting to take care of the horse.

Caleb dismounted before the sorrel had even come to a complete stop and tossed the reins to the teenager. He then ran the rest of the way to the house, busting through the door to find Clayton looking out the windows with his arms crossed, and Abby pacing the floor.

"About time," his sister said when she spotted Caleb.

Caleb glanced at Clayton, who had yet to turn around.

"You're scaring me. Is something wrong with one of the kids? Is it Shane?"

"They're fine," Clayton stated.

Caleb stared at his brother-in-law's back until Abby said his name. Caleb swung his gaze to her. "Someone better tell me what has both of you so riled."

"Audrey," Abby said.

One word. That's all it took for Caleb's stomach to drop, and his heart to beat double-time. Blood rushed through his ears so loudly, he could hear nothing else. It was obvious by Abby's and Clayton's attitude that something had happened.

Caleb took a step back and then another until he ran into something. He put his hand back and felt cold, smooth stone beneath his palm. The island. He'd run into the island.

"She's fine," Abby said.

Clayton turned then. "For now."

Abby wrinkled her nose as she glanced at her husband. "She doesn't know we're here."

Now, Caleb was confused. "Why? And why didn't she come to me herself? Wait. First, tell me what happened."

"A horse at the Hopkins' stables was poisoned," Clayton said.

In one sentence, Caleb was able to piece it all together. Someone was doing their best to ruin Audrey's career. It hurt more than he wanted to admit that she hadn't come to him, but at least she had gone to someone.

"What do you need me to do?" Caleb asked.

Clayton smiled. "Audrey already made a list of all the equine vets in the area."

"She also went through each one, telling us why she thought they might or might not be enemies," Abby added.

Caleb listened to everything they told him. "This won't stop until we find out who's doing this to her. They'll keep getting bolder and bolder."

"I agree," Clayton said.

Abby moved to one of the island stools and sat. "I called Danny."

Caleb exchanged a look with Clayton. "That probably wasn't the wisest action."

"As I already told her," Clayton stated.

Abby rolled her eyes. "He's a friend. But, I admit, it wasn't such a good move. The sheriff's department has already been to Robert Bremer's."

"Audrey didn't do it," Caleb stated.

"Of course, she didn't," Clayton replied.

Caleb frowned, his mind racing. "Audrey took some vacation days. She wasn't at Bremer's."

Abby's face fell. "That's the thing. Someone says they saw her."

"Audrey denies it," Clayton said. "And Maddy backs up her story that they haven't left the house since they returned from the horse rescue."

Caleb shrugged. "Then she's fine."

The silence that followed his statement made Caleb uneasy. When Abby didn't reply, he looked at Clayton and waited.

His brother-in-law removed his hat and set it softly on the coffee table as he sat on the sofa. "Somehow, Bremer knew about what happened at the auction house. That left Danny little option but to connect the two crimes."

"And the only one associated with both is Audrey," Caleb stated.

Abby took out her ponytail and ran her fingers through her hair. "It doesn't help that Audrey took time off."

"But she saved the other horses." Why didn't anyone else see that?"

Clayton glanced at the floor. "Abby said the same thing to Danny when he interviewed her at our place. His response was that someone is claiming that Audrey is doing this and then miraculously finding the toxin to make herself look good."

"Which gets her more clients and more money," Abby added.

Caleb shook his head. "Surely, Danny sees it's all a lie."

"He's following the evidence," Clayton pointed out.

"Danny has to follow the rules," Abby said. "If her alibi checks out, she'll be marked off as a suspect."

"But the damage to her reputation might not be so easy to wipe away." Caleb shook his head. He should've gone to see her.

Instead of worrying about what to say, he should've just driven out there and talked to her. Maybe then, she would've come to him for help.

Caleb fisted his hands. "It's time Danny has more evidence."

Abby jumped from the stool and smiled at her brother before she went to Clayton and gave him a kiss. Then she headed for the door.

"Where are you going?" Caleb asked her.

She stopped and looked back at him. "You're on board with helping Clayton."

"That's why you came?"

"Well," she said and gave him a hard look, "I wanted to make sure you didn't let another day go by without talking to Audrey. I like her, by the way. She's not just a pretty face. She'll keep you on your toes."

"Wait. What?" But Abby was already gone.

Clayton pushed to his feet. "Don't even bother. Abby is already on her way to check on Brice and Naomi before she returns to the ranch."

"I can't believe she's not trying to get involved in this."

Clayton let out a loud snort. "It's your sister, Caleb. Of course, she's in the middle of it. She's doing background checks on the list of names Audrey gave us."

Caleb should've known. Their family stuck together, no matter what. A reminder that his family didn't leave him.

Caleb looked at Clayton. "We need to start at the beginning. Everyone else is going to be looking at this latest poisoning, but I suspect it goes back further than that."

"I agree. I've already called David. He's waiting for us at the auction house."

Caleb was the first out of the house, swiping his keys as he left. Once on the road, he couldn't drive fast enough. "Where is Audrey now?"

"Back at her place. I tried to get her and Maddy to stay at the ranch, but Audrey was having none of that. She said she needed to reclaim her place after Maddy's attack."

"She's stubborn. And independent."

"You obviously care about her."

Caleb slowed just enough to turn safely onto another road. "I do. Did she say anything about us not talking over the last several days?"

"Not a word."

Damn. That hurt. Caleb had hoped that Audrey would try to get some sort of information about him from his family, but he should've known better.

"She did ask about you, though."

Elation swept through Caleb. He couldn't contain the smile when he glanced at Clayton. "Really?"

His brother-in-law grinned. "Really."

By the time they pulled up to David's, Caleb's happiness had turned to anger over someone targeting Audrey. He shut off the engine and got out of the truck. His gaze went to the stables before he looked at the burned building in the distance. By the time his attention turned to the office, he knew that nothing would stop him from finding who was after Audrey.

And God help whoever it was, because Caleb was coming for them.

Chapter 33

The sunrise was beautiful. Stunning, actually. But Audrey didn't really see it. Her mind was once more stuck on Caleb—and she quite liked it there.

It was a much better place than thinking about the crimes she was being accused of and questioned by the authorities. She could do nothing but proclaim her innocence and wait for them to check her alibi.

If she let herself, her mind would sink into an endless pit of negativity as she looked for anything that might help her find a connection to who was doing this to her. So far, that had gotten her nowhere.

Which turned her thoughts to Caleb.

After a brief attempt at sleep, she'd given up and spent the rest of the night at the kitchen table. She'd tried to go over the names she and Maddy had compiled again, but she didn't want to think about someone hating her.

Instead, she'd rather think of how it had felt to be in Caleb's arms. How, five days later, her stomach still quivered at the thought of him and the memories of what they'd shared.

The mug of coffee heated her hands as she stood outside to take in the sky streaked with red and gold. It was going to be a scorcher of a day if the morning heat was any indication. It was funny how refreshed she felt by taking a few days off, but now that she'd been fired from one job, she didn't know what to do with herself.

It was odd that Bremer hadn't been in touch with her. She'd left him a few messages, but she didn't think it was a good sign that he hadn't returned her calls. Honestly, she was surprised that he hadn't fired her, as well. He might be an asshole, but his first priority was his horses. He wouldn't let anyone he believed might harm them near the animals.

Could he actually think she was innocent? More importantly, would she be allowed to see the horses she'd taken care of for the last few years?

She turned her head at the sound of a vehicle approaching. It was barely dawn. Who would be coming out so early? Her heart jumped, thinking it might be Caleb. But the emotion died a quick death when she saw the police car.

Audrey wasn't sure what to think when Danny Oldman got out. Was he here to arrest her? She got even more confused when the passenger door opened, and Clayton stepped out.

"Mornin'," Danny said as he shut the door and walked to her.

She gave both men a nod. "What brings you two out here so early?"

"Why don't we go in and sit down?" Clayton suggested.

Audrey shook her head and threw out her coffee. "I'd rather not."

Danny drew in a deep breath and blew it out as he rested his hand on the butt of his gun. "Robert Bremer's wife said that he was upset with you last week. That the two of you were yelling on the phone."

Audrey's eyebrows shot up. "If we were on the phone, how would she know if I was yelling or not? Besides, anyone who knows Robert knows that he yells at everyone for anything."

"That's what I said," Clayton added.

Audrey glanced at him before returning her attention to Danny. "Robert wasn't happy that I missed a few days at his stables. My attention was on the poisoned horses at the auction house. Once I got them sorted, I called both Robert and Ted and took a week off."

"Why?" Danny pressed.

Audrey blinked, taken aback by his question. "Oh, I don't know. Maybe because I never take time off? I'm a workaholic. Ask anyone. But what happened at the auction house made me reevaluate things, and I realized I needed a vacation of sorts."

"The timing of all of this doesn't look good." Danny shook his head as he briefly looked at the ground. "Not good at all."

"What doesn't?" Audrey asked. "Someone says I poisoned a horse at the Hopkins' stables. It's a lie. I told you where I've been for the last two weeks at any given hour."

Clayton looked away, but it was the concern on his face that worried Audrey.

That's when she remembered that the poison was slow-acting. The sinking feeling in her stomach intensified when she realized that she had gone to Ted's to check on the horses once before taking time off.

"You think I did it," she said to the men. "You think I

went to the stables and injected that poor horse with poison before I took my days off. That way, I could say that I didn't know it was sick so I couldn't treat it. Since I was the only vet treating those at David's, no one else would know what to look for."

"No one is saying you did it," Clayton replied.

But Danny didn't utter a word.

Audrey looked skyward and tried to control her rising anger and fear. "Why would I do this? I love horses. They're my life."

Danny shrugged. "The why is what I can't figure out."

"Because I didn't do it," she stated. "Check what's left of my clinic for evidence of the poison. Check my SUV. And if I *had* harmed the horses, don't you think I would have turned the blame on anyone but myself? Right now, based on what you've told me, everything points to me and only me."

"Someone else said the same thing to me just a few hours ago. I believed them then, but now. . . ."

Audrey frowned when Danny trailed off. "What changed?"

"Robert Bremer is dead. His wife found him in the stables with a needle sticking out of his neck. It was full of the poison."

"I was here. All night," Audrey stated, her stomach churning at the surrealness of it all. "Ask Maddy."

She didn't wait for them to agree. Audrey spun and rushed into the house and straight to her sister's bedroom. As she threw open the door, Audrey's gaze landed on the empty bed.

Without a word, she pushed past Clayton and Danny in the narrow hall and ran outside to see Maddy's car in the driveway beside her SUV.

Audrey's head swiveled in the direction of the clinic. She jogged to the door and went inside. Every bit of glass and all the broken objects were gone. But there was no sign of Maddy. Audrey then went to the back room, where she found her sister tying off a garbage bag with her head bobbing to music through her one earbud.

For just a moment, Audrey allowed a sense of relief to pour through her. Then she called her sister's name.

Maddy spun around, yanking the earbud out of her ear.

Maddy's gaze moved past her shoulder. Audrey didn't need to turn around to know that the men had followed her inside the clinic.

"What's going on?" Maddy asked.

Audrey's heart thumped in her chest. "Robert is dead. Killed with the same poison as the horses. They think I did it, but I told the sheriff that I was here all night. And that you can verify that."

"Yep. I can," Maddy nodded as she looked at Danny. "She was here."

"And you were with her?" Danny questioned.

Maddy nodded again.

Audrey slowly turned to the men. She wasn't stupid. She knew what the next question would be, and there was no way she could outrun the answer.

"If you were with Audrey all night, why didn't she know you were in here?" Danny asked.

Maddy started to answer, then paused and looked at Audrey. "I went to bed shortly after my sister, but I couldn't sleep. I didn't want to clean the inside of the house and wake her, so I came out here, thinking I could get this place squared away for her."

Danny sighed. "You've been out here all night?"

"I have."

"With your music on?"

Maddy pressed her lips together. "Yes."

And just like that, Audrey's alibi went up in smoke. It was her word against whoever was framing her.

"Which means, Audrey could have left, and you wouldn't have known," Danny said.

"How long has Robert been dead?" Audrey asked.

Danny shrugged. "The coroner hasn't given me that information yet."

Audrey might not know much about the law, but she wasn't going down without a fight. And if she had to use every last bit of information she'd gleaned from the crime shows she watched, then that's what she would do.

She faced Danny, her gaze including Clayton. "I don't know how much poison was given to the horses. What we do know is that it takes a couple of days before symptoms begin showing up in them. Horses weigh significantly more than humans, so, depending on the dose given to Robert, it could have affected him immediately."

"Someone else pointed that out," Clayton said, a slight smile upon his lips.

Audrey grew more confident. "Which means, if he died before midnight, then my sister can account for my whereabouts, which was inside my house, where I've been since Maddy drove me home from the East Ranch yesterday afternoon. And if you need additional information, talk to the pizza delivery guy who arrived last night at eight thirty. I paid him."

"Ha," Maddy said and crossed her arms over her chest as she raised her chin confidently. "Take that, lawman."

Danny raised a brow at Maddy. "I'm not out to get your sister, Ms. Martinez. I'm simply after the truth. I have to follow where the evidence leads."

"I'll do whatever it takes to prove I'm innocent," Audrey told him. "Whatever you want of me."

The sheriff's lips twisted. "I wish I could say that would be enough, but I've seen myself that sometimes the evidence outweighs everything."

"Then we need to make sure that doesn't happen," Maddy stated.

Clayton looked at Danny. "If you don't mind, I'd like to have a talk with the sisters, please."

"Sure," Danny said. He tipped his hat at them and left the building.

Audrey was so nervous, it felt as if someone had poured ice water in her veins. Her hands shook, and she couldn't seem to catch her breath.

"All Audrey has done was work. She's worked her ass off," Maddy stated angrily. "And now, someone is doing their best to make sure the life my sister built for herself is ripped away, piece by piece."

Clayton caught Maddy's gaze. "I'm here to make sure that doesn't happen. You have friends, Audrey. Remember that. We're all doing what we can for you."

"And I appreciate that," Audrey told him. She swallowed then as she realized just how much the evidence was stacked against her. "You and your family are respected in the community. Perhaps you should rethink your association to me."

"Audrey," Maddy said with a gasp.

Clayton stared at her for a long time. "You've not been a friend to the Easts and Harpers long, so you wouldn't know that we don't scare easily. We stand together when things get tough. And we're standing with you."

Audrey had to look away as tears filled her eyes. "Thank you," she mumbled.

Maddy wrapped an arm around her and squeezed. There were no words needed. She and her sister had been through their mother's death and their father's disappearance. It might have torn some families apart, but they had grown closer.

Because they only had each other.

"Audrey," Clayton said.

She composed herself enough to look at him. His light green eyes were filled with determination.

Clayton shot her a quick smile. "It's going to be all right. You're going to have to trust me on this."

"It was luck that brought our families together. I don't think I'll ever be able to repay the kindness you've shown me or Maddy."

Clayton chuckled softly and shook his head. "You earned our friendship. Never forget that."

"What about the sheriff?" Maddy asked. "You're friends with him. Can't you do something?"

Audrey glared at her sister. "Forget she said that, Clayton."

Clayton walked to the door and stopped before exiting. He shifted to the side to look at them. "Danny is one of the most honest and honorable men you'll meet. He does everything by the book. He allowed me to come because we're friends, but the only thing that will convince him of anything is the evidence."

"Then we have work to do," Audrey said.

Clayton nodded. "Yes, ma'am, we certainly do."

Chapter 34

Caleb lay on his stomach and looked through the scope of his rifle to where Audrey and Maddy walked Clayton back to the patrol car and Danny. He'd heard the entire conversation between them thanks to being on the phone with his brother-in-law.

All Caleb wanted to do was go into the clinic and pull Audrey into his arms. He'd heard the apprehension in her words, but when her voice broke, it nearly did him in.

"Did you get all you needed, Caleb?" Clayton asked over the phone speaker once he was inside the car.

Caleb shifted so that the microphone on the earbuds he wore was unblocked. "Yeah. She didn't sound good."

"She didn't look good either." Clayton fastened his seatbelt. As Danny started the engine, Clayton asked, "Are you sure about this, Caleb?"

"He better be," Danny said.

Caleb watched the sheriff as he drove off. "Don't worry, Danny. I've got this."

Clayton snorted. "I still think you should've told Brice what was going on."

"No," Caleb stated. "He and Naomi need some time alone."

"I'll check in later. Oh, and just so you know, you're not out there alone."

Clayton hung up before Caleb could figure out what his brother-in-law meant. A heartbeat later, his cell phone buzzed. Caleb pulled it from his pocket and read the text from Cooper that said, DON'T SHOOT ME.

Caleb lifted his head and looked around. A moment later, he heard something behind him and glanced over his shoulder to find Cooper making his way toward him.

"What the hell are you doing here?" Caleb asked.

Cooper shot him a flat stare as he lay on his stomach beside Caleb. "I'll overlook the fact you didn't call me or Jace to help you out this time. Next time, I'm going to kick your ass."

"Seriously. What are you doing here?"

"I can't believe you even have to ask that."

Caleb stared into Cooper's green eyes for a long moment. Then he blew out a breath. "Thanks, man."

"After all the shit we've been through, you and Brice still try to do things on your own."

"Habit."

"It's a good thing Abby called us," Cooper said. "Otherwise, your ass might be out here on your own. Jace is at the front near the entrance to the drive. He'll alert us if anyone comes."

Caleb blinked away the sweat that trickled into his eye. "That's if they come by vehicle."

"I can set up to the west. There's a section of the drive that will be out of sight for both of us, though."

"It'll have to be enough."

Cooper shifted so that he squatted next to Caleb. "You think they'll come for her? Danny only has circumstantial evidence."

"I'm not leaving anything to chance. Whoever is after Audrey just might get cocky enough to show their face now that they think she's been backed into a corner."

"That would make things easy for us. I'll be ready regardless."

Caleb gave Cooper a nod before his friend disappeared into the brush. With his eye once more looking through his scope, Caleb searched for any sign of Audrey. He caught movement through a window of the house, but he wasn't sure if it was her or Maddy.

The hours stretched on as the sun climbed, and the heat became oppressive. Caleb didn't move. Not even when a rattlesnake slithered five feet in front of him. As he scanned the area for any movement, his mind went over and over everything in his head.

Time and again, his gut kept bringing him back to the auction house. After he and Clayton had met David there the day before, he'd tried to find something that would lead him to the men responsible for the poisoning. Because if he found them, then he could discover if they'd done this on their own or if someone hired them.

But no matter how hard he looked, Caleb didn't find anything. Once Danny was done, Caleb had questioned David for hours, to no avail. It wasn't until he, David, and Clayton were sitting around drinking beer that David had let something slip about how there had been a vet who offered their services to him a month before the horses got sick.

It was just something David said in passing, but Caleb knew immediately how important the information was—and he pounced on it. Within minutes, he not only knew who the vet was, but he'd also discovered their connection to Audrey.

Near three that afternoon, his phone vibrated. Caleb put the earpiece in his ear and answered the call when he saw that it was Clayton. "Well?"

"You were right. Unfortunately, it's taken Danny all day to track down your hunch. Patty Duncan did visit the Hopkins' ranch. Apparently, she and Robert Bremer were having an affair. Phone records show her texts, threatening to tell Bremer's wife about them if he didn't hire her on as the vet."

"Patty believed the reason she didn't get the job was Audrey," Caleb said.

"Pretty much. Also, the guy Brice shot at the auction house was taken to the hospital because his wound became infected. He told Danny everything. Including how he got the poison from Patty. Danny and his men are on their way to Patty's house to arrest her now. They've already arrested the other two men involved."

Caleb frowned when a text came through. He stilled as he read it. "Clayton, I don't think Danny is going to find Patty. She's pulling up to Audrey's now."

"Shit. I'll let Danny know."

Caleb hung up and jumped to his feet. He grabbed his rifle and called Jace. As soon as his friend answered, Caleb said, "It's Patty. She's the one Danny is after. Get to the house."

He hung up without waiting for a reply, but Caleb knew that Jace would call Cooper and fill him in. Caleb ran as fast as he could to the back of the house. He needed to get there before Patty because he wasn't sure if she realized that the police were on to her.

Or what she might do.

Caleb reached the back of the house at the same time he heard Audrey's voice call out Patty's name. He hadn't made it in time. Fuck. He got to the back door and slung the strap of his rifle over his shoulder. Then he slowly turned the knob. The door opened with barely a creak.

Once inside, Caleb flattened himself against the wall. He heard Maddy grumbling to herself in the kitchen at the sink. Caleb leaned around the doorway and whistled softly.

Maddy's head swung around. As soon as she saw him, her eyes widened. Then she looked over her shoulder to the front door. Caleb put his finger to his lips to keep Maddy quiet.

She wiped off her hands and came toward him. "It's Patty, isn't it?"

He nodded.

"I knew it. I never liked that bitch," Maddy said, more to herself than to him.

Caleb caught her gaze, thankful that she seemed calm and determined. "I don't know what she's capable of. Can you get out the back? Jace and Cooper will find you and stay until the sheriff arrives. Don't worry. I've got Audrey."

Maddy gave him a quick nod and left out the back.

Caleb slowed his breathing as Audrey and Patty walked into the house.

Audrey didn't know if it was the tight smile on Patty's face or the fact that she suspected Patty might be the one doing all of this that instantly put her on edge the moment she realized who had arrived.

"I'm surprised you're here," Audrey said as they entered the house and she looked for her sister.

"Why do you say that?"

Audrey heard the higher-than-normal pitch in Patty's voice. The woman was usually calm, but she seemed wound tight and teetering on the edge of losing it.

Audrey wasn't a suspicious person by nature, but it didn't look good that Patty was there. Was that why she suddenly noticed these things?

Audrey really didn't know what to think. She needed to feel Patty out more. Though Maddy wouldn't be happy to learn that Patty was there.

"Um," Audrey said when she realized that she hadn't replied to Patty. She was stunned to find Maddy gone. Most likely, her sister was hiding out in her room. Audrey faced Patty and motioned to the breakfast table. "Sorry. It's been a weird day. Have a seat. Would you like some coffee?"

"Do you have something stronger?"

"Oh, yeah." Audrey pulled a bottle of tequila from the cabinet and held it up to Patty, who nodded.

She got two glasses and set them on the table before pouring a shot into each. Only then did Audrey sit and look across at the redhead who she had believed was a friend— who could very well be the enemy.

Patty tossed back the liquor and laughed as it slid down her throat. "Whoa. Just what I needed," she said as she pushed Audrey's glass to her.

Audrey wrapped her fingers around it. "Why have you come? We've known each other a long time, but it's not like we hang out."

Audrey watched Patty drink another shot. She downed her own before she pressed the back of her hand against her lips as the liquor burned down her throat.

"I came to show my support. I can't believe what's being said. You're too nice, Audrey. You would never hurt an animal."

Audrey arched a brow. "You think I'd hurt a person?"

"Of course not," Patty replied with a laugh.

Audrey joined in, but the laugh was forced. She began second-guessing herself. Perhaps she'd been wrong about Patty. Maybe she *was* a friend.

Audrey watched as Patty poured two more shots. "Who do you think did it?"

"I trust the police. They'll find who did it." Patty flashed a smile.

Audrey drank the tequila in her glass. "How is the mare we worked on at the rescue?"

"Oh, she's good. You should go see her." Patty wrinkled her nose. "Well, when you can. I'm sure the authorities asked you to stay away from any animals until this nastiness is over."

Audrey ignored the next shot that Patty poured. There was something about the unmistakable glee she heard in Patty's words that made her gut twist. "Why are you really here?"

The back door closed then. Audrey didn't move, expecting it to be her sister.

"Hey, babe. Damn, it's a hot one today," Caleb said as he came up behind her.

Audrey's heart leapt into her throat, a mixture of surprise and relief. She was unsure what was going on, but if Caleb was there, then the shit was about to hit the fan. Audrey smiled up at him and put her hand atop his. "Hey. I don't think you've met my old friend. Patty, this is Caleb Harper."

"Oh, we met," Caleb said, his smile easy. "She came out when Brice and I were looking for equine vets."

Audrey didn't miss the way Patty's face tightened, though there was no indication on Caleb's face that anything was wrong.

Patty's smile dropped. "I didn't know you two were . . . together."

"It's new," Caleb said with a bright smile. "We've not really had a chance to tell anyone. But once I saw Audrey, I couldn't resist."

"You and everyone else," Patty said, malice dripping from her words.

The mask Patty had been wearing slipped, letting Audrey and Caleb see the viciousness that the woman had hidden from everyone.

Caleb's hand tightening on Audrey's shoulder warned her to remain calm. The anger rolling off Patty was hard to ignore, much less keep from reacting to.

Daggers shot from Patty's gaze as she stared at Audrey and leaned back while crossing one leg over the other. "You don't remember, do you?"

"Remember what?" Audrey asked, truly perplexed.

"Rodney Smith."

The name sounded familiar, but Audrey had to search her mind until she pulled the memory. "He was in our high school."

"He was my cousin. And utterly in love with you."

Audrey licked her lips. "I didn't know that."

"The hell you didn't." Patty sneered. "The summer of your freshman year at college, you came back home. It had taken Rodney years to work up the courage to ask you out.

He was over the moon when you said yes. It was all he could talk about for days."

Audrey felt sick to her stomach. She had a feeling she knew exactly how this conversation was going to end, and it wasn't good. "Rodney was a nice guy."

Patty laughed coldly. "Yes, he was. But that wasn't what you wanted, was it? You let him take you out, let him get his hopes up, and then you took him to your bed. After that, you blew him off."

"I did that to several guys. I didn't mean to hurt Rodney."

"There was more than my cousin?" Patty asked, eyes wide. "Why am I not surprised?"

Audrey took a deep breath. "It wasn't a good time in my life."

"Did you know that Rodney died by suicide?"

It was a good thing Audrey was sitting down. Otherwise, her legs would've given out on her. "I-I didn't know."

Patty raked her eyes over Audrey. "I don't see what it is everyone likes about you. There's nothing special at all. And yet, jobs fall in your lap." She glanced at Caleb. "And, apparently, so do men."

"So you decided to get your revenge," Caleb said.

Patty smiled smugly and shrugged. "It wasn't just for Rodney. It was for myself and every other person Audrey has managed to screw over."

Audrey started to reply, but Caleb tightened his grip on her shoulder. She wisely kept silent. Out of the corner of her eye, Audrey spotted movement outside the house through the window. When she looked, Danny and several sheriff's deputies surrounded the building.

"How do you think things will go from here?" Caleb asked. "You've let me know your plan."

Patty lifted one shoulder. "I'm resourceful."

Caleb twisted his lips. "I admit, you've made sure to look pretty good in all of this, but your time is up. You didn't just tell me," he said and pulled his cell phone from his pocket that was on speaker.

Patty jumped to her feet the same time the front door slammed opened, and police stormed the house. Audrey's gaze remained on Patty, so she saw the woman pull a needle from her pocket and lunge toward her.

Audrey shoved the table forward just as Caleb grabbed Patty's arm and twisted. The woman let out a cry of pain, and the needle fell to the floor.

With her heart hammering and adrenaline pumping through her, Audrey could only watch as Danny quickly put Patty in handcuffs while a deputy Mirandized her.

"Hey," Caleb said as he bent to look at Audrey. "Are you all right?"

Audrey looked into Caleb's brown eyes and threw her arms around him. When he straightened, bringing her with him, she clung to him harder, burying her face in his neck as he wrapped his arms tighter.

Chapter 35

He might have needed to be a part of the group that took Patty down, but now that Caleb had Audrey in his arms, nothing else mattered.

It felt right to have her against him, as if she belonged there. Whenever he thought about what could have happened had he not been there, his arms tightened. None of the missions he'd been on as an Army Ranger came close to the fear that had gripped him.

No one said anything to them. In short order, the deputies led Patty outside and into a patrol car. Danny gave him a nod and left with them.

A moment later, Maddy, Cooper, and Jace appeared in the front doorway, but the trio quickly backed away and softly shut the door behind them.

For days, Caleb had gone over in his head what he would say to Audrey when he saw her again, but now that he was with her, his mind was blank. All he knew was what was in his heart. He couldn't go wrong with following that, could he?

But he didn't know how to begin. Instead, he simply held Audrey until her grip finally loosened. He closed his eyes because he knew anything could happen over the next few moments. But he knew one thing for sure—he wasn't walking out of this house without having Audrey as his.

And not just for a few weeks or months. Caleb wanted her for eternity.

He'd discovered how great it was to have her in his life. And he found out how lonely and dull it was without her. She made him face his past, made him take a cold, hard look at himself.

And what he wanted.

He'd discovered that everything he needed was her.

She leaned back, her dark gaze meeting his. No longer was she open and smiling. The beginning of a wall was there, and Caleb couldn't blame her.

"How are you here?" Audrey asked. Then she shook her head and answered her own question. "Clayton."

Caleb's fingers clenched when she took a step back, separating their bodies. He couldn't help but feel as if she put distance between them for more than one purpose. Hell, he'd done it on so many occasions, he knew exactly what she was doing.

And it hurt.

"I've been on your property since four this morning," he said.

"I see," she mumbled.

Caleb swallowed. The fear that had held him so tightly in its grasp loosened the longer he looked at her. Knowing she was all right, knowing that the danger had passed relieved him. But just being near her gave him the peace that had been absent the past few days.

"Before I get started on this, you need to know that I

wasn't the one who put your things in your truck. That was Brice. He thought he was helping me out. He didn't know that I wanted you to have a reason to come back to the ranch. To . . . me."

Of all the things he thought Audrey might do or say, just standing there staring at him wasn't one of them. This was going to be much harder than he realized.

Caleb cleared his throat. "Clayton and Abby told me you came to them about what was going on. They knew I'd want to help. Abby went home to do background checks on the names you gave her, while Clayton and I went to the auction house to talk to David."

"Why?" Audrey asked.

"Because it started there. I knew I'd discover some kind of connection if I looked hard enough. It wasn't evidence to find, but rather to hear."

Audrey's brow furrowed. "I don't understand."

"We searched the entire place from top to bottom, going over everything again, but we found absolutely nothing. In the wee hours of the morning, David pulled out some beers. He and Clayton talked, while I had this nagging feeling that I'd missed something. I was so engrossed in my thoughts that I nearly missed when David said that a vet had come by to offer their services but that he'd politely refused. Not only did he already have two on the books, but he would always turn to you if he was in a bind. A month later, the first horse showed signs of the poisoning."

Audrey wrapped her arms around herself. "I'm guessing David told Patty that he not only had two vets on call but then mentioned something about me."

"Exactly," Caleb said with a nod. "He spoke about how close he and your family were. David being the talkative person that he is, even mentioned how you offered to do jobs for only a third of your regular rates, but that he demanded you bill full price."

Audrey threw up her hands. "He's a family friend. I've known him my entire life. And why should Patty get upset at that? I wasn't even David's on-call vet. He has someone that he's used for years."

"That was my thought, as well. Turns out, my sister is good at digging into people's lives. Patty is drowning in debt. She kept trying to get more jobs, but everywhere she turned, you were there, offering to do the job for little to no money."

"So I'm to be punished because I can manage money better than her?"

Caleb took a step toward Audrey but then stopped. "That was part of it. You became someone she could pin all the blame on."

"I didn't know about Rodney," Audrey said, blinking back tears.

He hated that she was torn up over something that had happened years ago. "Don't blame yourself."

"How can I not? He committed suicide because of me."

"I doubt you were the only reason."

"There is nothing that you can say that will make this better. Patty was right. I use men, and I get away from them as fast as I can. I . . . I do it because,"—she paused and shrugged—"because I'm scared of getting close to someone. Because I want the kind of love my parents had. Because . . . it's all I know how to do."

Caleb listened to her confession, hearing the heartbreak and loneliness he knew all too well in her voice. "I use women. It's why Brice took your things. I've never brought anyone to the house before. I don't want to hurt anyone, but sometimes, the idea of being alone is too much. Then, when I'm with a woman, I know it's a mistake. I don't want to hurt them with the truth, so I lie and disappear from their lives."

"What a pair we are," Audrey said with a half-smile.

"I was going to call."

Her gaze shifted away. Caleb inwardly winced at how lame his words sounded. This wasn't the way to win Audrey over. It was time for the cold, hard truth.

He took a deep breath. "I've never been in this situation before. I don't know what to do here. I know how to leave. I know how to make women hate me. I don't know how to stay. I don't know how to make one . . . want me." He'd wanted to say *love*. He didn't know how to get a woman to fall in love with him.

His stomach dropped when she didn't look his way. Naomi had been wrong. Watching all those romantic movies had done nothing to help him. He'd poured out his heart and told her the truth. He'd confessed things he'd barely been able to admit to himself.

And for what? None of it was doing a damn bit of good. It felt as if some unknown force were viciously, violently shredding his heart.

And there wasn't a goddamn thing he could do about it.

Caleb stood, watching helplessly as everything that had been building between them slowly faded away.

"There was something between us. You can't deny that," he told her.

When she still wouldn't look at him, Caleb knew that he had two options. He could keep talking and try to convince her to give him another shot. Or, he could leave.

He didn't want to walk out that door because he knew if he did, he'd never see Audrey again. But he also knew that he could stand there talking until the end of time, and she wouldn't change her mind.

She'd told him herself that she walked away from men, just as he did with women. It was his turn to understand what it felt like to fall for someone who didn't return the feelings. And quite frankly, it sucked balls.

Caleb retrieved his rifle from the back room and came to stand near her. He tried to find something to say, but he couldn't muster anything worth a damn. So, he walked away. It was something he'd done countless times before, but today, his heart stayed behind.

He wasn't three steps out the door before Jace and Cooper were beside him. Maddy looked from him to the house, her brows furrowing. Then she ran inside to her sister.

"My truck is this way," Jace said.

Neither asked Caleb what had happened. It must have been written all over his face because for the first time since they'd become friends, neither demanded details.

Caleb wouldn't know what to tell them if they did ask. He wasn't sure he understood the implications of everything yet. When it finally hit, it was going to knock him on his ass. But right now, he was still taking it all in.

On the ride back to his ranch, his friends talked about anything and everything just to fill the silence. When they reached the house, Caleb got out of the truck and didn't invite them inside. He wanted to be alone to wallow in his failure.

Except when he walked into his house, Brice stood in the kitchen. Caleb paused before shutting the door behind him. He propped up his rifle before he made his way to Brice, who held out a glass of bourbon.

"What are you doing here?" Caleb asked before draining the liquor and pouring more.

Brice set down his glass and leaned against the island. "I came to kick your ass for not cluing me in on what was going on, but one look at your face tells me that needs to be put on hold. For now. Things with Audrey didn't go well?"

Caleb shook his head. "They went as badly as I'd hoped they wouldn't. I don't know how to be . . ." He waved his hand at Brice. "Whatever you and Clayton are to your women."

"Husbands? Lovers? Friends?" Brice offered, his brows raised.

"I can't be any of that. I've spent too long being the opposite."

"That's not true."

Caleb swirled the amber liquid. "If I wasn't meant to spend my life alone, then I would've said the right things to her. I was too scared to call her, too afraid to admit how I really felt. And I fucked things up."

"You ne—"

"The thing is, I got a taste of my own medicine today. All those women I tossed aside? This was Karma coming to laugh in my face."

Brice shook his head as he frowned. "No way. I saw how Audrey looked at you. There was something there."

"If there was, I destroyed it. Just like I do everything else."

Brice pushed away from the island and moved to stop Caleb when he tried to walk away. "Take a look around," he said, motioning outside. "Look what we've built together. Then look further than that at the years we were with Clayton and Abby. What did you destroy there?"

"I know what you're doing, and I appreciate it. The simple fact is, if I love something too much, then I lose it."

His brother paused for a heartbeat. "You love Audrey?"

Caleb blinked, unsure where that comment from Brice had come from until he realized what he'd said. He laughed dryly and shook his head. "Apparently, I do. How fucked up is that? I finally fall in love, and I lose her."

"Did you secretly want to lose her?"

Caleb finished the bourbon and put his glass on the island. "I can't even get angry at that question. I would have a day ago. I don't want to talk about Helen, but our mother screwed us up. I won't ever forget asking her to stay as she walked out the door—"

"What?" Brice asked, his voice pitched high. His face was a mask of shock and concern.

There was no point in hiding it now. Obviously, Fate wanted Caleb to air all his secrets. "I woke up and saw Helen packing. I followed her down the stairs and asked her to stay as she was leaving. She looked back at me, then left without a word."

"Goddamn it, Caleb. Why didn't you ever tell me or Abby?"

"Why? What good would it have done? We all had our shit to carry."

Brice tossed aside his hat and ran a hand through his hair as he turned away. He spun back to face Caleb. "I understand things about you better now. Had Abby and I known earlier, we could have helped."

"There was nothing anyone could do." Caleb clapped his brother on the shoulder as he walked past. "At least Audrey is safe now. Patty is in custody and will be charged, and thanks to you shooting Zeke, we have the other men, as well."

"Should you have stayed with Audrey?"

Caleb didn't stop on his way to the bathroom. "She didn't want me there."

He pulled off his sweat-soaked shirt and wadded it up to throw it aside. Then he paused, looking at it, knowing it was the last thing he'd worn that Audrey had touched. He'd never look at the shirt the same way again.

And every time he wore it, he would think about her.

He'd be thinking of her for the rest of his life—right up until his last breath.

"You shouldn't give up on her."

Caleb jumped and whirled around to glare at his brother, who stood with his hands on the doorjamb. "What the hell, Brice? I thought you'd gone."

"You're not going to get by without replying."

"She made it very obvious that she doesn't want me. I've had so many women beg and plead with me to try and change my mind. It's a horrible experience. I didn't want to do that to her."

Brice cocked his head to the side. "What if it would've made a difference?"

"Then I would've gotten on my knees and said whatever she needed to hear."

"I know you well enough to say that if you don't try with her again, you'll regret it, always. She's your match in every way. If you love her, don't give up on her."

He didn't say anything as Brice walked away. It was only after the front door closed that Caleb realized he hadn't asked how his brother and Naomi were handling things.

Caleb threw the shirt into a corner and turned on the shower.

Chapter 36

"You've lost your ever-loving mind," Maddy said as she paced back and forth.

Audrey couldn't disagree. She still didn't know why she hadn't stopped Caleb before he left her house. Every word that fell from his lips struck her right in the heart—and it terrified her.

Now, three days later, she could still see Caleb standing in the kitchen, still hear the pleading in his voice as he spoke. She could still see the hope in his eyes.

Maddy stopped in front of her, causing the image Audrey had created of Caleb to vanish. She blinked and focused on her sister's angry face.

"You had the thing you've been searching for," Maddy said, her voice laced with frustration and a bit of ire. "The love you read about, one that you thought would never find you. Well, it did."

Audrey pushed the uneaten food away. She couldn't stand the smell of it right now. "You don't know that."

Maddy snorted loudly. "You haven't slept properly since you stayed the night with Caleb. You haven't eaten in three days, and don't think I haven't seen you repeatedly filling your wine glass. You haven't even been to work, despite being cleared by the police. Nor have you returned any of the messages people have left for you to see to their horses."

"Stop," Audrey mumbled.

But Maddy shifted so that she stayed in Audrey's line of sight. "Face it, sis. You're primetime, one hundred percent in love with Caleb Harper."

Audrey stood and pushed passed Maddy. She couldn't hear any more from her sister because it was the same things she'd been saying to herself.

"Why did you let him leave?" Maddy asked, following her.

Audrey stopped as she entered her bedroom. She turned and grabbed the doorframe. "Because I'm terrified of letting myself love him," she said and closed the door.

Comfortably numb.

That's what Caleb had been for three days thanks to his stock of prime bourbon. He hadn't left his house or answered his phone—although he looked each time it buzzed to see if it was Audrey.

And every time it wasn't her name on his screen, another dagger pierced his already shattered heart.

He'd even barred the doors so that his interfering family and friends couldn't get in.

Persistent banging pulled him from slumber. He pushed up on his hands and winced at the pounding in his head.

"Fuck," he murmured and rubbed his eyes.

The knocking intensified.

"I'm coming!" Caleb shouted as he rolled into a seated position on the bed.

Whether whoever banged on his door heard him or not, they didn't let up. He stood, swaying before he stumbled out of his bedroom.

Caleb used the walls to hold himself up as he squinted and shuffled to the door. The closer he got, the louder the pounding became, making his head feel as if it were going to explode.

"If you don't stop, I'm going to shoot you," he growled.

Immediately, the knocking ceased. Caleb pressed his head against the door then looked through the peephole. The bright sunlight that met his eye felt like a needle to his brain and caused him to jerk back.

"Who is it?" he demanded.

"Your brother and sister," Abby stated.

Caleb heard the anger in Abby's voice. In fact, he was surprised that it had taken her this long to try and talk to him. "Go away."

"Open the fucking door before I break it down," Brice threatened.

Caleb leaned a hand on the wall and squeezed the bridge of his nose with his thumb and forefinger. "Give me a few hours, and I'll come see y'all."

"It's going to be now," Abby replied.

Caleb straightened and shook his head. "No."

He turned and took three steps before his door was kicked in. When he spun around, he had to lift his hand to shield his eyes from the light that seared his retinas. "What the fuck?"

"I warned you," Brice said as he walked past.

Abby gave Caleb a shove. "Get some clothes on. And why the hell does it look like it's night in here?"

"He lowered the blinds."

Caleb lifted his head at the sound of Clayton's voice. Damn. So much for it just being Abby and Brice. Now, Caleb had to deal with his brother-in-law, as well.

"Ugh. I've never seen the place so dirty," Naomi said.

Caleb rolled his eyes. If he thought he could make it to his room, he'd head there immediately. But it was all he could do to stand upright. Apparently, he'd drunk much more than he realized.

Of course, it didn't help that he hadn't had any food in . . . he'd lost track of exactly when he'd last eaten.

"We got this."

Caleb squeezed his eyes closed when he heard Jace's voice. And if he was there, so was Cooper.

Caleb was unceremoniously grabbed by the arms and dragged into his bathroom. He opened his eyes long enough to see that it was his friends. He didn't even have time to try and break free as they threw him into an ice-cold shower.

Which sobered him immediately.

Caleb glowered at the duo from beneath the spray. "One day, I'll pay each of you back for this."

His friends weren't smiling. Jace turned and walked away.

Cooper ducked his head for a moment then met Caleb's gaze through the glass. "We'll be waiting in the living room."

When he was alone, Caleb removed his briefs and threw the soggy underwear into the sink. He turned up the heat and scrubbed himself. By the time he dried off, the headache no longer made his stomach sour, but it still throbbed in time to his heartbeat.

Caleb put on a pair of jeans and the first shirt he found

before he walked out of his room to find the others sitting solemnly in the living room and kitchen. He looked around at the six individuals who made up his family.

Naomi couldn't sit still. She picked up empty liquor bottles and trash. As she straightened, she was the first to see him. There was a wealth of pain in her chestnut eyes that might never go away. It was the same anguish he saw in Brice's gaze.

"There you are," Abby said as she brought Caleb a mug of coffee.

He accepted it but didn't bring it to his lips. "If you're here because you think I'm going to do something stupid, I assure you, that's not the case. I just need some time."

"That's not it," Brice murmured.

Caleb looked around, but no one volunteered any information. "Then I think someone needs to tell me what's going on."

Clayton took Abby's hand and gave it a squeeze. It was a small gesture, but one Caleb had seen him do a thousand times. It was Clayton's way of giving Abby courage to do or say something she found difficult.

Caleb suddenly had an uneasy feeling. He didn't want to know what it was they had all come to say, because it couldn't be good if all six were there.

"Don't," Caleb told Abby.

She drew in a breath. "You need to know."

It had to do with Audrey, Caleb was sure of it. The thought that she was hurt—or worse—was too much. He held up a hand. "Don't say another word."

"It's about Mom," Abby said at the same time.

Caleb felt as if he'd been kicked in the stomach. In a heartbeat, his panic turned to fury. "Then you've all wasted your time. I don't want to hear another word about Helen."

"She's dying," Brice said.

Caleb pointed to the door that hung by one hinge. "Get out. All of you."

Naomi walked to him and simply hugged him. She said nothing, and it was her lack of words that touched him. Her embrace told him that she understood his hurt and was there for him, but that she stood with the others. Then, his sister-in-law walked out.

Jace rose and came to Caleb. "Hear them out. Please."

Cooper was next. He nervously ran a hand over his jaw. "You may not be my brother by blood, but you're still family. Understand that everything we do is because we love you."

No sooner had they walked away than Clayton took their place. He put a big hand on Caleb's shoulder and squeezed. "I'm not going to pretend to know what you've gone through, but if you want a future, you have to put this behind you."

"It is," Caleb ground out.

Clayton's lips twisted ruefully. "You and I both know that for the lie it is." He gave Caleb's shoulder another squeeze before looking over his own at Abby and following the others.

Caleb walked to the sink and set the mug on the counter. "I know what you're going to say."

"No, you don't," Abby said.

Caleb faced her. "You're going to tell me that I have to say goodbye to the woman who left us."

Abby shook her head. Her blue eyes were red from crying. "I wish you had told me that you tried to stop Mom from leaving. I hate that you've carried that around all these years alone."

Caleb shrugged because there was nothing to say.

"You think because she left that you did something wrong." Abby walked to him and cupped his face in her hands. "You weren't the problem. None of us were. *She* was. You are kind and generous and loved more than you could ever know. Never forget that. *Never*," she said, emphasizing the word.

Caleb felt emotion choking him. He gave her a nod because words wouldn't come.

Abby smiled at him and leaned up to kiss his cheek. Then she quietly walked from the house.

"I think she practices what to say to bring us to our knees," Brice said into the silence that followed.

Caleb was grateful for the respite of brevity, but it was just for a moment. "They left you for last?"

"We didn't plan any of this, though I told them it wouldn't work."

"Is this where you convince me to go see Helen?"

Brice sighed as he rose from the barstool. "I'd planned on it. Abby and Clayton saw her two days ago. The hospital notified them when Helen was brought in via ambulance. Someone found her unresponsive at the motel and called 911. Yesterday, Abby and Clayton brought the kids to meet her."

"I wouldn't have."

Brice shrugged. "I don't think I would have either, but it wasn't my call."

"Did you go see her?"

"Yeah."

Caleb wasn't surprised. His brother was the most forgiving out of all of them. "And?"

Brice blew out a breath. "She has cancer. The doctor's say her body is riddled with it. She never got treatment, so it's just a matter of days before she's gone."

"And she came home to say goodbye? To ask for for-giveness?" Caleb quipped.

"I don't know. I don't care. This isn't about her. Naomi helped me see that it's about me, about my future with my wife."

Caleb rubbed his temple. He walked to the cabinet and pulled out two aspirin before taking them with the luke-warm coffee.

"I think it's something you should think about," Brice said.

Caleb cut his eyes to him. "Going to Helen?"

"Your future."

"That's all I've been thinking about."

Brice issued a bark of laughter. "I'm not sure how you could do much of anything with the amount of liquor you've consumed."

"The pain was too much. I needed to numb it."

"And did dulling it help?"

"No," Caleb said with a shake of his head. "It made it worse.

Brice walked toward the mudroom. "We're not going to force you to come with us to the hospital. That's a deci-sion you have to make on your own. But think about this. What if you don't go? What if you don't get to tell Helen all the things you want to say? How can you go forward with anything? You need closure. And this is your only chance to get it."

His brother's words rang in Caleb's head long after everyone had left. Caleb drank some coffee and three bottles of water before he made some peanut butter toast. And all the while, he was determined to remain at the house.

Yet he found himself putting on his boots, grabbing his keys, and setting his hat atop his head before heading to his truck. He had no idea where he was going until he pulled up at the hospital.

And when he walked into the room where his mother's frail body lay hooked to numerous monitors, he knew this was exactly where he needed to be.

"Caleb," Helen said and reached out a bony hand to him.

He walked to her bed but didn't get near enough for her to touch him.

Helen's eyes filled with acceptance. "I'm so sorry for leaving. Every night in my dreams, I see your face and your big brown eyes staring at me from the stairs. Then I hear your soft plea for me to stay. That's haunted me all these years. I was a horrible mother, and I thought leaving would be for the best."

"We needed you," Caleb said.

His mother nodded slowly. "I realized that too late. I had no right to come back here, but I wanted to see all of you one last time. I needed to see the beautiful people you've grown into. You three were so strong. You still are. Look at what you've done," she said with a watery smile.

Abby came up on Caleb's right and took his hand. Brice moved to Caleb's other side and put a hand on his arm. The three of them stood together—as they always would.

"Please, forgive me," Helen begged Caleb as a tear slipped down her cheek.

All the horrible, hateful things Caleb wanted to say to her vanished. None of it mattered any longer. He nodded slowly. "I forgive you."

Her smile was bright as she looked at each of them.

Then she closed her eyes. One of the monitors began beeping loudly. They moved as nurses rushed into the room, but Caleb knew that his mother was gone.

He stood with his siblings, friends, brother-in-law, and sister-in-law as Helen Harper was pronounced dead. And during it all, Caleb realized that he felt different. Healed.

All the anger and bitterness that he'd carried with him all these years was gone.

And the future looked brighter than ever before. There was a piece missing, though. A vital bit that Caleb was now ready to fight for.

It was time for him to win Audrey's heart.

Chapter 37

Audrey stood inside her clinic. New supplies had already begun arriving thanks to Maddy. There were so many things she needed to do. Tom Hopkins had called, asking if Audrey would return. Even Mrs. Bremer had left a message, wanting to discuss the future.

But Audrey didn't want to work with either of them. Her mind was stuck at the Rockin' H Ranch with Caleb. Worse, she feared it always would be.

"Weren't you going to check on the mare at the rescue?"

Audrey blinked and turned to face Maddy. "I did. Whatever else Patty was, she was an excellent vet. She did a good job with the mare."

"You were part of it."

Audrey turned away and blew out a breath. Soon, the empty cabinets would be full again. If she wanted, she could pretend that none of the past week had even happened.

"What are you going to do?" Maddy asked.

She knew better than to ask what her sister was referring

to because she knew Maddy meant Caleb. But Audrey couldn't think about that. Not now.

Possibly not ever.

"I think I'm going to spend some time at the rescue. And helping individuals. I have a lot of money saved up. I don't need to find a job right now."

Maddy sighed loudly. "I always thought you were the smartest person I knew. You had a goal and never let anything or anyone stand in your way. I envied you that."

Audrey spun around to look at her sister. Maddy had never spoken to her about anything like this before, and she was completely taken aback by all of it.

"What are you talking about?"

Maddy briefly looked at the ceiling. "You had life figured out early. You knew what you loved and what you wanted to do. You got the grades and saved every cent you worked for. You managed to maintain a four-point-oh GPA in college while interning with an equine vet. Successful doesn't even begin to describe you. How could I ever compete with that?"

"Compete," Audrey repeated. She gave a confused shake of her head. "I-I *never* knew what would happen from one day to the next. There were times that I didn't think I would get through the week. While you," Audrey said, motioning to Maddy, "wake up with a smile and find the good in everything. You don't worry about the mundane, stupid things I do. You live freely and, because of it, wonderful things happen to you."

Maddy grinned. "You mean like a sister who lets me live with her and not pay rent?"

"Exactly that," Audrey said with a laugh. She was suddenly overcome with emotion and wiped away a tear that fell onto her cheek. "When I focus on things like my schooling or career, I can forget that I'm so lonely that the ache feels as if it'll swallow me whole."

In a blink, Maddy had her arms around her. Her sister squeezed Audrey tightly. "You don't have to be lonely anymore. There is an amazing cowboy who has fallen hard for you."

Audrey closed her eyes and cried harder—because she knew that her sister was right. Caleb was all she had ever wanted. Why had she let him walk away from her?

But she knew the answer. It was easier to be alone than to give her heart to someone and take a chance that it might not work.

As if reading her mind, Maddy said, "Take a chance. Something wonderful could come of it. But you'll never know unless you take that leap."

Audrey leaned back and sniffed. "What if he doesn't want me now?"

"Oh, trust me. He does."

"Did you talk to him?" Audrey asked hopefully.

Maddy shook her head. "It was the look on his face when he walked from the house."

"Oh." The tightness of Audrey's stomach mixed with her nervousness. It would help if she knew for sure that Caleb missed her, but in the end, it boiled down to how much she was willing to risk.

The best days of her life had been with Caleb. Even with all the danger, his being there had made all the difference. And then, when they made love. . . . The very thought of him touching her could make Audrey's stomach quiver with desire.

She wiped her face and raked her hands through her long length of hair. "I'm going to find him."

"Um. Not to rain on your parade, but you might want

to take a shower first. You've been in those clothes for two days."

Audrey looked down and grimaced. Once again, Maddy had saved the day. "Thanks," she said and rushed past her sister into the house.

She'd never taken a shower and changed so fast before. It wasn't until she was in her SUV and driving off that she had time to think about what she would say to Caleb when she saw him.

After the way she hadn't looked at him, or even responded to the things he'd told her, she might have to go to extremes to make Caleb realize that she knew she was an utter fool but that she had finally seen the light.

Her nervousness grew as she ate up the miles. When she finally turned onto the drive that led to his house, her smile disappeared, and she actually feared she might throw up, she was so anxious.

She stopped the vehicle and put it in park. As she turned off the ignition, she looked around for some sign of Caleb's red truck, but she didn't see it. Still, she got out and went to the house. When she spotted the busted door, she got worried.

"Caleb?" she called.

There was no answer, so she tentatively stepped inside. It didn't take her long to confirm that the house was empty. She walked to the barn, but once more, there was no sign of Caleb. She did find a teenager bringing feed out to the paint stallion, though.

"You lookin' for Caleb?" he asked.

Audrey nodded. "I am. Is he around?"

"He took off a few hours ago. Not sure when he'll be back."

Audrey started to reply, but the teen turned his back to her to continue his work. Not wanting to bother him, Audrey made her way back to her SUV.

Inside, she set her hands on the wheel and asked herself, "Now what?"

She could wait at his house, but that seemed . . . almost stalkerish. She could go to Brice and Naomi's or even try Abby and Clayton's, but she didn't really want anyone else around when she saw Caleb for the first time. Especially since she wasn't sure what would happen.

Audrey shook her head and started the vehicle. She should just go home.

"What do you mean she's not here?" Caleb asked Maddy.

The younger Martinez sister sighed dramatically. "If you would only lis—"

"I thought she'd be here," Caleb said. He'd driven straight from the hospital to Audrey's. It had never dawned on him that she wouldn't be there. He'd just, well, expected it.

"—ten to me. I'm trying to tell you that she wen—"

"Don't tell her I stopped by," he said and turned on his heel.

"Caleb!"

He jerked to a stop after three steps and whirled around to face Maddy. He'd hadn't known her that long, but he had never heard that angry tone in her voice before. "What?"

"What?" she asked, eyes wide. "What?!"

He swallowed and glanced around him nervously. "Did I say something wrong?"

Her eyes grew even bigger. "Unbelievable."

Caleb frowned then. "What is?"

"I've been trying to tell you since you knocked on the door that Audrey isn't here because she went looking for you."

A smile erupted across his face. "Did she really? Why didn't you tell me?"

"Oh, God," Maddy said forlornly while rolling her eyes. "I think I might hit you."

Caleb wrapped her in his arms for a quick hug. "I'm going to find her."

"Just stay here!" Maddy called after him.

But he didn't want to take the chance that Audrey was waiting for him at the ranch. Caleb had the truck in drive before his door was even shut.

Audrey drove, all the while wondering if she should have stayed at the ranch. All she had to do was call him, but after what had happened, their first conversation shouldn't be on the phone. It needed to be in person.

A pedestrian along the side of the road caught Audrey's attention. As she passed him, she turned and looked over her shoulder. There was something about him that looked familiar.

Without hesitation, she turned around on the road. As Audrey drew closer, she realized why the man seemed familiar. It was his walk. The same slight limp that her father had from being kicked by a horse.

She pulled up behind him and put the vehicle in park, but she left the engine running as she opened the door. The man had no idea she was there. He kept walking, his thick black hair hanging over his face.

He carried a frayed brown backpack and had on clothes that had seen better days. Even without seeing his face, Audrey knew this was her father.

"Dad?"

The man stilled, his head snapping up. Slowly, he swiveled to face Audrey. The moment his dark eyes met hers, Audrey started to cry.

"Where have you been?" she demanded. "How could you leave like that?"

He walked toward her as cars zoomed past. He didn't stop until he was a foot in front of her.

"Audrey," he said, a small smile on his lips. His fingers briefly touched her face. "You and your sister have so much of your mother in you."

Audrey couldn't believe how thin he was. He looked horrible, but his eyes weren't as haunted as they had been after her mother's death.

"I'm sorry," he continued. "I shouldn't have left you or your sister. I just couldn't go on without your mom. And I couldn't take my own life."

"So, what? You wanted the land to do it?"

He nodded. "That's what I hoped for. But your mother wouldn't let me die. I got sick this past winter after being caught in the snow, and some homeless people saved me. I stayed with them for a time, but I knew I had to come back to my girls."

"Oh, Dad," Audrey said and threw her arms around him.

He held her against him. "I was selfish. So selfish. I thought I couldn't survive without my wife, but I never thought about you or Maddy going on without your mother or me."

"It's over," Audrey said, crying harder. "You're home now."

"I have much to make up for."

"And you can," she said and leaned back to look at him.

"Come. I'll take you to my place. You can tell Maddy everything."

Audrey was leading her father to her SUV when she glanced to the left and saw a red truck parked on the opposite side of the four-lane road. Leaning against the vehicle was none other than Caleb Harper.

"Who's that?" her dad asked when he caught her staring.

"I'll be back." She took her eyes off Caleb long enough to check and make sure no one was coming before she began to cross the road.

She didn't make it halfway before Caleb met her in the middle and pulled her back to his truck. The feel of his fingers linked with hers made her want to shout with joy.

Audrey couldn't stop looking at him. He'd always been a hard one to read, and she still wasn't sure what it was she saw in his eyes. He wouldn't have stopped if he didn't have feelings for her. Would he?

She hated not knowing.

"I'm such a fool," she said.

At the same time, he said, "I can't stop thinking about you."

They shared a laugh.

"Go ahead," he said.

Audrey licked her lips. "I don't know where to begin. I'm sorry for the other day. I thought it would be better to remain alone than risk giving you my heart. But these past few days have shown me that I don't want that. I want you."

"I saw my mother today."

Audrey had thought he might respond to what she'd just confessed, but since he didn't, she asked, "Is that good?"

"I forgave her. Right before she died."

"Oh, Caleb."

He shook his head and took both of her hands in his. "It made me see that the pain I held in my heart stopped me from allowing myself to love anyone. She left us, but I thought it was because of me. I didn't think I could be loved."

"That's not true," Audrey stated.

Caleb's brown eyes crinkled at the corners. "I know that now. You helped me see that. It was you who paved the way for me to see that, in order for me to move forward, I had to forgive her."

Audrey was shocked. "Me?"

"You," he said with a chuckle. "Don't look so surprised. You're an incredible person. I knew you were different from the first moment I met you. I don't know when you took my heart, but it's yours if you want it."

Fresh tears rolled down Audrey's face. "I do want it. I really do."

"I don't want to scare you off, and perhaps I should wait, but I want you to know all of it. I love you, Audrey. You are the light in the darkness, a blaze so bright and fierce that it will never go out. It called me home. To you."

Audrey cupped his face in her hands. "If I'm the light in the dark, you are the rock that steadies me. You offer shelter and stability. Your touch, your kisses showed me what it was like to be loved. And to love." She smiled up at him. "I love you, too. With all my heart."

They clung to each other. Two battered hearts who had found comfort and healing in each other's arms.

Life couldn't get any better.

"Who is that man?" Caleb asked.

Audrey pulled away and looked across the road to her dad, who watched the events with a smile on his face. "My father."

"Let's get him home then." Caleb lifted her hand and kissed it. "Together."

"Together," Audrey said.

As they crossed the road, Audrey knew that these were their first steps as a couple. There would be ups and downs, but they would fight for the love they'd found until the day they breathed their last.

Epilogue

Caleb lit the last of the candles and stepped back to look at the space. There were rose petals scattered on the floor from the kitchen into the bedroom and even up on the bed.

He cleared his throat and looked outside at the darkness. He caught a glimpse of his reflection and straightened his tie. The first time he'd worn a suit, he'd seen the way Audrey had looked at him—as if she wanted to devour him.

Pretty much the same way he'd looked at her when she wore the slinky red dress with the slit up her thigh.

Caleb felt his pocket where the ring was. He'd been thinking of this night for months. Every day with Audrey was full of love and adventure. They argued, but sometimes simply so they could have make-up sex.

As if they needed a reason for that.

He grinned, thinking about it. Audrey was his entire life. It boggled his mind that he had lived so long without her. Though it had only been just over six months since they met, it felt as if they had known each other for eons.

Caleb checked the champagne that sat in its bucket of ice. Audrey was due back any moment. She had taken over as the vet for both the Rockin' H and the East ranches, which kept her busy. But not so busy that she didn't spend time at the rescue or with other individuals' horses.

The front door opened, and Caleb's stomach clenched with nerves. He faced the bedroom entrance and waited for Audrey. Within moments, she stood there.

Her long hair loose about her shoulders, she took in the dozens of candles lighting the room and the rose petals. Then, her eyes landed on him.

"Oh, my," she murmured appreciatively when she saw him in the suit. "And I look like this."

He didn't care that she was in jeans and a T-shirt. To him, she looked beautiful in anything. "Hello, sexy."

She walked into his arms and smiled up at him. "Hello, handsome. This is . . . I can't find the words to tell you how wonderful it is to come home to this."

He smiled inwardly. Audrey had only moved in two months ago, but it hadn't really been much of a change since she spent nearly every night with him anyway. The only difference was that her clothes took up the other side of the closet now.

"I just wish I looked as good as you," she said.

He gave her a soft kiss. "You always look great."

She rose up on her tiptoes and locked her arms around his neck. "You are a pretty spectacular man, do you know that? I'm so glad you're mine."

"I'll always be yours."

Her dark eyes searched his face. There was a slight frown on her lips. "Is everything all right?"

"It's perfect," he said. Then he stepped away from her and went down on one knee, withdrawing the diamond ring from his pocket. "Audrey, you're the love of my life. I've never known happiness as I have these past six months. I want to spend the rest of my life with you as my wife. Will you marry me?"

She looked from him to the ring and back to his face. Her expression was blank. He worried that he might have rushed things. They had talked about marriage, so he knew she wasn't against it. At least, he didn't think she was.

A tear rolled down her cheek. Then another. And another.

"You always know what to say and do," Audrey said as the tears came faster, now accompanied by a smile. "Yes. Yes, I'll be your wife."

His hands shook as he tried to put the blue diamond on her finger. Once it was on, she was in his arms—and the suit came off.

Caleb forgot all about the champagne as they lost themselves in each other. Tomorrow, they could celebrate and plan their future. Tonight, well, that was for loving.

Don't miss more titles

by DONNA GRANT